The time for evasion was over.

She had almost fallen apart when she feared he was gone for good. Nina was searching for a brand of healing she suspected he knew how to give. She would not risk losing him again.

David looked at her with a soaring expectancy he had not experienced in a long time.

He threw his keys on the couch, took her by her hand, and proceeded directly to the bedroom. She walked out of her clogs, climbed up on his spacious bed, lay back, and let him pull her tight jeans from her slender hips. His eyes never left her as she reclined completely nude and unashamed.

A dark mahogany ceiling became their canopy, enclosing them in a world of quiet promise. . . .

By Amanda Wheeler
Published by Fawcett Books:

ARMS OF THE MAGNOLIA
BEYOND THE FIRE

BEYOND THE FIRE

Amanda Wheeler

FAWCETT GOLD MEDAL • NEW YORK

A Fawcett Gold Medal Book
Published by Ballantine Books
Copyright © 1996 by Amanda Wheeler

http://www.randomhouse.com

Library of Congress Catalog Card Number: 95-90822

ISBN 0-449-14934-X

Manufactured in the United States of America

First Edition: April 1996

10   9   8   7   6   5   4   3   2   1

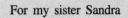

For my sister Sandra

Chapter One

Berkeley 1972

SHE SPOTTED HIM, cruising past her in a top-down, T-Bird convertible. A tilt to his floppy cap, bushy hair peeking out the back added flavor to his laid-back good looks.

She was checking him hard, pretending she wasn't—doing that I'm-too-cool, you-think-you're-cute, girl thang. Shoulders back, head high, she counted seconds before he'd accelerate and disappear. Nina's heart, already beating like a tom-tom, did a flip-flop when he slowed to a crawl.

Brake lights flashed red. He pulled over and waited for the sassy sister stepping out of his dreams.

At first, she pretended not to notice him, as he trailed patiently along beside her. Nina glided down Shattuck Avenue like Gumby in high gear.

"Somebody's in a hurry. Need a lift?" he asked, leaning over to open the passenger door. "I'm David, and I don't bite."

"In that case I may keep on walking." Nina smiled, then introduced herself.

"Where you headed, Nina?"

"To the law school. I'm late."

"I saw the way you were hattin' up around the corner."

Nina tossed her backpack and sank slowly, dramatically into the weathered leather seat of his 1956 Thunderbird.

Her head bobbed to the beat of funky music jamming on the car radio. She caught him looking at her when she was looking at him. In unison, they broke out laughing.

1

"What's on your mind? I can feel you thinking," she said.

"Your hair."

"It's just an afro."

"No, it's more than that. It's symbolic of your exotic, liberated nature. Nina, with hair like a lion's mane—bountiful, wild, with sunlight peeking through it."

"You're quite lyrical for so early in the morning."

"You inspire me. Did you like it?"

"Yeah, I liked it." Nina nodded.

"What do you do when you're not studying?"

"Cool out with my girlfriends, part-time work here and there."

"That's no life for a woman fine as you."

Nina looked away self-consciously, breaking the second rule of hitchhiking. Never let the driver get next to you. She broke the first rule when she gave him her real name.

"I wasn't hitting on you. Just making an observation," David explained.

She changed the subject quickly. "I like your car. It suits you nicely."

"How do you know that?"

"Some things you just know," she said, adjusting her position.

Nina's fringed denim cutoffs, ending just south of heaven, made David's eyes work overtime. His long, graceful fingers tapped nervously on the steering wheel. He punched every button on the radio, gave up, and turned it off.

"Am I making you nervous?" she asked.

"A little bit. There's a lot I want to say to you, but you back up when I get personal."

"I'm not being evasive, it's the circumstances. . . ."

"Let's pretend we didn't meet on the street."

"But we did. There's no way to change that."

"We can ride back to the diner on Shattuck. Sit in different booths, if it makes you happy. I'll drink coffee and eat sugary doughnuts until you're ready to talk to me."

"I wish I had time, but this is where I get off." Nina motioned toward the building. "Let me out here."

David pulled up to the curb at Boalt Hall School of Law, overlooking the U.C. Berkeley campus. A group of pranksters lined the sidewalk, hawking women and making lewd comments.

Nina mumbled, "Not this, first thing in the morning."

"Is there a problem?" David asked.

"No. Just a bunch of lightweights searching for their manhood," she answered, referring to T.J. and his cohorts. For them harassment was a form of entertainment.

She turned her back on the snoops and said to David, "Thanks for the ride. I really appreciate it."

"Enough to give me your phone number? I'd like to finish our conversation."

For the moment, Nina forgot about the pranksters straining to get in her business. She was caught up in hypnotic eyes that begged, Come on, baby, give me a chance. Two seconds before surrender caution overruled her instinct.

She pulled up out of the low-riding T-Bird and hoisted the overstuffed backpack on her shoulder. Regretfully, Nina explained to David, "I don't feel comfortable giving my phone number to a stranger. Maybe next time. Thanks again." She closed the car door and sashayed past her observers. They were quieted by Nina's panache.

David watched from the street until she disappeared inside the law school.

Eight-fifteen. The door squeaked as she entered the huge lecture hall. Two hundred eyes stared at the towering woman who dared enter Professor Collins's class fifteen minutes late. The wooden heels of her six-inch platforms clanked with every step. " 'Scuse me," she said, climbing over two students slouched in their seats. Professor Collins paused, glancing at his watch and seating chart.

"Now that Miss Lewis has joined us, I'll continue with the lecture. In case you were distracted by Miss Lewis's lack of common courtesy, I will summarize the points covered so far."

Nina sat mortified through the remaining forty-five minutes of class. She kept waiting for him to call on her to discuss cases she hadn't read or even considered briefing. Periodically Collins glanced at the seating chart, intensifying her anxiety. This was not the way she wanted to begin her final year of law school. At the end of class the professor let her get as far as the door before calling her back for a parting shot.

"Miss Lewis, may I have a word with you?"

She was tempted to rush out the door, but it was too late. Collins knew she heard the summons.

"Yes, Professor Collins." Nina turned to face him.

"The next time you're running late, spare yourself the embarrassment. Skip it." Collins glanced over the top of rectangular bifocals to emphasize the point.

"Understood. No problem." Any attempt to apologize or explain would have further stirred his wrath.

In the hallway Nina commiserated with Sheila, the first friendly soul she encountered. "Collins stone cold busted me for being late. I missed my bus and had to walk for days until this really interesting brother gave me a lift. I wanted to keep on riding."

"He must've been fine."

"To the max and then some. His skin was smooth like warm, melted chocolate. It wasn't just his looks. He was different, kinda jazzy."

"He had you goin'. Did you hook it up?"

"No, girl. He tried to rap in front of T.J. and the hot-nosing crew. I couldn't handle it."

"What a drag. Come with us to Golden Gate Field."

"The track? It's nine o'clock in the morning and you're thinking about gambling?"

"We're not going until after two. We'll grab some munchies and hang out until then."

"Count me out. You're the reason I didn't get to class on time. Stayed up half the night playing bid whist. I don't even like card games. I'll be in the library till ten, then I'm going home to study. You also have a class, Sheila."

"I'm not going. If they don't see me, they won't know I'm not there. Smart, huh?" Sheila tossed loose curls from around her face—the face of an angel. It was the perfect cover for her gangster moll soul. Walking away, Sheila remembered what she intended to ask Nina. "You're coming to T.J.'s party, aren't you? School has you going in circles."

"T.J. makes me uptight."

"Don't let the boy's bad attitude make you miss a happenin' party. We can make it a girls' night out. I'll pick you up—and your roommate too, if you insist on dragging her along."

"Depends on how desperate I get. I'll call you tomorrow and let you know."

"Whatever's right. We'll be at Maxwell's, in case you get a panic attack in the library." Sheila flitted away in a burst of gum-chewing energy.

Only two weeks into her final year of law school and the grind was wearing heavily on Nina. Sheila was right about Nina going in circles. The pressure was blowing her mind. Their situations were entirely different. Sheila could waste time and party all she wanted. Her boyfriend, Derrick, could hustle enough cash to get them over, in or out of law school. Nina was on her own, proud and independent. As she got closer to graduation, independence was losing its shine.

She rushed out after her ten o'clock, hoping to keep the world at bay. Still planted outside the entrance was T.J. and his entourage. It was too late to change directions without being obvious.

"Hey, pretty lady. You planning on reading all those heavy books in one sitting?" T.J. laughed at her, initiating a chorus of heckles. It was their usual routine.

" 'Scuse me, but I think I was minding my own business. Why don't you do the same? Or even better, try going to class every now and then. It might do you some good."

"Check this out, fellows. Lady law student telling the master how to handle his studies. I'd be happy to take a few lessons from you."

"Not in this life," Nina shot back, and kept walking.

"You got no time to talk to brother T.J.? All your time taken up by that hippie I saw you with this morning?" T.J. shouted after her.

"Who're you calling a hippie with your trashed-out, mismatched clothes? Take a bath before you talk to me," Nina countered, still moving.

Law school was a three-year endurance race that everybody wanted to win. What began as an adventure rapidly transformed into a burden. Nina hit the wall of aggressive, cutthroat competition. It wasn't just T.J., who was obnoxious, but manageable. Hostility permeated the air.

Nina missed the comfort of Mills College, where she completed her undergraduate studies. Competition had been keen at Mills, but not vicious. At the all-women's college, Nina had advocated allowing men in the classroom. She even signed a petition in favor of coed education. Now that she was surrounded by men, she wondered what had been on her mind.

She walked past People's Park on the way to Telegraph Avenue. Not a single blade of grass sprouted in the barren earth that was once the site of a major student movement. No tear gas wafted through the air, burning eyes and steeling youthful resolve. Now the noxious smell of debris rose from the fires of homeless squatters sprawling in gray dust. A shirtless man, chest drooping with age, sang shrilly above the music of a badly tuned guitar. Had she imagined that this was once sacred ground?

A maze of competing activities awaited her on Telegraph. A woman with hair stiff as cardboard argued loudly with a man selling hashish pipes outside her boutique door. Street vendors selling, crowds milling, dogs barking, tourists gawking, the threat of bedlam lurked on every corner.

Nina loved this street, but not today. It was getting to her. She broke into an all-out trot, lunging for the bus as it pulled away from the curb. She banged on the rear end with her backpack, screaming at the driver "Stop! Let me in." The bus screeched to a halt. Her coins clanged into a glass meter. Slowly she walked to the back of the bus.

"This institu-shun is but a symbol of the oppres-shun that the White man has used to enslave our Black bro-thuhs and sis-tuhs in Mozambique, South Africa, Guinea Bissau, and in this country—yes, in this country that we call America." T.J. spoke in the rhythmic speech pattern made popular in the sixties by Black militants. Sweeping hand movements punctuated every syllable.

"We called this meeting of the Black Law Students' Association of Boalt Hall to dispel the notion, particularly for you first-year students, that what you learn here is in any way relevant to what's happening in our community. You must take from this situation what little there is to be taken—that is, a J.D. certificate and the opportunity to face the next White man's trick, the bar examination."

Sheila nudged Nina, sitting next to her, and whispered, "What is this fool talking about?"

"Now be nice, you know he can't help himself."

T.J. continued to speak, unperturbed that he had lost three-quarters of his audience. Nina squirmed in her seat, upset that she hadn't sat close enough to the door to escape unnoticed. She had run four blocks from the sandwich shop for the lunchtime meeting that was turning into a T.J. side-show. Sheila cracked gum with abandon, a clear signal that she was ready to bolt. Nina occupied herself by unwrapping her sandwich. Brown avocado sat on limp, warm tomato smothered by a mountain of wilting sprouts. Nina grimaced and closed the paper. First T.J., now her sandwich was ruining her appetite.

"Hold on a minute, brother T.J., that might have been your purpose in coming together, but some of us have a different, less heavy purpose." Sanford Washington, president of the association, interrupted.

"Brother man, if you think you can do better, then you're welcome to take a shot at it." T.J., clad in a rumpled army

jacket, defiantly folded his arms and stared intently at
Sanford, who was unmoved by T.J.'s aggressiveness.

"Easy, bleed. I'm not trying to steal your thunder, but
you're coming on a little strong for our first meeting. We
veterans know where you're coming from and can appreciate your intense, political perspective. But for our new
members, it may be too heavy. We should start by welcom-
ing them into the organization."

Nina and Sheila relaxed a bit, thankful that Sanford had
injected a voice of reason. Every year they went through
the same ritual—the struggle to control the politics and
minds of the new students.

Sanford stroked the uneven hairs of his goatee and continued. "Next we should give them a chance to ask any
questions they might have. You remember how intimidating
it was when you arrived here. Dean Wilbur gave his annual
speech: 'Look to the left, look to the right. One of you
won't be here by the end of the year.' That can be some
scary shit when you're new."

"Man, I didn't come here to baby-sit. I came here to rap
about the serious problems facing our community. If we
won't be dealing with relevant issues, me and my boys can
split and let you carry on with your agenda."

"It's all relevant, T.J., but as president of this organization, I'll decide the order in which we discuss things,"
Sanford answered.

"Right on, brother," Nina's roommate, Estrellita, chimed
in from the back of the room.

With order restored, Sanford returned to his written agenda. T.J. alternately wisecracked and looked sullen for the
balance of the meeting.

"Our special guest today is Attorney Roland Hill. As
some of you already know, Attorney Hill is a graduate of
Boalt Hall, he's been a guest lecturer here on many occa-
sions, and he's currently running for mayor of Oakland. Attorney Hill has been a friend and supporter of our
organization for many years, and the Executive Committee
felt it appropriate to allow him to address the group. It's not

our policy as an organization to endorse any candidate for office. However, if you, on an individual basis, like what you hear today, I encourage you to get involved in this worthy campaign. Attorney Hill . . ." Sanford yielded the floor to the candidate.

"Thank you, Sanford. Every time Sanford refers to me as Attorney Hill, I look over my shoulder to see who he's talking about." The audience laughed and Hill continued. "Seriously, I've known Sanford for most of my adult life and believe it or not, he's almost as old as I am." They laughed again. "For some of you, this is the second time around with me. I owe my election to the Board of Supervisors to the volunteers who worked tirelessly on my behalf and on behalf of a cause that we all believe in—quality management of our resources. I appeal to you today to help me continue that cause by elevating it to a higher level. I see one of my supporters over there—Nina Lewis. Nina, stand up."

Nina stood and mustered a weak smile.

"Nina and several other young women from Mills College gave my campaign the boost it needed to be successful. For those of you who haven't had a chance to get to know her, watch out for this dynamic young woman. . . . Now it's time to move to an even larger arena. Becoming mayor of the City of Oakland will allow me to oversee and direct policies relating to city finances, crime control, health and sanitation services, and numerous other issues of vital importance to this community. To win this election, I need the support and creative energy of students like you. Right now we're gearing up for the primary in June. I promised Sanford I wouldn't hog the mike, as politicians tend to do. Two of my campaign workers will be available after the meeting to sign up volunteers and to answer any specific questions you might have."

"I have a question." T.J. stood up. "You talk about crime control. How do you propose to control these pigs on the street committing crimes against innocent brothers?"

"T.J., Attorney Hill didn't ask for questions from the floor," Sanford interrupted.

"Bourgeois niggers never do," T.J. shot back, to the embarrassment of almost everyone.

"Hold on, Sanford." Roland Hill jumped into the fray. "The brother asked a legitimate question, which I'm prepared to answer. I don't particularly care for being labeled a bourgeois nigger by someone who doesn't know me, but I hope that, given proper education, my brother can overcome that. . . . The question of illegal police behavior or unnecessary force is one that I've grappled with as an attorney and as a Black man living in an urban center. I believe it's critical to have properly trained personnel so that they deal with all suspects without regard to race. As a practical matter, we live in a racist society, and people bring to the job their own backgrounds and beliefs. I can only say that, as mayor of Oakland, I will ensure that our men receive adequate training and will deal decisively with complaints of police misconduct. Let me also say that, as a representative of this community, I will not tolerate lawlessness or individual agendas that conflict with the safety and common good of all the people."

After the presentation, most of the audience applauded generously. A few people were afraid to express an opinion. T.J.'s group stalked out. Nina approached Candidate Hill and extended her hand. He brushed it aside in favor of a quick hug.

"I apologize for some of the less-than-classy people who squeeze their way into law school," Nina said.

" 'Nuff said. It sure was good to see a friendly face out there. How've you been?"

"I'm makin' it. I see you've got a little gray in that beard?" Nina teased, touching his beard lightly.

"It's a disguise. Someone told me that mayors need to look distinguished. Make an old man happy, sign on with my campaign."

"I have to think about it. Everything is up in the air."

"I don't want to hear that. The Nina I know is always up

for a good fight—and this is definitely a fight. Don't make me start singing 'Please, please.' You know I can't sing."

"That's an understatement." Nina laughed, remembering how Roland used to break the tension by singing loudly, off key. "Okay, okay. You got me."

Roland placed his hands on her shoulders. "That's a definite, not a maybe?" he asked, looking her in the eye.

"It's a definite."

Chapter Two

TWO DAYS LATER Nina attended her first meeting at Roland Hill's campaign headquarters. She looked forward to getting involved in something that could take her mind off the law books that were dogging her, even in her sleep. It seemed the more she studied, the less she retained.

She was not quite ready for Hill's campaign manager, Austin Greene, a slight, light-skinned brother with oxblood-colored hair and freckles around his nose. Austin was a man of few words, prone to short, robotic responses that many interpreted as a sign of high intelligence. Nina thought he was just rude. She could tell, from the jump, that it would not be easy working with this man who knew he had all the answers.

Austin's background as a former navy pilot was well known in local political circles. No one knew anything about his social life, which was either well hidden or nonexistent. Rumor had it that Austin had been rejected by all the major law schools on the West Coast. Law students were not his favorite people.

Austin made a career out of managing political campaigns. Getting jobs was easy in an area where everyone was involved in politics on one level or another. The man's personal politics, however, were as elusive as his personal life. He had the ability to change his philosophy conveniently, depending on which candidate was willing to employ him. He seemed a strange choice to manage Roland, whose campaign was sorely in need of direction.

Roland's campaign was caught in the middle of a

transformation. The sixties' political activists were turning into mellowed-out, security-seeking adults. Some of their fervor had spilled over into the seventies, but it seemed more symbolic than substantive. Voting attitudes were changing along with the face of politicians who were quietly becoming more moderate in their positions.

While the citizenry in urban enclaves swooned with the sedative of sixties liberalism, much of the country had taken a decided turn to the right. Caught in an uncertain period of political adjustment, politicians like Roland Hill found it difficult, if not impossible, to please anyone. Their campaigns could be made or broken by a single event over which they had little control.

After Austin presented his plan for the next major fund-raiser, Nina commented, "I think that's an excellent strategy for getting grass-roots people involved in the campaign, but what about the rest of the city, you know, the ones with the money?"

Austin glared at her. "Little sister, this is a grass-roots campaign, in case you hadn't noticed. Our primary goal is to bring power to the people. The folks you're talking about can write checks."

"That's cool and all, but I thought the primary purpose of a fund-raiser is to bring money to the coffers. I don't think it's wise to dismiss the rest of the community as mere check writers. You're running a major, citywide campaign here, not organizing a Friday night fish fry. If we expect to win, and I assume that's the primary purpose, we have to bring in all elements of the community. The city is fifty percent Black, but not all of us will vote. With other Black candidates in the primary race, the vote will undoubtedly be split. We need to concentrate on garnering a majority of the voting population, not just the Black population."

"Teach, baby, teach," an unidentified male voice chimed in from the sidelines. Nina turned to see who was seconding her opinion but was blinded by a flashbulb exploding before her eyes. Momentarily unable to focus, she missed seeing Austin rolling his eyes at the newcomer, who had pissed him off royally. Nina could not make out the voice of the speaker but did recognize Roland, who had walked in on the tail end of the discussion.

"This is what I like to hear. New ideas being tossed around. Nina may be on to something."

When her vision cleared, Nina recognized the man standing next to Roland. It was David, the man in the T-Bird. He was taller than he had appeared sitting down. His broad shoulders filled the camouflage T-shirt he was wearing. Every woman in the room was mesmerized.

"I'm sorry to interrupt the meeting, but these people are with the Oakland *Sentinel*. They want to take pictures for an article Mr. Hamilton is writing about the campaign. You don't mind, do you, Austin?" Roland asked.

Austin's frail arms folded defiantly across his scrawny chest. He was clearly unaccustomed to being challenged. "No, I don't mind. Interruptions seem to be the name of the game today," he said, his eyes beaming right through Nina.

Roland pulled Austin aside as the meeting began to break up. Unintentionally, at their first meeting today, Nina had gone toe-to-toe with the dictator. She couldn't sit back while Austin's questionable tactics squeezed every ounce of life out of the campaign.

David directed the photographer to snap pictures of Roland's supporters. "I see some new faces. Get a shot of the sister over there," he said, pointing to Nina.

Embarrassed by the attention, Nina dropped her binder on the floor.

She walked over to David and asked, "What are you doing?"

"Taking pictures of the volunteers."

"You're putting me on the spot."

"The way I heard it, you were putting yourself on the spot. You'd better watch out for Austin. He doesn't like being upstaged."

"Are you a supporter?" Nina asked.

"No. I'm doing profiles on all the candidates. I try to

stay neutral, but it's not always easy. I'm surprised you remember me. The last time around, you treated me like the big, bad wolf."

"It wasn't like that. I didn't know you from Adam."

"Now you know who I am, what I do, and where I work. All I know about you is that you have the prettiest brown eyes I've ever seen. We should remedy the inequity in the information exchange. Do you agree?"

"Yes, I agree," Nina answered without fully realizing what she was committing to. The photographer moved on to other subjects and David saw his opportunity.

"What are you doing tonight?"

"I'm busy."

"You're a hard one to figure. You have this bold exterior, say exactly what's on your mind, but you clam up when I try to get to know you. Are you afraid of me?"

"I probably should be, but that's not it. I have a party to attend tonight." Nina seized upon T.J.'s party as an excuse, not sure why she needed one. "Can I get a rain check?"

"You can get almost anything you want from me," David said, standing so close she could feel his energy. "You're taller than Amazon woman."

"Amazon woman was white."

"That's the Hollywood image. I'm talkin' 'bout the real deal. The long, lanky sister strolling through the jungle like she owns it."

"It's my platform shoes and hair. They make me look taller."

"Since you won't give me your number, let me give you mine. Call me when you're ready to hang out with someone other than your girlfriends."

"I'll do that." Nina took his card and quickly gathered her things, hoping to avoid any further confrontation with Austin. She had almost made a clean getaway when someone called out, "Nina, wait up."

She was relieved to see that it was Roland and not Austin trying to get her attention. Roland caught up and said,

"Listen, I'm glad you spoke up in the meeting today. We desperately need new blood in the campaign. I hope you won't let Austin discourage you. He can be aggressive sometimes, but once you get to know him, you'll see that he's basically good people. I agree wholeheartedly, we do need to broaden our base of support. Will you be at the next meeting?"

"I definitely plan on being there," Nina said, then strolled out of the office, thinking about shopping for clothes she could ill afford. The urge to look good was upon her, but she controlled it and boarded the bus toward home. Seeing David again had given her a major boost. The excitement showed on her face as she nervously fingered David's business card, stuffed deep inside her pocket. His rare magnetism was messing with her mind. A derelict seated across the aisle from Nina assumed her glee was directed toward him and began feverishly manipulating below his belt. Nina sprang from her seat and moved up front, directly behind the driver.

Disgusted, she said, "This is getting ridiculous." The bus chugged and lurched its way to the next stop, making it difficult, but not impossible, to meditate on David.

T.J. lived in the bottom half of a refurbished Victorian house in West Oakland. He commandeered use of the upstairs unit by bribing his neighbor with a little ganja and a lot of high-minded bullshit. By the time Nina arrived at the party, fashionably late, they had been at it for hours. People were everywhere: on the sidewalk, in the yard, hanging out of windows, and peeking over the rooftop like sentries in a castle. The house bulged with bodies, sweaty from dancing and primed with enough herb and spirits to spontaneously combust.

"Hey, get out and come on in. This party is outta sight." A classmate rapped on the hood of Estrellita's orange Volkswagen, hopelessly trapped in an unmoving line of vehicles. An impatient driver detoured around the congestion by driving over the curb and routing stunned pedestrians from the clogged sidewalk.

Nina said, "Maybe we should let this slide." The noise from the party was so loud that Estrellita couldn't hear her.

In the backseat Sheila bounced to the music, taking the last hit off a joint. She shrieked, "Dammit, I burned my fingernail. Park this raggedy piece of shit and let me out."

"Don't start tripping with me, Sheila. You were the one who didn't want to drive your precious little Triumph. Sit your black ass down and wait like the rest of us," Estrellita said.

"Look who's calling me black—El Chicana herself."

Daggers darted from Estrellita's mascara-lined eyes. Sheila had struck a raw nerve.

"We're all a little edgy. Let's not ruin the party before we get inside. Peace, my sisters," Nina said soothingly.

After circling the block for fifteen minutes, Estrellita squeezed the Volkswagen between a fire hydrant and driveway clearly marked "Do Not Block Driveway." They bailed out onto pavement that vibrated with the downbeat of the music, blasting two blocks away. Sheila was back to being her bubbly self, but Estrellita sulked as they approached T.J.'s house. Navigating the crush of bodies lining the sidewalk was the next major challenge. Luckily, Sheila's boyfriend, Derrick, spotted them from his vantage point on the porch and beat a path through the crowd to rescue them. Once inside, Nina couldn't imagine why she wanted to be in a room filled with elbow-to-elbow funk, hemmed in by hyper strangers.

Within seconds she was pulled to the floor by a man wearing a leather aviator skullcap pulled down over bushy eyebrows that crowned bulging eyes. He assumed, without asking, that Nina wanted to dance. It always happened to Nina. Every weirdo zeroed in on her as if she wore a sign that read: "Try me." Nina moved her feet lackadaisically to a beat muffled by blistering sound. The visual assault from a flashing strobe light made her head spin, but fortunately she was tall enough to catch whiffs of air above the heads

of the other dancers. When the song ended, aviator man
thrust his face ominously close to hers and started rapping.
"What's yo' sign, baby?"

Nina backed away swiftly, making excuses. "Thanks for
the dance, but I have to find my friend. She's barely five
feet tall and might get squashed under somebody's army
boots."

She spotted Estrellita huddled beneath the armpit of a
tall, dashiki-clad brother wearing dark sunglasses indoors at
night. Maybe his eyes needed protection against the strobe
light shooting neon rays in random patterns. Nina didn't
want to disturb Estrellita, so she made a bee-line for the
back porch. The tiny yard backed up to an alley filled with
overflow from the party. The smell of reefer hung heavy.
T.J.'s party had usurped the floors, walls, roof, sidewalks,
and streets and was now taking over the airways. It was too
much for someone not in the mood. The blame was on her.
She could be somewhere else getting cozy with David instead of pretending to have a good time.

Nina elbowed her way outside the chain-link fence. She
was tempted to keep walking, but common sense said, Tell
them you have to split.

Bracing herself, she reentered the madhouse. The pace
had slowed considerably. Al Green was singing "I'm Still
in Love with You." Couples plastered together on the dance
floor made her feel like a reject from Noah's ark. From
across the room aviator man was looking. Nina's search for
Estrellita intensified.

Estrellita had been replaced under the armpit of the tall
brother by another equally petite woman. Nina felt a tug
from behind and spun around, expecting to see Estrellita.
"Oh, shit," she said out loud, intending to only think it. It
was T.J.

"What's happenin', pretty mama?" He grabbed Nina by
the arm, pulling her along.

She argued, "I gotta go."

"Get with the program, baby. We're just startin' to
groove."

T.J. waltzed through the doorless entry to his bedroom and ejected the couple about to "get down" on his water bed.

T.J.'s buddy was pissed, protesting, "Say, man, why you wanna bust me like this?" as he pulled up his jeans. Embarrassed, his woman friend ran out without saying a word.

"Naw, man. Not tonight. I'm trying to rap with this sister and we don't want company," T.J. said.

With her head shaking and hands on hips Nina asked, "What do you think you're doing?"

"Slow down, slow down," T.J. insisted. "I'm not getting fresh. I wanted to apologize for the misunderstanding we had. Sit—" He motioned toward the bed.

Nina flopped down on a bean bag chair. Her knees buckled as her arms flew up; her back sought nonexistent support. She zeroed in on the beaded curtain, still swinging and clinking in the doorway. The room reeked of incense burning in a small metal holder. Powdery gray ashes dropped continuously on a bare spot in the matted, gold shag carpeting. It didn't seem to bother T.J. so she didn't let it bother her.

"You embarrassed me in front of my boys."

"You said you wanted to apologize."

"I do. I'm not accustomed to being ragged on like that."

"And I'm not accustomed to being heckled by a supposedly enlightened Black man."

"I was trying to be friendly."

"Being friendly doesn't include making obscene gestures."

"Let's call a truce. What I really wanted to talk about is your support of Roland Hill. As you know, I'm supporting Donna Dixon for mayor. The brothers and sisters at the law school are confused by all this divergent information being thrown at them. I think it would be a good idea if we united behind a single candidate."

"I think so too. Roland would be delighted to have your support."

"Come off it, Nina. Roland Hill is too soft to fight The Man. He'll punk out the second they put pressure on him."

"That's unfair. Roland may not have the macho facade, but he's a good man and a hard worker. Roland's work on the Board of Supervisors gave him access to the people who run this city. He has a direct line to the Port of Oakland. He's an advocate for senior citizens and a proponent of women's rights."

"What's his agenda when it comes to Black folks?"

"All those things I just mentioned directly impact the lives of our people. We need jobs, not unworkable theory. Roland may not be strong on revolutionary rhetoric, but his heart and his vote have been in the right place on every critical issue. On the other hand, your candidate has never held public office. She was slamming the system until she decided to run for mayor."

"So were you. We marched around the Alameda County Courthouse together, participated in the same demonstrations," T.J. reminded her.

"That's right. I don't see my past as inconsistent with my present stance. We all have to evolve, like Donna Dixon. This election is not about who can scream the loudest. The man or woman in the mayor's office has to pull together a coalition to make positive change. Roland is the only one who can do that."

"You're dreaming, baby."

"You're the one who's dreaming," Nina responded in a huff, struggling to get up from the collapsed bean bag. When she found her footing, she added, "You know as well as I do that Donna Dixon is a puppet for the People's Liberation Party."

"Everybody has to answer to somebody. You got a problem with the PLP?"

"No. I admire a lot of what they're doing. I do have a problem with some of the tactics, especially as they relate to women."

"Watch yourself. You're not turning into one of those feminists, are you? The Black man has been oppressed for so long, sometimes we resort to extraordinary measures to gain control of our community."

"Black women have been oppressed too."

"I use the term 'man' in the universal sense."

"I'm not so sure of that. How is it that we agree on the fundamentals but can never get together on specifics?"

"Your problem is, you don't understand the complexity of the situation."

"School me."

"If we subscribe to divisive ideology, the strength of our movement will be diluted to the point where we can no longer move forward."

"I'm hip to that, but I will never accept abuse from my own Black brother as a necessary corollary to progress."

"If you're down for the struggle, your personal comfort is subordinate to the greater good of the people."

"How does a man's fist in my face translate into the greater good of the people?"

"Now we're going in circles. Accept the fact that men and women are endowed with distinct yet equally deadly forms of power. Men have physical power and women have pussy power. It's as simple as that."

"That's it. End of conversation."

"You seem uptight. You need a good man to unruffle your feathers."

"I don't see one here." Nina blew past T.J. and out of the room so quickly that he had no chance to think of a comeback. She passed Sheila on the way out and yelled that she would meet them in the car.

Nina sat alone for an hour on the hood of the Volkswagen Beetle, waiting for Estrellita to show up with the car keys. It took that long for Sheila, who was riding home with Derrick, to track down Estrellita. By the time Estrellita appeared, Nina was shaking from the cool night breeze that attacked her bare midriff and chilled the tip of her exposed toes.

"Girl, you are really bodacious standing out here by

yourself at night. Do you know how dangerous that is?"
Estrellita asked.

"The most dangerous person out here tonight is me.
Open the car door before I demonstrate."

Nina held out the parking ticket she had removed from
the windshield of the car.

"What's that?" Estrellita asked.

"A parking ticket. What do you expect when you block
somebody's driveway?"

"Toss it under the seat with the rest of 'em. There should
be a law against giving more than one ticket a month to the
same driver," Estrellita answered nonchalantly.

When they were almost home Estrellita announced, "I
hope you don't mind, but I invited a friend over this evening."

"Evening! It's almost morning." There was no point in
protesting. Sometime before daybreak a zoned-out stranger
would stroll into their apartment, drink Nina's last bottle of
wine, and camp out in Estrellita's bed. For at least a week
Estrellita would be fatally in love, write bad poetry to her
African prince, then slip into a deep blue funk when he
dumped her after borrowing her share of next month's rent.

Dear God, don't let him be a squatter, Nina prayed si-
lently.

Estrellita's most recent conquest—his name was Amir—
moved in his record collection first, followed quickly by his
unwashed wardrobe and a stinky sheepdog that lay in the
doorway all day and all night. Nina suggested, after a week
of co-op existence, that their flat was getting crowded.
Estrellita went ballistic. She didn't regain her senses until
Amir disappeared and left the dog as a going-away present.

"No, I don't mind if you have company," Nina lied, "but
please don't blast the stereo and wake up the neighbors. My
name is on the lease and I like having a place to live."

Nina quietly contemplated how to survive the inevitable:
the sound of Estrellita's headboard banging against the
wall, her roommate's catlike wailing at the slightest hint of

stimulation, and, worst of all, the feeling that she was the only woman in Oakland not getting any. The combination could set Nina's nerves on edge for days—and it did.

Chapter Three

KNEE-DEEP IN drafting a constitutional law paper, Nina came up for air. She sprawled spread-eagle on the carpet and let her pencil fall to the floor.

"Should I call the ambulance?" Sheila asked.

"No. My back needed relaxing. What do you think about what T.J. said?"

"Give it a rest. You and T.J. were the only people at the party talking politics instead of dancing. You're like little kids. Squabbling one minute, playing games the next."

"The stakes are too high to play games."

"That's why I don't get involved in politics anymore. It used to be fun, now it's work. There's nobody to get excited about. My heroes are dead, in exile, or marked as false prophets. The politicians out there now are like—like . . ." Sheila stammered to complete the analogy.

"Like Roland. I know Roland isn't the perfect candidate, but neither are the others. He's the only one addressing the issue of Black economic development. Donna Dixon doesn't stand a snowball's chance in hell with her antibusiness rhetoric. Half the people shouting 'right on' at her rallies won't bother to go out and vote. It's sad. Roland's head is in the right place, but he's too moderate to appeal to the hard core. The white, middle-class vote is solidly backing McFarlane."

"Sounds hopeless to me. Why bother?"

"I have to get fired up about something. I feel numb inside. Nothing's wrong and nothing's particularly right. I've

24

spent all this time getting educated, and I want to see something positive happening in this city."

"Roland's solid, but he's not the kind of guy to create a
lot of sparks."

"That's the problem. He's too solid. The man needs a
makeover—add a little jive talk and a lot of street savvy.
It's like trying to teach someone to slow-dance. You can
show them the basic steps, but unless they feel it, they end
up looking stiff."

"If anyone can make him over, it's you. You've got your
work cut out for you though."

"Roland's a challenge, but he's open to suggestion. Austin Greene, his campaign manager, is the main problem."

"Is Austin still giving you the blues?"

"That's an understatement. Every time I enter headquarters I put on my hard hat. Speaking of which, let's
finish this paper. I have to see how much damage Austin
did today."

Austin's contempt for Nina intensified with each encounter. He remained a rigid, intimidating presence determined
to get rid of her. The tension came to a head when Austin
accused Nina of undermining his orders.

Austin flew into headquarters wearing perfectly pressed
khakis and a short-sleeved, button-down shirt. He stood directly over Nina's chair, and asked, "Who gave you the
authority to redirect my workers?"

"What are you talking about? I haven't redirected anyone." Nina wanted to stand up without brushing against
him, but there was no room.

"You sent Mike over to some computer lab instead of
letting him address the envelopes like I told him." By now
Austin's shoulders were squared like a boxer ready to
thump.

"A friend of mine who works with computers offered to
train one of our volunteers to speed up the mailing process. We're still addressing things by hand while our com-
petitors are using machines. I figured we could free up the

volunteers for more useful work, like making phone calls and walking the precincts."

"You've been doing a lot of figuring lately without consulting me." Austin's index finger wagged furiously within centimeters of her nose. Nina's chair was pushed up against the wall. She had nowhere to go, except under the desk. Several people were watching, but no one said anything. A split second before D-Day Roland sailed out of his office and grabbed Austin by the arm.

Roland asked, "What the hell is going on here? I can't believe what I'm seeing."

"This creature is trying to take my job. That's what's going on. She's decided the way we've been doing things isn't good enough anymore." Austin's deadly stare remained fixed on Nina, who had managed to free herself from behind the desk.

"Are you talking about the computer, Austin? Nina mentioned that to me and I told her it was a good idea. Mike went over to check it out. No final decision would have been made without consulting you," Roland explained.

"Since when do we have money to buy computers?"

Nina's heartbeat had slowed enough to allow her to speak. "I'm not suggesting we buy computers. My friend offered to input our mailing list on his system and run labels in his spare time—at no cost to us. Eventually he could train Mike to handle everything. He's doing us a favor."

"Who is this friend and how do we know he's not working for the opposition?" Austin asked.

"Okay. I give. Do it your way, Austin, even if it ruins the campaign. I know when my suggestions aren't appreciated." Nina threw her hands up in exasperation, grabbed her sweater, and started loading her backpack.

"Don't go, Nina. We need you," Roland pleaded with her.

"Well, somebody is going. Me or her," Austin said, looking defiantly at Roland.

"Austin, I want to see you in my office. We're disrupting

the entire operation and creating the kind of disunity that my opponents love to hear about. Wait just a minute, Nina. I want to talk to you before you leave."

Nina was too hyped to get back to work and too smart to be trapped behind the desk again. Austin, the shrewd manipulator, cast himself as the victim to gain support from gawking volunteers. They soaked up every word of the confrontation. But he underestimated Nina. Behind her courteous facade, she had a reservoir of street smarts to fall back on. She couldn't be intimidated by finger-pointing and a raised voice.

Nina sat on the front of her desk opening mail, trying to appear calm. She picked up a curious-looking eight-by-ten package addressed to her personally. Two glossy black-and-white photos of her were inside with a note: "Do law students get lonely too? I know I do." The note was signed /D/.

She grabbed the phone and dialed the number, which she had memorized. Several times she had picked up the phone to call David, but chickened out before the first ring. Now the phone rang five times before it was answered.

"Hello, may I speak with David, please?" Nina whispered into the receiver.

"Who?" a man on the other end bellowed.

Nina switched the receiver to the other shoulder, trying to prevent the others from eavesdropping, and spoke a little louder. "David Hamilton. Is he in?"

"Uh . . . He's somewhere around here. Let me check."

Nina could hear him asking people around him if they knew where David was. The man came back on the line. "Somebody said he was up in the copy room. Can he call you back? Gimme your number."

She pictured the man waiting impatiently on the other end with his pencil poised to write. Maybe this wasn't such a good idea. "N-no. I'm going to be in and out. I'll call him later."

"Okay . . . Oh, hold on a second, he's coming in the door right now."

"Hello." David came on the line. His deep, sexy voice made her fidget.

"Uh, hi, David. This is Nina."

"Nina. What took you so long to call?"

"I've been busy with schoolwork, the campaign and all."

"I'll accept that answer if 'and all' doesn't refer to a husband or a steady boyfriend."

"No, nothing like that." Nina wanted to say something clever. Wittiness escaped her when she needed it most.

"Did you get the pictures?"

"Oh, yeah, that's what I was calling about. They're great. I love them. Thanks."

"Would you like to see the rest?"

"Sure. We'll have to get together sometime."

"Why do I get the impression you're putting me off again?"

"I didn't mean to give that impression. We're both busy people and sometimes it's not easy coordinating schedules."

"My schedule is free tonight. What about yours?"

She took a deep breath and swallowed. "I'm free."

"What time shall I pick you up?"

"Where are we going?"

"No place in particular. Can I make you dinner?"

"Sounds good . . . Dinner would be fine, but why don't I meet you, say, at seven."

Nina jotted down David's address and hung up quickly. She smiled, pressing her lips together to keep from grinning too hard. Austin blew past her like a speeding bullet, grabbed his bag, and split without saying a word.

"You look awfully happy for someone who came within inches of getting pummeled," Roland teased her.

"Some things I let roll off my back." Nina made a waving gesture with her hands.

"I assured Austin that no one is threatening his position and you'll check with him before making any decisions. Can you live with that?"

"No problem. I don't understand why he's so resistant to everything I say."

"He works hard. You know, the perfectionist type. Austin hates it when anyone, including me, proves him wrong."

"I'm not trying to prove him wrong. I want you to win. Anyway, I've got midterms coming up and I could use more time to study."

"You're not deserting me, are you?" Roland looked concerned.

"No chance. I'll be back with a vengeance ... oops, poor choice of words. I'll be on the case as soon as exams are over. I would've talked to Austin myself, but he didn't seem to be in the mood. Gotta boogie. Catch you next week."

Roland watched intently as Nina floated out of the office. Two volunteers caught him gaping. They exchanged suspicious glances, then pretended they hadn't noticed.

Chapter Four

NINA TRIED ON three different outfits before finding something appropriate. She wanted to look alluring without being too provocative. The distinction was beginning to blur. The flowered skirt looked contrived and dowdy; a low-cut midriff blouse revealed all she didn't have. Halfway into a printed dress with puffy sleeves, the Flying Nun with afro stared back in the mirror. Nina settled on flared white jeans with thin black stripes that made her eyes cross when she focused for too long.

She borrowed a wide leather belt with metal studs from Estrellita and painted her fingernails bloodred. At the last minute she fretted that lint balls on her mock turtleneck made her outfit look cheap, which it was. She laughed at herself for worrying about what he would think. From the look of his eclectic clothing, she and David probably shopped at the same army-navy surplus store.

Estrellita's Bug backfired ominously as they pulled away from the curb. Nina wondered if she should have allowed David to pick her up, but immediately rejected the thought. Estrellita could hang around for a few minutes while she scoped out the situation.

Her right knee jerked continuously, symptomatic of her nervousness. To further heighten her anxiety, Estrellita talked nonstop as they rode the freeway to the Oakland Hills.

"What did you say he does for a living?" Estrellita asked.

"He's a journalist."

"He must have big bucks living in a neighborhood like this. How old is he?"

"I don't know exactly, but he's older than me."

"Girl, you dating an old man?" Estrellita asked point blank.

"Not an old man. An older man," Nina clarified.

"Let's go over the signal again. You say What time is Jamal picking you up? And I say Oops, I'm late already. Gotta run. What if you don't like the vibe? What happens then?"

"We'll figure that out in the unlikely event it occurs."

"Don't forget to find out his birthdate. I can check his astrological chart to see if he's worth the effort. There's no point in wasting a lot of time on the brother if the stars say the relationship is going nowhere. If I'd listened to the stars when I met Abdul, I could've saved myself a lot of grief."

"When did you ever listen to anything except the message between your legs? Slow down and pull over. I think that's the house on the right." Three columns of stairs zigzagged up a steep, ivy-shrouded hillside. A shallow, softly lit front entrance created an illusion of mystery.

Nina adjusted her clothes nervously before they began the trek to the top. She knocked softly and then a little harder. There was quiet music playing inside.

David answered the door wearing loose-fitting pants, tapered at the ankles, and a flowing matching tunic. The rich detail of the fabric, together with his handmade leather sandals, gave him the appearance of a Moroccan prince. In a flash Estrellita brushed past Nina and started stroking the silky fabric of his tunic.

"Wow! This is outta sight," Estrellita gushed, running her hands over his clothing with a familiarity that embarrassed David. He stepped back and extended his hand to the bold stranger. Nina stared open-mouthed at her roommate's behavior. David broke away and greeted Nina with a friendly hug. He smells good too, she thought.

"Come in and have a seat." David gestured toward the

sparsely furnished living room framed by a high-beamed ceiling and intricate wood moldings. An area rug covered gleaming hardwood floors that gave the house a cool, open feeling.

"You have a very nice place here," Nina said. Estrellita was so busy doing a visual survey that she nearly stumbled over Nina.

"Thanks. What can I get you ladies to drink?"

"I'll have some wine," Nina answered.

"And you?" David turned toward Estrellita, who was interrupted by Nina before she could answer.

"What time is Jamal picking you up?" Nina arched her eyebrows and glowered to make sure her roommate, acting totally dense, read the signal properly.

"Uh . . . Jamal . . . Now. He's picking me up now. I'm late. That's right. I'm late. Well, it was a groove meeting you, David. You guys have a nice evening. Call me if you need a ride home."

"That's okay. I can drop her off," he offered.

The minute Estrellita cleared the premises, they broke out in spontaneous laughter.

"I'm sorry," Nina managed to squeeze between chuckles. "I know my roommate is a little wacked, but I had no idea she would act like that."

They drank wine from beautiful crystal goblets and chatted amiably to break the ice. All the while he kept looking at her the same way he had when they first met. Out of the clear blue he asked, "For someone who hitches rides with strangers, you sure are being cautious with me. Why is that?"

Nina had no answer. She only knew that when she looked at him, she had trouble collecting her thoughts. It was an exciting but scary sensation, one that Nina wasn't accustomed to.

David approached her while she was standing by the fireplace. He took the wineglass from her hand, set the glass on the mantel, and drew her to him. He kissed her easily, without haste or awkward groping. Nina sank deeper into his embrace, savoring the moment. Still holding her hand in his, David pulled back and looked at her.

"What is it?" Nina asked.

"I don't know. I guess you rattled my brains." David puffed out his cheeks and shook his head rapidly from side to side, causing his face to quiver like Jell-O.

Nina laughed and shoved him playfully.

David put his arm around her narrow waist and escorted her toward the dining room. "Let's eat, baby. My grits are gettin' cold and hard."

She was impressed when he poured more wine from a bottle that had a cork instead of a screw-off top. Nina realized that this was the first time a man, other than her father, had prepared a complete meal for her. He served grilled fish with pasta and a salad so delicious that she had seconds.

"All right. Now tell me who really cooked this food," Nina kidded him.

"I've been a bachelor all my life. I learned to cook to survive. I eat out most of the time, but at my age it's not too healthy. . . . Uh-oh. That look tells me you're dying to find out how old I am."

"It never crossed my mind," Nina lied. "But since you brought it up, tell me, how old are you, David?"

"I'm thirty-five and a half, as the kids say."

No wonder he knows how to kiss so well. He's had a lot of time to practice, she thought.

"And you, are you legal yet?"

"I'm twenty-three."

"Whew," David said, pretending to wipe sweat from his brow. "I was afraid I'd have to confiscate your wine. Feel like taking a walk?"

"Sure."

"You're lucky you didn't wear your platforms tonight. These hills can get pretty steep. Let me get you a jacket. It's probably cool outside."

They started out holding hands loosely and quickly progressed to arms around each other's waist. It felt natural

being with David, as if he had always been there. He talked
about things other men seemed uninterested in and he was
interested in her. As Nina leaned against his shoulder, he
kissed her forehead and let it go at that. There wasn't the
pressure she felt with other dates who pounced on her if
she gave them so much as a smile.

The last time she was alone with a man in the Oakland
Hills was a disaster. Her first lover, Lionel, had pinned her
under the steering wheel of his gangsta' ride and taken his
pleasure, oblivious to her physical and emotional discomfort. The steering wheel had been more memorable than the
sex, which, thankfully, was brief.

"What are you smiling about?" David asked, interrupting
her remembrance.

"Oh, nothing important." They reached the top of the
street that was once a hill and settled in an open area. City
lights glowed like candles in a cavern, sweeping the horizon as far as they could see. Oakland was transformed into
a peaceful valley—no horns, no sirens, no screams. She sat
down on a bumpy log, the fallen remnants of a tree. David
sat next to her, took her hand, and studied it with the intensity of a palm reader.

"What made you decide to go to law school?"

"It seemed like the best thing to do at the time. Lately
I've been wondering why I did it. I was a psychology major in undergraduate school but didn't see much future in
pursuing psych on a graduate level. I can hardly figure out
what I'm doing, let alone what someone is about. A couple
of my buddies at Mills were applying to law school, so I
decided to check it out. I was surprised to get accepted at
Boalt."

"A Mills girl, huh. Mom and Dad must have the bucks."

"Don't get your gold-digging shovel out yet. I was on
scholarship and worked two jobs for spending change.
Good grades in high school and a preppie appearance for
the interview got me over. I'm sure they were shocked
when I showed up on the first day with an afro bigger than
Angela Davis's.

"My mother was working as a maid when I started Mills, less than six years after my family migrated from Georgia. Daddy came first, then sent for us with money he earned washing dishes. Eventually, he got a job working in the shipyard.

"We traveled across country on a Trailways bus, my brother, sister, Mama, and me. I was twelve years old and all excited about coming to a place where everybody went to school together, regardless of race. When we boarded the overcrowded bus in Atlanta there were soldiers, Black soldiers, who gave up their seats to let us sit down. I don't know why, but for me their gesture was reassuring. The desegregation order had already been handed down in Georgia, but many Blacks still moved to the back of the bus. Here we were competing for seats with certain people who felt that we didn't have a right to sit down at all.

"That slow-moving bus sputtered, backfired, and stopped in every town that had a population of ten or more. Our friends had packed a shoe box full of fried chicken that tided us over until we left the deep South. The bus depots were still segregated, separate toilet facilities for White and Colored. Frequently, there was no place for us to buy food along the way. I remember one stop in Mississippi where the White bus driver begged them to let Mama buy milk, but they wouldn't. We made it anyway—all the way to the Golden Gate Bridge. I was disappointed that it wasn't gold but a strange hue of reddish orange." Nina paused. "I don't know why I'm telling you this."

"Go on. That's a fascinating story," David said.

"Enough about me. Where did you go to school?"

"I went to school in Virginia, then came to California to live with relatives. After high school I took a few courses in junior college and hit the work trail. I started in the mail room of the Richmond *Voice*—they're out of business—and worked my way up to the editorial page of the *Sentinel*. Do you read my column?"

"No, I'm ashamed to admit. I read the San Francisco

paper, but I promise to start checking you out. Do you like being a journalist?"

"It's cool, but it has it's drawbacks."

"Like what?"

"People deal with you in extremes. They either hate you or love you."

"Why do you stick with it?"

"It gives me a chance to say something important. That's all I've ever wanted to do. My dream is to get my novel published. I've been working on it for a while."

"Oooh. Tell me about it. Can I read it?"

David hesitated before answering. "Maybe someday. It's incomplete and I'm not ready to be read. . . . It's getting windy out here. We'd better head back."

Nina could tell that she had hit on a sensitive area.

When they reached the house, Nina asked to see the pictures David had promised to show her. As she followed him into his study, she had a chance to view the rest of the house. The rooms were huge, but few in number. There was a massive four-poster bed in the darkened bedroom. Nina refrained from asking for a closer look. He might get the wrong idea. French doors in the study opened to a balcony overlooking a canyon. The backyard was sloping and unfenced on the southern perimeter.

On the walls there were framed photographs from stories David had covered. None conveyed his personal life—no family or friends.

"You're very photogenic. Have you ever done any modeling?" he asked while opening an overstuffed portfolio of photos.

"Are you kidding? I hate being photographed." Nina reached down to grab pictures tumbling to the hardwood floor. He managed to pull her photos to the top of the pile. She was surprised by how relaxed she looked, not straining or grimacing as she usually appeared in pictures.

"Your photographer has a good eye. Can I look at the rest?"

She sat in the only chair in the room and flipped through

the pages of mostly black-and-white shots. "What's this?" Nina laughed, and held up a photo of a nude woman with a less-than-perfect body.

David grabbed the picture and slammed the book shut. "Oops. I forgot that one was in there. I'd better organize my book before I let you wander through it. Let's listen to some music. That might be safer."

He put an old Marvin Gaye, Tammy Terrell record on the stereo and pulled her up from the chair. It was a slow, slow song that gave them an excuse to get close.

"This is the only kind of dancing I know how to do. I can't jump around with you youngsters," he explained.

"This is the only kind of dancing worth doing," Nina answered before he leaned down to kiss her. He began with teasing brushes across her lips, graduated to slow, deep kisses, then nibbled at her neck until her mind cried out for mercy. David was in no hurry to get there too soon. He would squeeze and then release her, keeping the tension mounting at all times. His fingers must have had sensors; he knew what to touch and when to touch it.

Nina tried to calm herself by concentrating on the song lyrics. But Marvin was moaning and Tammy was groaning—not the easiest path to self-control. When David's hand traced the outline of her body, she was ready to scream, but the turntable beat her to it by repeating a high-pitched, nerve-tensing sound.

"Damn," David muttered, walking over to the record player and lifting the arm. "Don't move," he said, but by then Nina had come back to earth and was getting oxygen to the brain. David regrouped quickly as Nina joked that the record skipping was probably her mother using ESP to keep her in line.

"I can't believe a little fuzz on the needle interrupted a righteous groove."

"It's getting kind of late. I think you should take me home."

"Late? It's early and you don't have classes in the

morning. Can't you stay a little longer? You got me begging like Marvin Gaye." David laughed at himself.

"No, I should leave. I've got a lot of studying to do this weekend."

"Okay, I'll be a gentleman and take you home, even though I don't want to. Let me find my keys."

The lights were out inside when they pulled up to Nina's flat.

"Doesn't look like anybody's home. Can I walk you to the door?" he asked.

"No, thanks. I can find my way inside. Estrellita's probably holed up inside with who knows who. I had a wonderful time this evening. Maybe we can do it again."

"There you go being iffy. I'm counting on seeing you again. You gonna give me your number or keep me in suspense for the rest of my life?"

"Oh, I'm sorry. Here's the number." She jotted it down on a pad he handed her. "Call me tomorrow."

"No. I'll make you wait for a few weeks like you did me." He smiled then gave her a kiss that made her regret coming home.

Inside, the house was unusually quiet. Maybe Estrellita decided to go out. She hoped not, since she was anxious to get on her case for rubbing all over David.

"Lita, you in there?" she yelled toward the closed bedroom door. No answer. She heard sobs coming from inside. Nina pushed open the door and saw Estrellita crouched in the corner, crying. A single candle burning on the nightstand cast eerie shadows on the ceiling.

"What happened? Are you all right?" Nina asked, expecting major bad news.

"Nothing new. Same old shit, same old problems," Estrellita answered in a voice hoarse from crying.

"Get up off the floor and tell me about it. I'm turning on the light. Looks like a séance in here."

The gist of the problem was that Estrellita really didn't have a problem, just hang-ups plaguing her since long before they met. Caught between two cultures, Black and

Latino, she never felt she fit in. Estrellita was convinced that her mother, a striking woman of Mexican ancestry, hated her. Nina had met her once, when she drove up for Estrellita's birthday. To Nina, Estrellita's mother seemed very hip, which caused her to suspect that Estrellita might be jealous of her own mother. The father, a Black man, had disappeared years ago. Estrellita's mother mentioned, more than once, that except for the hair texture, Estrellita looked just like her father.

"Everything about me is wrong. I can't wear a natural because my hair is too straight. The Chicanos shun me because my skin is too dark. I'm a woman without an identity, a soul lost in the struggle to be somebody." Estrellita hung her head between her knees.

"I think you're being a dramatic, dear. You're a beautiful woman and you have a lot of friends." Nina tried to console her.

"Then trade hair with me. I'd give anything to have strong, nappy hair like yours."

"Now you're being ridiculous. Not so long ago I wanted hair like yours. You're misunderstanding the whole point of the cultural revolution. It's not about wanting what someone else has. It's about loving who and what you are. There are people with two Black parents who have hair straighter than yours. You need to get over this trip about your father. He didn't desert you because you're Chicana. He left because he was irresponsible."

"Don't you dare talk about my father like that," Estrellita snapped back.

"Well, shit. I'm sorry. I was just trying to help."

Estrellita calmed down. "You're right. I'm the one who should be sorry. Thanks for listening to me."

"Can I say one last thing?"

"Go ahead." Estrellita looked at Nina apprehensively.

"Don't try to find your father in your boyfriends."

"You're right. I'm trying to work it out. Speaking of men, how was your date?"

"I had a wonderful time."

"Cut the crap, Nina. You know what I mean. Was the brother any good in bed?"

"I wouldn't know. We didn't get that far."

"Was he queer or something?"

"No. Unlike yourself, Miss Hot Pants, I don't fuck everybody I meet on the first date." The moment it came out, Nina knew she had said the wrong thing. Estrellita started boo-hooing all over again despite Nina's attempts to apologize. Nina finally gave up and went to bed to the sound of Estrellita's stereo blasting "Papa Was a Rolling Stone."

What kind of person am I living with? Nina thought to herself. She's messy, loud, and could keep a staff of psychiatrists busy full time. Relief came around two-thirty in the morning when the upstairs tenants pounded on the ceiling and yelled, "Turn that shit off before I call the cops."

Chapter Five

WHEN THE PHONE rang the next morning, Nina was too exhausted to pick it up. Probably one of Estrellita's Lotharios, she concluded, before pulling the pillow over her head. The ringing ended abruptly. Nina dozed until she heard Estrellita chatting gaily in the next room. Lured by the force of her instincts, she got up to check it out.

Estrellita was perched in the middle of her bed dressed in pink shorty pajamas. She spoke in that whispery tone of voice she used when trying to be sexy. Coiled tightly around sections of her straight hair were a thousand pink plastic rods. She looked like a baby chick with a nest on its head. The girl was getting deep into the conversation when she looked up and saw Nina standing in the doorway.

"Oh, look who just woke up. It's David," Estrellita said, covering the receiver with her hand. "He is so fine," she squealed. "I was just telling him that you were still asleep."

"I'll bet" was all Nina said, giving her a cold look before walking to her room to take the call.

"Good morning. Did Estrellita entertain you?"

"That roommate of yours is a trip. Where did you find her?" David inquired.

"I'd rather not say." Nina laughed.

"Sorry I called so early. Are you a late riser?"

"Only when Tweety Bird keeps me up all night listening to loud music."

"Come ride with me to San Jose."

"What's happening down there?"

"There's a big rally at two and I'm covering the story."

41

"I'd love to, but I can't, David. I really can't. I have midterms all next week and I haven't done any studying."

"I've got a surprise for you," he said to entice her.

"You tempt me, but I've gotta say no. I've been spending too much time on the campaign and not enough with my law books. I've got to work miracles in the next two days or start planning another career."

"I'm disappointed, but I understand. When are your exams over?"

"On Thursday."

"I'll call you Thursday. Later."

He sounded let down. The second she hung up she wanted to call him back, but she knew that doing so would mean surrendering the rest of the weekend to nonacademic pursuits.

"What the hell am I thinking about?" Nina said out loud, then reached for a textbook and started reading. It took an hour before each paragraph stopped ending with the name David.

By Thursday she was a basket case, exhausted from studying and lonely as hell. She literally ran home and waited for David to call, but the phone never rang. She phoned his office with shaking hands. He was on assignment and not expected in the office until Monday. She couldn't survive until then.

Nina set up operations next to the telephone. A bottle of Boone's Farm wine, a week's supply of reefer, and a box of saltine crackers kept her company as she dialed and redialed his home number. "What did I expect?" she asked herself. "Was he supposed to sit around and wait for a silly girl to finish her homework? Stupid, stupid, stupid."

"I've never seen her like this," Estrellita confided to Sheila when she called. "Her room is a disaster zone. That's not like Nina. She's been watching television all weekend, especially the news. She cries over every story. Nina cried over Watergate, she cried about the upcoming presidential election. When Shirley Chisholm came on, I thought that would pep her up. Instead she started preach-

ing about how she's sick of symbolic progress. 'I want real,
tangible change. Something I can feel,' Nina said. I think
she's frustrated and not just politically.

"So I asked, What about George McGovern? She looked
at me and said, 'You know as well as I do, Nixon is going
to win, no matter what we do. The sixties are gone. Dead.
There's nothing to look forward to. Reactionary politicians
are taking over the world.' Maybe it's the herb. She's acting
paranoid."

"Is she trying to smoke?" Sheila asked.

"Yes, and you know how she gets."

"Put her on the phone. Let me see what I can do." Sheila
waited a full two minutes before Nina picked up the phone.
"Hey, girl, let's check out a movie."

"Ain't nothing worth seeing," Nina said.

"Sweet Sweetback's Baadasssss Song is replaying downtown."

Dead silence.

Sheila said, "So much for that. You suggest something."

"I suggest you leave me alone. I'm tired and I've got the
blues. Only an earthquake could move me from this bed."

"I take it you didn't get in touch with David."

"Don't say his name. It might push me over the edge.
He's probably holed up with some big-bosomed woman
who won't let him up for air. I bet he doesn't remember my
name. Twenty years from now I'll be a spinster, chasing
ambulances to get clients and still living with Estrellita."

"Leave my name out of it," Estrellita yelled from the
back room.

Nina ignored Estrellita's hot-nosing. "I appreciate you
trying to cheer me up, but I have to ride this one out. I'll
talk to you tomorrow, Sheila."

As darkness fell on the city, Nina descended into the twi-
light zone. She was beyond thinking about how she blew it
with David. She was beyond thinking at all.

"Nina, wake up. He's here, he's here." Nina unsealed her
right eye enough to see Estrellita jumping up and down like
a Jack-in-the-box.

She wanted to get up and knock this silly woman out, but her body would not cooperate. Estrellita persisted in shaking and rattling what was left of Nina's brain. Nina pushed up and rested on one elbow, certain she could kick some butt, if she could just get her eyes to focus.

"David's here. He's in the living room. Do you want me to bring him in here?" Estrellita looked around and, despite her warped sense of judgment, determined it was not a good idea.

"Okay, okay. You get in the shower and I'll keep him company until you come out." Nina rolled her bloodshot eyes at Estrellita, who understood completely. Even in her debilitated condition, Nina would react harshly if Estrellita got out of line.

Nina sat on the floor of the shower and let hot water flow over her head. The steam released some of the toxins ingested during the preceding seventy-two hours.

Estrellita came in to check on her. "How's it coming?"

"I'm getting there. I feel so stupid for doing this. It's not just him, you know. It's everything," Nina rationalized.

"Um-hmmm." Estrellita grunted sarcastically.

"How does he look?" Nina asked in a whisper.

"Good. No, better than good."

From the floor of the shower, Nina hugged her knees and found her smile.

After a full fifteen minutes she stood upright and turned the metal faucet from hot to cold. Her body shivered in shock, but it was the only way to exit the shower semi-sober. The mistake she made was looking in the mirror. There was not much she could do about the circles under her eyes. A stale film plastering her tongue and mouth convinced her to move on to phase two. She brushed her teeth and gargled repeatedly before feeling presentable.

Estrellita was an angel and had laid out clothes for her. The shock of seeing Nina so vulnerable for the first time brought out her mothering instinct.

David waited patiently on the homemade couch, a twin bed covered with fake reptile fabric purchased at Kmart. He was so pensive that Estrellita dared not intrude, except to reassure him that Nina was getting dressed as quickly as possible. David stood up when Nina entered, a long forty-five minutes after he had arrived. Nina walked into his arms and buried her head in his chest, holding on as if he were a soldier returning home from war. She would have cried, if she had any tears left.

He was surprised by the warmth of her reception. "Come home with me, Nina." David said the right words. Although he didn't know it, she wanted him as much as he wanted her.

Estrellita handed Nina her purse and jacket.

In the car David explained that he was unexpectedly sent to Monterey on assignment. "I wanted to take you with me, but I knew you had exams. Did you miss me at all?"

"Yes, I missed you," she answered candidly, then kissed him on the cheek. The time for evasion was over. Nina was searching for a brand of healing she suspected he knew how to give. "I'll show you how much when we get to the house."

David looked at her with soaring expectations. The T-Bird flowed a little faster down the street.

He threw his keys on the couch, took her by the hand, and proceeded directly to the bedroom. She walked out of her clogs, climbed up on his spacious bed, lay back, and let him pull her tight jeans from her slender hips. Nina eased her poncho over her head, unveiling firm, uplifted breasts that ached to be touched. His eyes stayed with her as she reclined completely nude and unashamed.

Boldly he undressed in front of Nina. She marveled at his gifts from Mother Nature.

"You have the most beautiful body I've ever seen," he said, lying down and pulling her on top of him. He squeezed her buttocks, well defined despite her leanness. She raised up on her forearms. Her breasts dangled above him like succulent black cherries. David took one in his mouth and kissed it tenderly, then with an urgency that set her soul on fire.

He slid a pillow beneath her as they reversed positions. His power, though long anticipated, made her tremble when their bodies joined. At first he moved slowly and considerately, making sure she was in sync with him. They quickly locked into the proper groove. David shifted into overdrive. Trapped in the eye of a hurricane, Nina was swept away with the force of its wind.

His muscles relaxed. Nina thought the storm was over until he moved in a new direction. She came again and kept coming for an eternity. David cried out, exploding under pressure.

Mesmerized and exhausted, Nina breathed slow and deep.

A dark mahogany ceiling became their canopy, enclosing them in a world of quiet promise.

When he tumbled away, Nina scampered to the bathroom. Sitting on the edge of the claw-footed tub with her head resting in her hands, she asked herself, "Was it as good as I think it was, or am I tripping?"

She looked in the mirror. Aside from being flushed, she looked the same but felt reenergized. Nina closed her eyes and breathed in her satisfaction.

"Are you okay in there?" David asked, knocking on the bathroom door.

"Oh, yeah, I'm fine. Coming right out."

"I'm not rushing you. If you need towels or anything, look in the cabinet."

When she finally emerged, David was sitting in an overstuffed chair wearing a robe. One muscular thigh hung over the arm. She slipped into a terry cloth robe he had laid out for her on the bed.

He motioned and said, "Come sit with me." Nina sat on his lap and put her arms around his neck.

"You're a complex woman. Do you know that? This is the second time today you made me wait while you hid in the bathroom. Did I do something wrong?"

"No, David. It's not you, it's me. It feels strange being with you."

"Good strange or bad strange?"

"Good. Very, very good." Nina kissed him.

"This is different for me too."

"You're kidding. You probably do this all the time."

"I don't get attached, the way I feel attached to you, all the time."

Good answer, even if it was evasive, she thought to herself.

David continued, "I thought about you all week. I wanted to call you, especially when I was in Monterey, but I stopped myself. I was worried you didn't want to see me. On my way home from Monterey the T-Bird took on a mind of its own and ended up outside your door. I sat there for several minutes until I found the nerve to knock. I was afraid you might be entertaining some hard leg with his boots parked under your bed."

"I'm too embarrassed to tell you how I spent my weekend. I can say that it was very lonely."

He slipped his hand underneath her robe and stoked the fire, which landed them back in bed for round two. At eight o'clock the next morning David could barely move, but he had to. Three days away from the office had put him behind. His story had to be on the editor's desk by the end of the day.

"Nina, I have to go to the office for a few hours. Why don't you sleep in?"

Unable to budge, Nina grunted her consent.

"Call me if you need anything. I'll get back as soon as I can. I'll call around noon to make sure you're alive."

Nina burrowed underneath the covers until she felt buried under layers of hot lava. Finally she pushed the covers away and came up for air. Disoriented, she maneuvered close to the clock. She had missed two out of three classes and was at risk of missing the third. If she could get up, get dressed, and catch a ride to the law school, the day might be salvaged.

"Naw," she said, "enough of that crap." After rummaging through cabinets in the kitchen, she located the essentials for a cup of tea. The temptation was strong, but she resisted the urge to prowl through the rest of the house.

Wrapped in the terry cloth bathrobe, Nina basked in the afterglow of love. A clear day in the Bay drew her to the balcony. With her feet resting on a wrought-iron table, Nina scanned old copies of the *Sentinel* for David's column. Her finger traced the features of his expressive face—strong chin, high cheekbones, and a marvelous mouth. Of course, faded newsprint couldn't convey his disarming charisma.

His column, called "The Bay Beat," was free-flowing, political commentary. He came down hard on politicians who took inconsistent positions or no position at all. Fashioning himself as a maverick journalist, David didn't mind telling it like it was.

Nina read through several back issues before concluding that he must know everyone in town. She saw his potential for developing into a major syndicated columnist. Nina pulled back, realizing she was inserting herself in areas where she had no right to be. The last thing she wanted to do was to alienate David by being pushy.

Intense purple and pink bougainvillea climbed a white wooden trellis and trailed along the edge of the balcony. Nina experienced a sense of wholeness previously missing from her life. She prayed that this was more than a one-night stand. After David, making love with anyone else would only be a downer.

The phone rang, shattering Nina's misty-eyed musing. She ran inside to answer it, thinking it was David.

"Hello," Nina answered cheerily.

"Uh ... Hello. Is this, uh ... Sorry, I must have the wrong number." The woman caller hung up abruptly.

Ten seconds later the phone rang again. Nina answered, more slowly this time. At the sound of Nina's voice the caller disconnected.

"Hmmmm. She sure didn't want to talk to me," Nina said. "Maybe I shouldn't answer his phone. And why not?

He said he'd call at noon and it is noon. I'm wigging out over a phone call and talking to myself."

Nina tried to recapture the feeling. The mood was broken irretrievably. What if he has another woman? I should have asked that before I went to bed with him.

She dressed quickly and struggled to write a note for David. Nothing sounded right. "Thank you for a nice evening" was trite and impersonal. "Hope to see you soon" hinted desperation. Half a note pad and fifteen minutes later she settled on "Have a class, had to dash. /Nina."

Nina trotted to the main intersection, intending to hitchhike, but she couldn't get into the groove. This was no time for chitchatting with strangers. She had too much on her mind. After boarding a bus carrying profanity-spewing, dope-smoking teenagers, her tolerance for public transportation hit an all-time low. The long ride gave her a lot of time to think. Maybe she expected too much, too soon from a man she had known less than a month—less than twenty-four hours, in the biblical sense. Discomfited, jealous, and confused, Nina sulked at the back of the bus.

Chapter Six

"AM I GLAD to see you!" Roland reached out and grabbed Nina the second she entered campaign headquarters.

Surprised by his enthusiasm, Nina said loudly, "Gee, it's nice to be missed. What's happenin', people?" The volunteers appeared unusually frantic.

"Everything. Come inside. I need to talk to you." She was rushed into Roland's inner sanctum. "Have you been following the polls?"

"Not too closely. I finished my exams last week and kind of took the weekend off. Is there a problem?"

"Problem ain't the word. I'm trailing McFarlane citywide and only two points ahead of him in predominantly Black precincts. The word is not getting out to the people. A lot of folks are still unsure of me. McFarlane's people are using propaganda and scare tactics—quite effectively, I might add. His speech changes according to the group he's addressing. My campaign manager isn't helping the situation by issuing weak press releases that rarely make the news. His bad attitude is turning more people off than he's recruiting to the cause. We've got to turn this around somehow."

"Pardon me for asking, but how did you select Austin as your campaign manager?"

"It's a long, involved story, but to cut it short, we thought he would be a major asset. This is all confidential, of course. Austin has a reputation as a strong campaign organizer, but for some reason he hasn't been effective. It's like he's dragging his feet. I'm running out of time. Austin wasn't my first choice. Joe Landers was supposed to run the campaign. Two weeks before the campaign kickoff, Joe had a major falling out with key members of my organizing committee. He opted out and took a job as head of a company owned by none other than the crafty Michael McFarlane. You have to help me, Nina. I've been listening to you in the meetings and you seem to have your head on straight. Everybody else is jockeying for position in the new administration that may never come to pass. I don't know who to trust anymore. I want you to take a more visible role in the campaign. Pick the title and I'll take care of Austin."

"You gonna hog-tie and drop him in Lake Merritt?" Nina laughed at the thought. The expression on Roland's face suggested that the idea was not beyond the realm of possibility. She straightened up. "That's a lot to digest. I'm flattered, but I'm not sure I can handle it with my schoolwork and all."

"Maybe you could take a leave of absence," Roland suggested.

"I don't know about that. The way I'm feeling about school, a temporary leave might become permanent. Give me time to think. I can't decide something this big on the spur of the moment."

"Fair enough, but don't wait till I go down in flames before you make a move."

Overwhelmed, Nina walked out, shadowed closely by Roland, who wouldn't ease up. Her plan had been to come in for a couple of hours, stuff a few envelopes, and go home to study.

A recent volunteer patted Roland on the back and said, "Gimme some skin, brother." Roland plastered on his campaign smile and slapped hands with the man.

Then his attention diverted immediately to Nina and he whispered, "Austin's heart is in the right place, but he doesn't project a positive image. You, on the other hand, would be perfect."

"When did you become such a fan of mine?" Nina asked.

"I always admire strong Black women. I knew you were a star when I met you four years ago. You had the energy of a young kid but the focus of a mature woman. It was inevitable that someone would tap you to be a campaign organizer."

"Volunteering is one thing, running a campaign is another. I can barely keep up with my schoolwork as it is. Antitrust is giving me the blues."

"You're looking at the man who can help with that."

"How can you help?"

"I have an excellent hornbook that breaks down the concepts into simple language. You memorize a few critical cases and you're over. By the time the exams come around, you'll be cruising. There may be some new cases, but the black-letter law remains the same. Do you want to borrow it?"

"Sure. I need all the help I can get. That doesn't mean I'm agreeing to commit more time to the campaign."

"That's entirely up to you. I promise not to pressure you, just give friendly encouragement."

"Give me your address and I'll pick it up later."

"Better yet, if you hang on a few minutes, we can swing by the house and get it now."

Roland Hill lived in an exclusive, secluded area of Oakland. The house sat back from the street on a large lot surrounded by mature evergreen trees and lush foliage. Birds of paradise were planted at intervals, giving the yard a tropical look. It was the kind of house Nina had always dreamed about.

"I can wait in the car," Nina offered.

"Nonsense. I want to introduce you to my son."

A young boy ran out to the car and hugged Roland around the waist. He was so happy to see his dad that he barely noticed Nina, slowly exiting from the passenger side. The child talked incessantly, moving from subject to subject.

"Slow down, Matthew. I want you to meet someone. Nina, this is my son Matthew. Matthew, this is Miss Lewis."

Matthew let go of his father long enough to extend his hand and say, "Pleased to meet you, Miss Lewis."

"Oh, call me Nina."

Meeting a boy so well mannered was a rare treat. Matthew had the cutest chubby face and an innocence that was refreshing.

Nina paused at the entrance to the ornate living room, waiting to be offered a seat.

"Come on back," Roland insisted, and led her to the family room, which was far less formal.

"Where's Rosie?" Roland asked Matthew, referring to the baby-sitter.

"Rosie went home early. Mom's upstairs."

"That's a shock. Saks must have closed early," Roland responded dryly. "Nina, excuse me for a second. Let me run upstairs and say hello to Brenda."

Matthew went to work entertaining Nina. He pulled out a large box of baseball cards, perfectly organized according to team and player position. Matthew sat right under Nina and explained the significance of every card. He instructed her on how to handle them since damage, including fingerprints, diminishes the value of the card. The kid obviously inherited his father's entrepreneurial spirit.

Five minutes into Nina's baseball education, Brenda Hill, whom she remembered from the first campaign, made her grand entrance. Brenda posed and then descended the spiral staircase, carrying a long-stemmed wineglass. The scene was reminiscent of Loretta Young, or was it Marlene Dietrich? In either case, Brenda had flair to spare.

Roland made the introductions. "Brenda, you remember Nina, don't you?"

"Of course I do." Brenda extended long, lacquered nails toward Nina and shook hands limply. "Nina, can I offer you a drink?" Brenda asked while batting major false eyelashes. She was painted like a model posing for high-fashion photography. Heavy mascara and light frosted lipstick made her face look unreal. Every strand of her up-swept hair lay perfectly in place. Nina had never seen a woman this done up at home.

"Nothing for me, thanks. I overdid it last weekend. If I even smell alcohol, AA will impound my body." Everyone laughed, except Brenda, who was lost in a world of her own.

"You know, it's been years since I used that material," Roland murmured. "It might take a minute to find it."

"Brenda, I'm amazed we haven't run into each other down at headquarters." Nina tried to make small talk.

"I haven't been there," Brenda answered matter-of-factly and didn't bother to elaborate. "Roland's obviously very impressed with you. He says you're the glue that keeps it all together."

"Roland's very generous in his praise. You must hate all the time he spends away from the family."

"I'm glad he has something to keep him busy," Brenda said. "I'll excuse myself and let you two talk law, politics, whatever." She strolled off to another area of the rambling house and closed the door behind her.

Brenda's response seemed strange to Nina—but then, anything could be expected from a woman who walks around the house in high heels and stockings.

"Bingo, here it is," Roland exclaimed. "There's enough information here to ace any exam they put in front of you. Just remember—it's supplemental and not in lieu of doing the reading."

"Solid."

"Matthew, run and tell your mom I'm taking Nina home. I'll probably stop by the office for a few minutes after that."

"Daddy, Nina knows more about baseball than you do," Matthew said.

"That's not saying much. I'm afraid my son isn't im-pressed with my baseball know-how."

"Do you play baseball, Matthew?" Nina asked.

Sticking out his chest, Matthew answered proudly, "Sure do. I'm a catcher."

"Tell you what. Next time I come over I'll bring my glove and we can toss a few balls."

Matthew's eyes lit up with anticipation. "When, when, when?"

Roland interceded. "Don't pressure Nina right now, son. I'm trying to sponge off her time as it is. As soon as the campaign is over, we'll arrange something."

Matthew flashed a broad smile, displaying missing front teeth and lots of gum.

Roland rubbed the boy's head, spun him around, and closed the door. "He really took to you. I hope he didn't wear you out," Roland said apologetically.

"Are you kidding? I love kids. Your son is precious, a real joy."

"That's what I keep telling his mother, but he seems to get on her nerves all the time."

Nina let the subject drop.

On the way home, Roland asked if she was ready to say yes to his proposal.

"The more I think about it, Roland, the shakier I get."

"Why is that?"

"I didn't want to mention it before, but I have to find a part-time job. Financial aid isn't what it used to be and I'm self-supporting. As much as I want to work with you, I have to deal with reality."

"Why didn't you say that? You can work for me."

"Volunteers don't get paid."

"Legal assistants do. I can put you on the payroll at my firm. Of course, you have to actually do legal work. I don't want anybody accusing me of campaign violations. I usually hire a couple of students every year, but I've been too busy to deal with it. I have one girl who does research full time, but I can definitely use more help, especially while the campaign is in full swing."

"You're not just doing this to be nice?"

"Of course not, and I'll work your butt off to prove it.

In fact, I already have one assignment in mind. I was appointed by the court to represent a San Quentin inmate accused of murdering a prison guard. You can work with me on that case."

"Wow. I didn't expect anything that challenging. I'm used to doing dull research that nobody reads. You don't know how grateful I am."

"Grateful enough to help me out of my jam?"

"You're making it tough to say no."

"Good."

"Why'd you leave so soon?" David asked.

"I felt guilty lounging with so much work to do." Nina lied to keep from admitting that a phone call had set her off.

"You coming over tonight?"

"If you want me to."

"I want you to. Why don't I pick you up on the way home. Meet me outside. I'm too exhausted to deal with your roommate."

David had Chinese food in the car when he arrived at six. "Didn't want to waste time cooking," he said. They kissed at the first stop light, ignoring the horn honked and obscenities yelled by the driver behind them.

While she was chomping on a greasy egg roll, David laid a copy of a newspaper clipping next to her plate.

Nina almost choked. "Oh, God! Where did you get this?"

"I pulled it out of the archives at my office. I remembered reading about a student protest at Mills College a few years ago, so I checked to see if you were involved."

In a photo taken from a 1969 article, Nina was standing in the middle of a group of Black coeds, all wearing dark sunglasses. Their clenched fists were raised toward the sky. No one was smiling, except one woman in the back row, displaying a demented grin.

"This is incredible. It seems so long ago, but it's only been three years. Did we look tough or whuut?" Nina laughed at the blast from the past. "There's Sheila, she's at the law school now, and this is my friend Rita," Nina said, pointing at the photo. "And this . . . this is Tanya, looking crazed. She was the ringleader.

"The Black Student Union had met the night before the sit-in. We couldn't reach consensus on how to press our demands for an ethnic studies department. San Francisco State, San Jose State, U.C.L.A., and a lot of other campuses had already done their thing. The problem at Mills was that we were few in number and the sisters came from diverse backgrounds. Nobody wanted to be called an Uncle Tom, but a lot of girls were worried about what Mama and Daddy would say. Anyway, the next day we were supposed to be meeting for more discussion. Instead of talking, a core group, including me, bullied the rest of the girls into participating in a demonstration. A classic case of mob psychology."

"What's this part about a fight?" David asked.

"Well, that was when things got interesting. It was supposed to be a peaceful demonstration—take over the bookstore and close down operations until our demands were met. What we hadn't anticipated was that some of the White students objected strongly. When we got inside, the shopkeeper looked up, saw all these bushy-haired women, locked her register, and got the hell out.

"Most of the students who were shopping left quickly and quietly. A few even expressed sympathy for our cause. But there was this general's daughter and her group of friends who refused to leave. They started shouting that they had a right to buy their books without interference from 'you people.' Why did they say that? Tanya went off. Next thing I knew, I was in the middle of a shoving match, us against them, to see who would control the bookstore. Nobody was thinking, just reacting.

"The pushing and shoving escalated into punching. Shit was flying everywhere: books, toiletries, candy, whatever. Even the middle-of-the-road sisters were going toe-to-toe. I remember this mild-mannered woman from Alabama throwin' down with an umbrella.

"When it was over I could barely breathe. I hadn't been that worn out since my last fight in elementary school. I was so pumped, I couldn't stand still. We were inside with the door locked and they were outside, yelling, screaming, and banging against the door. The adrenaline slowed about ten minutes after the combat ended. We had to face the inevitable question, 'What now?' We hadn't planned for the aftermath, so there we were, with nowhere to go."

"If you'd been anywhere but Mills they would've sent the riot squad in and rousted you," David said.

"That is so true. At the time we didn't know what to expect. A couple of sisters panicked. They wanted to leave before the police came to haul our asses off to jail. We were too far down the road to turn back, so we sat down and waited. A representative from the administration finally showed up and agreed to negotiate under less stressful circumstances."

David shook his head and said, "I can't imagine you doing something like that."

"I can't imagine it either. It didn't hit me until it was over that I had taken a major risk. They could've pulled my scholarship like that," she said, snapping her fingers, "and I would have been out on my behind. My mother had a fit when she read about it in the paper. I had always been so well behaved. That's when we had our first woman-to-woman talk. She started laying down the law, as usual. I got real quiet, then calmly explained to her that I did what I had to do. For me, it was liberating, the first time I stood up for something important without thinking about the consequences. I was fighting for my dignity. I wasn't afraid anymore. My mother backed down, which was a real surprise. She looked at me and said, 'Maybe if my generation had done more, yours wouldn't have to fight so hard. Just be careful.' At that moment I felt closer to my mother than ever before."

"What happened after that?" David asked.

"We got our ethnic studies department and a commitment to recruit more Black students. More important, we got some respect. A lot of the students had never come into contact with Black people, and it showed in their attitudes.

"Fortunately, there were some hip White chicks who balanced out that kind of thinking. They were going through their own rebellions, rejecting many of the traditions that hemmed them in. The only thing I regret is that I was so busy resisting, trying to change the system, I didn't have the luxury of enjoying my surroundings. It was a world at the opposite end from my existence.

"Mills College was like heaven compared to Berkeley. Berkeley is so big and impersonal. You have to wait in line for everything, including a chance to be told 'No, you can't get any financial aid.' "

"Sounds like you got spoiled."

"I did. Mills had a definite impact, even though I couldn't see it. I had the time of my life. No worries, totally optimistic; the opposite of how I'm feeling now."

"What do you want that you don't already have?"

"Oh, I don't know. I could think of a few things. Can I keep this picture?"

"Sure. Do you have any more wild stories to tell?"

"No. That was the wildest, destined to remain a distant memory unless you keep dredging it up."

After dinner Nina changed into a floor-length, hooded caftan to get comfortable before studying. She made a final foray into the kitchen, allegedly for water.

"You don't expect me to sit here and work while you parade around in that outfit? Come here and let me see what's under it." David squeezed the off-white gauzelike fabric in his hands. "Just as I suspected, nothing but flesh, soft, tender flesh," he said, pulling her down on the couch beside him and pushing the caftan up to her waist.

Nina reclined, allowing her left leg to dangle to the floor and propping the right one against the back of the couch. He kissed the inside of her thighs, methodically working his way up until he reached the intended destination. David's mouth played her like an instrument.

When the song was finished he said, "I made you messy."

"Yes you did."

"I can fix it."

He filled the tub with gardenia-scented water, then led her upstairs to bathe by candlelight. Nina stepped into the bathtub, immersing herself from toe to chin. With a sponge David washed her back and every place he had touched her.

"Aren't you coming in?" she asked.

"No. This is for you."

"What did I do to deserve this?"

"You know what you did."

He blew away bubbles from chocolate rings around her nipples, watching them harden from the coolness of his breath. Then he lured her languid body from the water, dried her thoroughly, and took her to bed.

Lying in his arms, Nina made the announcement. "Guess what."

"What?"

"I got a job as a legal assistant to Roland Hill."

His body stiffened, creating a space between them. "I thought you were too busy with school and the campaign to take on anything else."

"That's true, but I have to eat. I thought you'd be happy."

"I am happy, but it's not wise to get too involved with him."

"What does that mean?"

"I don't want to see you disappointed."

"You don't think Roland will win, do you?"

"No."

"Can Donna Dixon win?"

"The numbers say she can't, but we've gotta have somebody to vote for."

"So you're saying you're voting for Donna."

"I'm not saying anything, and I'd prefer not to argue about it."

"We're not arguing. I'm asking your personal opinion."

"Okay. I don't think Roland will win because he's known to flip-flop when it's politically expedient. For example, Roland was slow to speak out for affirmative action until it was safe to get on board."

"I read him the riot act on that position. He's had questionable people advising him. Give him credit though—he *did* get on board."

"Belatedly. We don't need a mayor who checks the political pulse before he makes a move."

"He isn't like that at all," Nina said.

"You asked for my personal opinion. Maybe I'm wrong, but I don't think so. My advice is, don't let Roland monopolize your time."

Nina decided to wait to tell David about her expanded role in Roland's campaign. The mention of Roland had put a damper on the party. "I have to read a few cases before class in the morning. Can you survive without me?"

"I'll try." David looked concerned as she walked from the room.

Over strenuous objections from Austin, Roland rented the ballroom in a major downtown hotel for the biggest fund-raising event of the campaign. As Nina had predicted, ticket sales were brisk and the proceeds easily covered the initial outlay.

Nina was dazzling in her first new dress since high school. Bell-bottom jeans, assorted cutoffs, and an occasional skirt had rounded out her college wardrobe. She had seen the dress, costing a month's wages, in the Joseph Magnin display window. After two weeks of fantasizing she broke down, went inside, and asked to see it. With raised eyebrows the sales lady appraised her. Nina persisted. The satin low-back, glamour-queen dress looked strange with leather criss-cross sandals. But Nina had a vision of

herself—hair together, accessories right, perfect makeup—
gliding in on David's arm.

She plopped down her only credit card and prayed she
wasn't over the limit. The sales lady's attitude softened
when the transaction miraculously cleared.

"Shall we send your package or will you be carrying it,
Miss Lewis?"

"I'll be carrying it, thank you." Nina waltzed past the
perfumed ladies of Joseph Magnin with her dream dress.

The dream turned into a nightmare the minute David and
Nina entered the hotel. David was whisked away by a determined woman who seemed to know him quite well. Nina
had no time to complain. She was commandeered to take
care of nonglamorous details, such as paying the caterer
and finding seats for guests whose reservations had been
overlooked somehow. Sequestered in a dreary room with no
windows, she wondered what happened to the rest of the
committee. She suspected sabotage, but was too busy to
take on Austin. While the Black Napoleon retained the title
of campaign manager, he had dropped all of the grunt work
on Nina's shoulders.

During Nina's infrequent passes through the ballroom,
she glimpsed David huddled with a succession of people,
mostly female. He was in his glory, animatedly mingling
and obviously not the least bit concerned about her. She
even saw him dancing, to a fast song, with a woman bearing an amazing resemblance to the nude photograph she
had seen at his house.

"I must be seeing things," she convinced herself.

Nina watched as Roland and Austin posed with notables
from state government and the local community.

By midnight Nina was zonked. Her feet ached in new
shoes that matched her dream dress. Her head throbbed re-
lentlessly. She hadn't had a minute to relax or have a drink
to calm her frazzled nerves. Thankfully, the crowd was
thinning out. David was sitting at a table with two women
vying for his attention. During a break in his flirting, he
turned around, spotted Nina, and waved casually in her di-

rection. She gave him a smirk instead of a smile and was tempted to flash him the finger, but she managed to maintain her composure.

Alone in her misery, Nina started toward the bar, then realized that her purse was in the back room. As she hobbled out from the back, she ran into Roland, who pulled her aside.

"I saw you come in with David. What's goin' on?"

"I'm going to buy myself a drink, pray that God will have mercy, and end this party soon."

"That's not what I meant. David's a reporter, a very aggressive reporter. In case you hadn't noticed, he's been doing reconnaissance all night. I can't have him pumping you for inside information about the campaign."

"He's not pumping me for anything. We rarely talk about the campaign. Do I look stupid to you?"

"I know you're not stupid, but David's methods are very sophisticated."

"What are you talking about, Roland? I'm tired, my feet hurt, and I wish you would get to the point."

"Nothing. Just be careful with him. Maybe I'm being paranoid. Let me buy you a drink. That's the least I could do. I know you've been working nonstop all night."

David intercepted them as they walked toward the bar. "Hey, baby, where you been?" he had the nerve to ask.

Nina took a deep breath and kept moving toward the liquor.

"I know you're not upset with me. I was trying to keep out of the way," David explained.

"A glass of white wine, please. No, make that a gin and tonic." Nina addressed herself to the bartender, purposely ignoring David.

"Say, man, I see you're robbing the cradle." Roland turned to David.

"You wish you had a cradle to rob," David said.

Nina's mouth flew open. They were talking about her as if she weren't there.

"I guess Nina told you about her position as my special assistant," Roland said.

"She told me she was working as your legal assistant," David responded.

"No. I'm not talking about that. Nina has agreed to be my *special* assistant in the campaign." Roland stuck his chest out, like a man who had just gotten over.

"Is that right?" David stood there looking at Nina.

Nina was fed up with the word game in which she was apparently the pawn. "I don't know what the problem is between you two, but I'm tired. When you can break away from your entourage, David, let me know. I'd like to go home."

The arguing started the minute they hit the parking lot. David burned rubber in the T-Bird, speeding away from the hotel.

"Take me home," Nina insisted.

"What? To your house?" he asked.

"Yes, to my house."

"You're too fine to go home alone."

"Don't start that shit with me, David. I wasn't too fine to ignore all night."

"I don't get it. I thought I was doing you a favor by giving you space. As far as I'm concerned, we could've stayed home. You forced me to go."

"I didn't realize it was such an imposition."

"It's not that. I don't enjoy that kind of party."

"It looked like you were having fun to me."

"What was I supposed to do while you were holed up in the back room?"

"Ask if I needed anything. A drink, a glass of water, something to eat."

"The food was terrible. You wouldn't have enjoyed it."

"It would've been nice to decide that for myself."

"I admit, I'm a little jealous of the attention you've been giving Roland. When you're not in his office, you're on the phone talking to him. And now you're his special assistant. What does that mean?"

Nina "igged" him big time. She wasn't about to answer his question.

"I'm sorry, baby. You're entitled to your own opinions. Don't make me sleep by myself," he begged. David parted her legs and leaned over to kiss her. She relaxed and let his hand climb higher.

Nina was losing it and she knew it. She sat back, closed her eyes, and let him have his way.

Chapter Seven

"YOU'VE BEEN MOPING around, acting frosty. What is it, Nina?" Roland asked.

"You know what it is. I can't believe the way you and David carried on the other night." Nina laid down her pencil and made eye contact with Roland for the first time that day.

"That was just a man thang, Nina. Two old geezers kicking each other around. Don't let it worry you."

"It was more than that. You were hostile toward each other and disrespectful toward me."

"There was certainly no disrespect intended. I apologize if it came across that way. I'm concerned about you, Nina. I can tell by the way you look at him. David has your nose wide open. That can be dangerous for someone so young."

"Wait a minute, Roland. The fact that I'm working for you doesn't give you the right to monitor my personal life. I appreciate the concern, but I'm capable of taking care of myself. Since you're getting into my business, I might as well get into yours. I was surprised that Brenda was a no-show at the biggest fund-raiser of this campaign. You know how important public appearances are to a politician."

Roland hesitated, obviously uncomfortable. "She was there for a minute, but got a headache and had to leave. I might as well tell you now since it's bound to come up. Brenda and I are having problems, typical marital stuff. It hasn't helped that I'm away from home so much. She'll get over it."

"I hope so. We could use a devoted wife at your side

during public appearances. And Matthew, people will eat him up; he's adorable."

"I'll see what I can do on that score." Roland walked from behind his desk and put his hand on Nina's shoulder. "Regarding the other matter, I'll stop playing big brother and get out of your business. You know if you need me, Nina, all you have to do is holler."

Nina looked up at Roland. She put her hand on top of his and replied, "I know you mean that, Roland, and I appreciate it."

"Well." Interrupted by the sound of a woman's voice, Nina was surprised to see Brenda standing in the doorway, wearing a full-length red fox coat over blue jeans tucked into knee-high boots.

"Brenda, this is quite a surprise. We were just talking about you," Roland said.

"You missed a big party the other night," Nina chimed in, preparing to exit.

"Come in, sit down." Roland pulled a chair out for her.

"I hope I'm not interrupting anything," Brenda said suspiciously.

"Of course not," Roland answered.

"I thought maybe we could have lunch today, if you're not too busy," Brenda suggested, glancing toward Nina. "Can you spare him for a few minutes, Nina?"

"Of course we can. I could use the time to draft some letters. Listen, it's great seeing you, Brenda. I'll get out of the way and let you two have lunch." Nina hurried out of Roland's office.

Nina wasn't sure why, but Brenda made her nervous. It was a vibe coming out of nowhere, inexplicable and unsettling. Granted, she instantly felt like a frump in the presence of Miss Model Perfect, but that wasn't it. Overdressed women with static hair and globs of makeup never intimidated her before. She wondered if Brenda might be jealous of the time she was spending with Roland, but Brenda didn't fit the mold of an insecure wife.

Nina watched as Brenda walked over to Austin's desk

and warmly embraced the man. Nina had never seen Austin display so much warmth toward anyone. He fawned over Brenda, making a big deal about the fur coat, which was not the antique store variety most women were wearing. Brenda promised to stop and chat with Austin when they returned from lunch. Nina couldn't believe what she was seeing, a Black version of a bad soap opera—kissey, kissey, kissey.

Nina worked for another hour and a half before preparing to leave. She left a note for Roland and headed home to study. Austin barely grunted when she said good-bye on the way out the door.

Nina couldn't blame Austin for being resentful. She had tried to make amends, but their relationship was permanently strained. He hated her guts, no ifs, ands, or maybes. The wisest thing to do was to stay out of his way. Nina had insisted that Austin retain the title of campaign manager, but it was clear to everyone that Nina was the one Roland consulted whenever he made a decision. Nina sometimes felt uncomfortable in the office, as if she were being watched. Certain supporters loyal to Austin searched for ways to put her down.

It was always the same in every organization, everybody jockeying for position. When Roland had asked what spot Nina wanted in the new administration, she was honestly able to answer "None." She had decided to make a go of her legal career, even if it killed her.

After studying a few hours, Nina phoned David to see what he was doing.

"You coming over?" he asked.

"No, I get too distracted over there." They laughed. "What are you doing tonight?"

"I'll probably work on my article."

"Yeah, right. I hear you puffing on that joint."

"A man has to get into the proper frame of mind before committing to hard labor." David exaggerated the sound of exhaling smoke on the other end.

"Call me before you go to bed tonight," she said dreamily.

"Okay, baby. Study hard."

Addicted to lying next to him, it was a struggle to sleep in her own bed. She had to snap out of it and concentrate on the outline for community property, the class she dreaded the most. A simple subject, taught by a boring professor—it was hard to stay awake.

Estrellita was in the other room using a unique method of studying, transcendental meditation. If the nerves are calm, the answers will automatically flow into the brain, according to Estrellita. By midnight Nina was considering adopting Estrellita's study method. She had planned to stay up all night, break for a few hours, and study into the following evening. Despite good intentions, Nina's head kept inching toward the pillow.

"Lita, you have any No-Doz?" Nina yelled toward Estrellita's bedroom. No answer. She walked across the hall and found the meditation queen sacked out on the bed.

"I need No-Doz."

"I don't have any. The only drugs I use are pure and natural, of the herbal variety." Estrellita yawned.

"Let me borrow your car to run to the drugstore," Nina said.

"The keys are on the table." Estrellita turned over to do some serious sleeping.

"I hope there's enough gas to get me there," Nina said, grabbing loose change from the dresser. "I don't want to stop for anything." She jumped in the Bug and headed toward the drugstore, hoping to make a quick round trip. A few blocks from the house flashing lights barreled down from behind. She wasn't speeding, so she veered toward the curb to allow the police to go around her. Loud music playing on the car radio muffled the sounds coming from outside. The police car tailed close to her bumper. She pulled over and stopped to see what was up. Red, white, and blue lights whirled behind her. A second police car pulled directly in front, blocking her in.

"Get out of the car," she heard them yell amid the confusion. Nina reached for her purse but found nothing but empty space. A policeman with his hand on his holster tugged at the door handle, warning her to come out with her hands up.

Nina exited the car slowly. The policeman backed up two steps. His hand was planted on the handle of his gun, ready to clear leather.

"Officer, there must be some mistake. I wasn't speeding," Nina said.

"I didn't say you were speeding," he shouted back. "Go around and check the other side of the car. She was reaching for something," he said to his partner.

"I was looking for my purse," Nina tried to explain.

"Keep your mouth shut unless I ask you a question, understand?"

Nina was baffled by his behavior. She couldn't understand why going to the store for No-Doz could subject her to this type of treatment.

"Joe, you need any more assistance on this?" the policeman from the car parked in front of the Volkswagen asked.

"No, I think we can handle it from here. Thanks, buddy."

He turned to his partner who was busy searching the car. "Find anything?"

By now Nina was praying, hoping Estrellita hadn't left any contraband in the ashtray.

"Why didn't you stop when I flashed you?"

"I slowed down immediately. I thought you were after someone else," Nina answered.

Gruffly he said, "I don't know where you're from, but around here, we stop when a police officer turns his lights on."

The futility of the situation was sinking in. Nina shut up and looked at him.

"License and registration," he demanded.

"The registration is in the glove compartment. My license is in my purse, which I was looking for when you stopped me."

"Harold, you see a purse in the car?" he asked his partner.

"No purse in here," the partner yelled back, still searching.

"What's your name?"

"Nina Lewis."

"Sure. And my name is Howdy Doody. Estrellita Brown, you're under arrest for outstanding parking warrants." He started to read her her rights.

"Wait, wait. I'm not Estrellita Brown. I'm Nina Lewis. I borrowed my roommate's car to run to the store. I only live a few blocks from here. Take me to my house and I can show you my license."

"Turn around and face the car," he ordered.

The sound of handcuffs clamping on her wrists was the first shock. The only thing she could think about was her mother's advice: "Wear good underwear in case you get in an accident." Nina wondered if this qualified as an accident.

The unreality of what was happening took hold when she found herself riding in the backseat of a patrol car headed for jail. Strangely enough, she could not focus on her dilemma, but zeroed in on cryptic radio messages as they carted her off like baggage.

The police car came to an unnecessarily abrupt halt as they pulled in at the station. Without the benefit of hands to stop her movement, she lunged forward. The officer on the passenger side jumped out to open her door. He pulled Nina from the backseat with such force that she almost fell face forward on the ground. She wondered why she was being treated inhumanely, then remembered that she was now on the other end of the system, a criminal until proven otherwise. The policeman clutched her arm with such intensity that it grew numb.

"Lighten up on the arm. I can't run my best hundred-yard dash with my arms handcuffed behind me." He was annoyed by her attempt at humor. She started laughing to keep from crying.

By now Nina's head pounded repeatedly with jack-hammer force. At least she didn't need No-Doz. She was wide awake. Nina asked a policewoman walking by for an aspirin. She kept walking, as if Nina were invisible. A woman sitting next to her, also awaiting booking, lifted her head and spoke.

"You must be new here, honey. You ain't gonna get no aspirin until after they book you and then, only if you beg." The woman's matted blond wig was pushed to one side. She kept wiggling like she had an itch that needed to be scratched. "Damn, I'd give anything to get a cigarette. You don't have any cigarettes, do you?"

"No, sorry, I don't," Nina replied.

A constant flow of policemen moved through the narrow corridor, seemingly oblivious to the prisoners lining the hallway. Nina worried that someone she knew would walk past and see her restrained, like an animal, to a backbreaking hardwood bench.

Her resolve not to cry weakened. Tears began to form, but she was taken in for processing before fear could kick in full blast. Each finger was rolled across a blackened pad to make an imprint on white paper. The purplish dye embedded itself beneath her nails. When the flashbulb exploded, she thought of David and the time he had her photographed at campaign headquarters. Somehow, she didn't expect this picture to turn out as well.

As she was pushed inside a windowless room, she heard someone comment loudly, "I'd be willing to search that one. Whadya think, man? Heh heh."

"Listen, Officer, this is absurd. There's no reason to search me. You already took all my belongings. I have no way of hiding anything."

"Take off your clothes and be quiet," the Black policewoman ordered.

Nina turned her back and slowly began removing her blouse.

"You get butt naked in less than one minute or I'll have the boys undress you," she threatened, wielding a baton.

Nina was determined not to grovel. She wouldn't let them break her. When she turned around, the officer touched underneath each breast.

Nina said, "What are you looking for? May I ask?"

The officer circled around Nina, stepped back, and said, "Bend over and spread your legs."

"You expecting to find a gun up my ass, Officer?" Sarcasm was the only weapon Nina had left. Outside, she could hear people laughing. Her humiliation was a comedy in process.

The officer approached Nina's exposed flanks with a pocket-size flashlight and shined it up the most private of parts.

"Finished yet, Fraulein?" Nina inquired with as much dignity as possible with her head hanging between her knees. When lady cop was done, she allowed Nina to get dressed.

"You get one phone call." The policewoman dropped a dime in the slot.

"Just like in the movies," Nina mumbled while dialing David's number. No answer. She hung up and tried it again. Seeing the impatience on the officer's face, she decided to try Estrellita before the woman changed her mind. "Please answer, please answer," Nina begged. After what felt like an eternity, Estrellita answered the phone.

"Thank God. Lita, listen carefully. I'm in jail for parking tickets."

"What! Parking tickets? You don't have a car."

"I know that, but they don't. I was driving your car and I didn't have my license with me. They thought I was you."

"Where's the car? What about the car?" Estrellita asked.

"Fuck the car! Just come down here and get me. I need three hundred dollars for bail. I know you don't have the money, but call around and see if you can get it. I tried David, but he's not answering the phone. Are you writing this down?"

"Yes, yes." Estrellita fumbled. "I'm on it. I'll be there as soon as I get the money. Be strong, my sister, keep the faith, baby, *venceremos* . . ." Estrellita rattled off a series of slogans.

Nina cut her short. "Not now, Lita. Get up, get the money, and move quickly."

Nina was locked inside a cell with two other people, who were so out of it that they barely looked up when she entered. Hyperventilating, she had to slow her breathing to keep from freaking out. Nina had a mild case of claustrophobia, which she had discovered while trapped inside an apartment elevator crammed with people on their way to a party. All the cool had gone out of the cool people. Nina survived that ordeal by closing her eyes, standing very still, and pretending she was someplace else. She didn't know what was worse, being at the mercy of an elevator or at the mercy of Estrellita, who was probably turning in circles in the middle of the floor.

Giving in to negative thoughts would be disastrous. Stay calm, keep breathing, cling to sanity. She sat on the floor, crossed her ankles and turned her palms up to meditate. The steel bands squeezing steadily against her temples gradually loosened.

Her cellmates looked at each other, shaking their heads. A prostitute guessed, "She must be one of them hairy Christians."

"That's not what they're called. It's Hare Krishna," the other woman corrected her.

The prostitute lost interest, turned her back, and fell asleep.

Nina transcended the walls and felt cool breezes blowing. The ocean roared within arm's reach. Nothing could hold her, nothing could harm her. She was weightless, invisible, outside her body.

"Estrellita Brown." The guard's voice awakened her from deep meditation. She asked what time it was. It was five A.M. She had been inside this hellhole for hours.

"I'm not Estrellita Brown. I'm Nina Lewis," she answered defiantly.

"Well, whoever you are, you've been bailed out."

Nina rose quickly and followed the guard through two sets of security doors. They ended up in the same corridor where Nina had been handcuffed to the hardwood bench. The guard handed her an envelope containing her valuables and pointed toward the exit. Instead of racing out to freedom, she hesitated at the door. The trauma had made her knees weak. She broke out in a cold sweat as she walked through to the other side.

The second she appeared she was swallowed in a wave of angry students, shouting "Free Nina, Free Nina." There were Sheila, Estrellita, and at least ten others who alternated between congratulating Nina and shouting accusations at the police on duty. The desk sergeant warned them to leave quickly or face arrest. T.J. stood on top of a chair, shook his clenched fist, and led the group in a chorus of "Power to the People."

Nina was too drained for a repeat confrontation. Seeing that she was close to collapsing, Sanford forcibly yanked T.J. down from the chair. Two brothers helped him pull T.J. away, screaming "You muthafuckin' pigs haven't heard the last of this. We'll sue you for false arrest." The group trailed out to the parking lot. Hastily made signs that read "Free Nina" and "End the Oppression" were taped on a four-car caravan. Nina surprised herself when she laughed. She thought she'd never laugh again. Sheila ushered Nina to her car, refusing to let anyone else in.

"Give her a break, man. She's been through a lot," Sheila insisted. Nina heard Estrellita inviting everyone over to the house to celebrate.

"What do you feel like doing? You don't have to deal with this madness, if you don't want to. We can sneak away and go to my house where it's quiet," Sheila suggested.

Nina leaned her head back and took a few deep breaths. "I'm feeling pretty spaced right now, but it wouldn't be right to ignore them. They came down to help me out. I probably should go home."

"You sure?" Sheila asked.

"I'm sure. Thanks, Sheila." Nina started working on clearing her head.

Everything was exactly as she had left it the night before. The community property textbook was on the nightstand turned to the same page. Her purse was on the couch where she had left it.

The rest of the group streamed in within two minutes of their arrival. Music jammed on the stereo. Sheila cleared a table to get a game going. Sanford suggested breakfast, which started a fight over what to eat.

"I won't allow any hog to be cooked in my kitchen," Estrellita, the vegetarian, insisted.

"Listen to this shit, man. Madam Moonbeam's trying to tell everybody else what to eat. I want grits, eggs, and a big slab of pig to wash it down," T.J. proclaimed loudly.

"Let's get a variety of food. I promise to replace the pan soiled by the hog," Sheila said. "The big question is, who's paying for this?"

They looked around sheepishly. Nina felt guilty. They had probably pooled what little money they had bailing her out.

"Let me see what I have in my purse," Nina offered.

"Nonsense, you're the guest of honor," Sheila said, and started going from person to person, fleecing their pockets. "Give it up, people."

Nina pulled Estrellita aside. "Where did you get the bail money?"

"Don't worry about it," Estrellita said.

"But I am worried about it. You know I don't like to owe anyone anything."

"Well, I tried to raise the money among this group, but we came up short. T.J. had fifty dollars, but everybody else was pretty low on cash. So I called Roland."

"You *what*?"

"It was either call him or let you sit in jail until the bank opened this morning. We caravaned up to his house and then picked you up from jail."

Nina was mortified that Roland knew she was in jail.

"He was really nice about it," Estrellita continued. "He wanted to come down himself, but I told him it might not be a good idea with him running for mayor and all. T.J. tried to egg him on. I had to muzzle him, as always."

"Did Brenda hit the ceiling?" Nina asked.

"You mean his wife? I don't know. I didn't see her. Everybody except T.J. waited outside while I dashed in to get the money. His neighbors must have flipped when we pulled up in front of his house so early in the morning. Roland was really concerned. He wants you to call and let him know you're all right. Why don't you do that now? I can handle this group."

Nina went to the phone in her bedroom and dialed, hoping Brenda wouldn't answer.

"Roland, this is Nina."

"Nina, are you okay?" He sounded frantic.

"Yes, I'm fine. A little shaken, but fine."

"I was so worried. I've been walking the floor since Estrellita called. What happened?"

Nina started telling the story, unemotionally at first, then began reliving the nightmare all over. Suppressed tears, waiting for the right moment, fell uncontrollably. She was embarrassed but couldn't hold it in any longer.

"I'm coming down there right now. I should have come to the police station," Roland said.

"No. Please don't come. I was doing fine until I started talking to you, and then it hit me. I wanted to cry all night, but I couldn't. My friends are here, so I'll be okay. I wanted to thank you for bailing me out."

"That's nothing. You sure you don't need me? I could be there in fifteen minutes."

"No, that's not necessary. You've done too much already. Besides, I don't think it would go over very well with Brenda."

There was a long pause at the other end of the phone. "What she thinks is totally irrelevant. If you need me, just call. Don't worry about this little incident. I'll have one of the lawyers at my office on it first thing in the morning.

This will never go on your record, and I'll have them apologizing to you. Guarantee it."

"Roland, I can't thank you enough."

"You already have. Get some sleep and throw that bunch of rowdies out when they start getting on your nerves. I'll check on you a little later."

Reassured, Nina hung up and sat on the side of the bed. She was lucky to have a friend like Roland. Without him she might still be languishing in jail. Nina tried David's number again. Still no answer. She gave up and joined the party.

When the frenzy surrounding the food subsided, she stepped outside and sat next to a cactus shaped like a man carrying a tray. The streets were still quiet and the sun was slowly rising. Every breath of fresh air was a blessing. She inhaled deeply and thanked God for her freedom. Last night was the first time she had prayed in the years since she had shunned organized religion. She was glad she could still make a spiritual connection and even happier that God had not forgotten her.

T.J. came out to join her. "I—I'm," he stuttered. For once T.J. was speechless. Nina watched as he stood against the background of a purple and tangerine sunrise, searching for words to express his feelings.

She stood up, put her arm around his shoulder, and said, "It's okay. I'm fine."

"Aw, man, I came out here to comfort you and now my shit is shaky," T.J. confided.

"My shit's been pretty shaky too." Nina laughed.

"It hurts me when we can't protect our women."

"You did your best and I appreciate it. You had me scared in the police station, though. I thought you were going to start a riot."

"I would have, if the brothers hadn't held me back."

"They would've put you in jail and we'd be raising money for your bail. Thanks for chipping in on the bail. I'll pay you back next week."

"Don't sweat it. I would've blown the money on an o.z.

or some shit like that. . . . Getting back to the apology I started some time ago. I want to say I'm sorry for being abrasive at times. My mouth gets a bit grandiose, but I didn't mean any harm."

"I should record this for posterity." Nina laughed. "Seriously, your apology is accepted. Your concern means a lot to me."

Estrellita sailed out the door, interrupting their quiet conversation.

"What's this? A private party?" she inquired.

"No. What's goin' on?" Nina asked.

"I need a partner for Spades."

"You must be talking to T.J. You know how I feel about card games." Nina excused herself as T.J. obliged.

Time alone to sort out her feelings was what she needed. Nina wrapped her arms around her legs and rested her head against her thighs. She needed comforting, she needed healing. The man who could give it to her was nowhere to be found. Scenes from the jail kept recurring. I should have done this, I should have said that. Nina chided herself for not being more in control. She finally let go, knowing she had done the only thing she could do, which was to survive.

"You are dumber than I thought!" T.J.'s shouting jarred her from a light nap. For a split second she thought she was back in jail.

T.J. was yelling at the top of his voice. "How the hell can you be black and brown at the same time? That shit don't work."

Nina rushed inside to find T.J. and Estrellita at each other's throats. Estrellita was so flustered, she couldn't get a sentence out.

"The Chicanos are competing against us in the special admissions program and to get funding for their projects. Our budget was cut last year to make room for their demands. The administration isn't making more resources available. They're cutting up the pie into smaller pieces as more groups become active. Now the Asians are trying to get into the act. Who's next?" T.J. said.

"Are you trying to say that other groups don't have the same rights as Blacks to determine their own destiny?" Estrellita argued.

"No, but I am saying that we have to prioritize the needs of our people in this struggle against The Man."

"The struggle can be maintained on many different fronts, through individual action, group action, and through ethnic coalitions."

"You go in there talking about dealing with us, the Chicanos will kick your black ass out. The reality of this world is that you're either black, brown, red, yellow, or white, and never the twain shall meet."

"That's enough, T.J." Nina jumped in T.J.'s face, separating him from Estrellita. "We're all tired. It's time for everybody to go home."

"You don't have to take up for me," Estrellita insisted, edging her short, petite body in front of Nina.

"The sister's right. It's time for me to split." T.J. moved toward the door and the rest of the group filtered out behind him.

Sheila offered to help clean up the mess, but Nina said she would take care of it. At this point she just wanted everyone out. She could hear Estrellita taking out her anger on the pots and pans in the kitchen.

"I know you're not letting T.J. bum you out," Nina told Estrellita.

"That bastard disrespected me in front of everybody."

"You have to take T.J. with a grain of salt. He's highly intelligent, very energetic, and so wrapped up in himself that he doesn't make room for other people. He's a Johnny-come-lately to the struggle. T.J. never lived in the segregated South, but he condemns southern Blacks for 'allowing' Whites to discriminate against them. He never rode at the back of the bus, yet he disparages the nonviolent strategies used to integrate the bus system. T.J. never worked in the fields with migrant farm workers, but he knows everything about their plight."

"What do you know about farm workers?" Estrellita asked.

"In the early sixties I did a brief stint picking tomatoes in the Napa Valley. The media was paying a lot of attention to Mexican farm workers, called Braceros, who were brought into this country to work the fields. Some U.S. politicians got the idea that Americans should be doing the work. The only people they could get to do it were poor Americans like me. Every morning at five o'clock we were picked up at the unemployment office and driven to the valley to harvest fruits and vegetables. It was the worst job I ever had. We shivered as cold air whipped us mercilessly in the back of open pickup trucks. By nine in the morning the sun choked the moisture from the air, roasting us in a desert of dryness. We were paid according to the number of crates we filled and stacked. Thirty-five cents per fifty-pound crate. I remember wobbling through the trenches dazed by sun spots that turned rows of red tomatoes into one continuous sheet of yellow.

"The Braceros, men, women, and babies, worked with machinelike precision. They rarely looked up, never recoiled from the moldy mush of an overripe tomato, or complained about the stifling heat. After work they disappeared into shanties, their temporary housing, only to return the next morning before daybreak to begin the process again.

"By week's end I was too sore to move, my back was hunched into what felt like a permanent arch. My hands were severely blistered, bleeding around the cuticles. Acid from tomatoes had eaten into my skin. While the politicians sat and debated the impact of Braceros on the U.S. economy, I hurt and the Mexicans hurt, no matter how well they masked it. Politicians couldn't begin to comprehend the human impact of their decisions.

"I can't tell you whether T.J. is right or wrong. I do know that being pitted against each other over crumbs is stupid. T.J. made one good point. Our circumstances are unique because our ancestors were brought to this country in chains. That fact permeates every area of our existence."

"What would you do in my situation?" Estrellita asked.

"I can't imagine being anything but Black, but I'm not in your situation. Do what feels right to you and don't let anyone, especially T.J., dictate your choice."

Chapter Eight

NINA PACED FOR hours, unable to relax, unable to sleep. Incarceration had wound her into a coil that wouldn't release no matter how hard she pulled against it. She tried David's number one last time. This time she got a busy signal. She slammed the phone down, angry that he was unavailable when she needed him most.

By noon the weight of emotion came crashing down on her. She lapsed into a deep sleep, awakening to the sound of rain thumping against the window. Cold and confused, she squinted at the alarm clock. She had slept longer than she had intended.

Estrellita was bumbling around in the kitchen, concocting a blend of herbal tea. "Did you get some sleep?" she asked.

"I got sleep and then some. How long has it been raining like this?"

"A couple of hours. I thought it would sprinkle and stop, but it's been going steady. Want some tea?"

"Yeah, I could use some warming up. Did anyone call?" Nina asked.

"Roland called to check on you about an hour after you lay down. He said not to wake you. David called an hour ago. Said he'd call back."

Nina sipped her tea slowly. She felt outside herself, as if the events of the last twenty-four hours happened to someone else. Maybe she was still tired, but there was no time to be tired. The exam was happening tomorrow morning whether she was ready or not. She propped herself up on

the bed and started studying. An hour into it David called
again.

"Hey, baby, what's happenin'?" he said casually.

With an edge to her voice Nina responded, "How can
you ask me that? Didn't Estrellita tell you?"

"Tell me what?"

"I spent the night in jail, that's what."

"Run that past me again."

Nina related the harrowing events of the previous night.

"I hate that you had to go through that. You should've
called me," David said.

"I did call you. All day and last night. Where were you,
David? I was a wreck."

"Don't be mad at me. One of my buddies called after we
talked last night and invited me out for a nightcap. We
cruised around, hit a few night spots, and before I knew it,
it was morning. After I got home I took the phone off the
hook so I could snooze for a couple of hours before going
in. I'm sorry, Nina, but I had no way of knowing what was
happening. Are you all right?"

"Yes, I'm okay now. My nerves are still frazzled, but I'll
live."

"Why don't I pick you up?"

"I'd like that, but I have to bring my books with me. I
have an exam in the morning."

As always, David knew how to relax her. He massaged
Nina from head to toe, loosening her neck, lower back,
calves, and ankles. Circling the pressure points at the bottom of her feet, he eased the tension considerably. When
the pampering was completed, he cleared a space in the
study for her to work.

Several times while she was reading she heard him talking on the phone. David was a man of many voices. The
timbre of his voice ranged from loud and rowdy to soft and
sexy, the latter trailing to a whisper followed by a rapid dis-
connect.

He held her protectively when she joined him in bed that night. But Nina was restless, unable to lie still.

David tried to reassure her. "I hope you're not still angry that I wasn't home last night. You know you're my main squeeze, Nina. You don't have to worry about that."

Nina hated the term "main squeeze." It prioritized people as chattel, which is exactly what she felt like after her jail ordeal. Coming from David, it was meant as a compliment. She let it slide until it started to bug her.

"I'm not worried about my ranking in your system of priorities."

"That's not what I meant."

"That's how it sounded."

"It's only a phrase, not the basis for an argument."

"You don't understand. Last night really shook me up. My life is so insecure, anything could've happened. If it wasn't for Roland, I'd still be in jail."

"What does he have to do with this?"

"He put up most of the bail money."

"So that's what this is about? You want me to be more like Roland—safe, secure, and predictable."

"There's nothing wrong with predictability. Roland has a beautiful home and a wonderful family."

"Everything looks good on the surface," David said.

"What's that supposed to mean?"

"You don't know Roland as well as you think."

"He was there when I needed him and you weren't."

"Quit comparing me to Roland. No matter how much you glorify him, I won't turn into a clone of Roland. That's not my bag and you know it."

"So what is your bag, David? What is this about?"

"Uh-oh. Here we go with twenty-one questions. Are you asking me to declare my intentions? You women . . ."

"Don't give me that 'you women' stuff. My name is Nina."

"It's too late for a heavy discussion. No matter what I say, it'll be the wrong thing. Can I have time to think before I put my foot in my mouth?"

"Take all the time you need." Nina jumped out of bed and grabbed the comforter. She tossed one corner over her naked shoulder and let the rest trail behind her down the stairs.

Bewildered, David asked, "Where're you going with the cover?"

"To the couch."

"You gonna leave me hanging like this?"

"Yes," Nina answered curtly before curling up on the living room couch.

During the ride to school the next morning, they exchanged barely two words. Nina had gotten up early enough to catch the bus, if necessary, but heavy rain made the prospect unpleasant. David knew better than to let her fend for herself when the weather was as foul as her mood.

Nina grabbed her book bag and exited the Thunderbird without a kiss or a good-bye. They arrived at the same time as Sheila, who whiffed Nina's attitude from twenty yards away.

"Girl, what is the matter? You didn't look this pissed after spending the night in jail," Sheila said.

"I don't know, maybe it's just me. Why do I always get involved with the wrong kind of man?"

"If there's such a thing as the right kind, please let me know." Sheila laughed, then heeded the dour expression on Nina's face. "Hey, you're getting pretty serious about David, aren't you?"

Nina looked down, shook her head, and decided not to answer. "It's too complicated to discuss right now. I have to take this stupid test. Call me later."

"I can give you a ride. I'm done at noon. You look like you need to talk."

"That sounds good. I'll meet you in the library."

For the first time in Nina's memory Sheila showed up on time.

"How was the test?" Sheila asked.

"Not as bad as I expected. There were no trick questions

and I knew most of the answers." Nina hesitated and added, "Maybe I'm too dumb to know what I don't know."

"Don't start making up stuff to freak out about. You wanna get something to eat?"

"I'm really not hungry. Maybe something to drink."

"I've got just the thing for you. Let's swing by the house while we think about it."

At her apartment Sheila pulled a bag stuffed full of weed from underneath the couch.

"Damn, Sheila. You've got enough reefer to service an army," Nina commented.

"Derrick picked this up last night. Roll us a joint while I scavenge up some wine."

Nina sat down and went about her task. She knew getting high in the middle of the day was bad news, but she felt like being bad. She pulled two papers from the package of ZigZags and glued them together. The bud was still clinging tightly to the stalks. She spread a little on the magazine to clean it before she rolled.

Sheila walked in, acting impatient. "You're not finished yet?"

"No, and if you don't like it, you can do it yourself," Nina warned.

"You know I can't roll worth a damn. Derrick has to roll mine for me."

"I have never heard of a dope dealer's woman who couldn't roll a joint," Nina kidded her. "Where is Derrick? I haven't seen him at school in ages."

"He's out and about. I'm getting concerned about him. He's spending more time dealing with this shit than going to class." Sheila grabbed the bag to make her point. "Derrick's problem is he's too smart for his own good. He can read through an outline and take a test with no sweat."

Nina sighed. "I wish I had that problem."

"Fire it up." Sheila tossed the matches.

Nina moistened the joint by running it through her lips, then leaned back and lit the end twisted the tightest. She took a hit, inhaled deeply, and held the smoke inside until she started coughing and gagging.

"What kinda shit is this?" Nina asked, choking.

"Derrick says it's Hawaiian. Whatever it is, it's a bomb. Don't hog the joint." Sheila took a few short puffs and blew ringlets from her mouth with the smoke.

"What are we doing, Sheila?"

"Gettin' high."

"No. I mean, what are we *really* doing?"

"I ask myself that question every morning and then I just get up and do what I have to do. It's not school that has you worried, is it?"

"No."

"I've never seen you like this. You were the calm, pragmatic one with all the answers until you met David. Admit it, Nina, David has your mind messed up and you can't stand being out of control."

Nina couldn't help but laugh. Sheila knew her better than anyone. "Yeah, you got me down cold," Nina confessed.

"I saw you getting out of the car this morning. Why were your lips all poked out?"

"I don't know. I'm mad at the world, especially David, and I'm not sure why. I want him to do something, but I don't know what. He's been good to me, but there's no sense of security."

"Security? What do you want? A deposit, nonrefundable in case of damage?"

"Don't make fun of me. This is serious business."

"I'm sorry. It's the herb talking."

"Maybe it's the age difference. I always feel tentative with David."

"With men it's always something—other women, work, sports, drugs, whatever. They can't exist without distraction. You haven't been together that long, so quit worrying," Sheila said.

"Every time we're together I wonder will it last. We're so different. David says 'go with the flow.' Whatever feels good. I act crazy sometimes, but I'm kind of old-fashioned."

"Kind of!" Sheila underscored the point and fell out laughing. Nina threw a pillow, then started laughing too. The sound of the key turning in the lock was drowned out by their rowdiness. In walked Derrick with a compact man wearing dark sunglasses, a black leather jacket, and a wide-brimmed leather hat.

"Sounds like you two are having fun. Ladies, this is Keith. Keith, this is my woman, Sheila, and her friend Nina."

Keith pulled narrow rectangular sunglasses below the bridge of his nose and said, "It's a pleasure to make the acquaintance of such exquisite lovelies."

Sheila and Nina nodded in his direction, trying hard to control themselves. Keith strutted into the back room with Derrick.

The coast was clear. They rolled on the floor in hysterics, covering their mouths to keep from being heard.

Wiping tears, Sheila asked, "What was that?"

Nina hunched her shoulders and shook her head. While Derrick and Keith conducted business in the back room, they downed goblets of sangria garnished with oranges.

Sheila's mood turned suddenly somber. She spoke in whispers. "You see the kind of shit I have to put up with. Strangers parading in and out of my house. I never know if they're a friend or someone to watch out for. This business of his is getting on my last nerve."

"Maybe I should go," Nina said.

"No, don't leave. They'll be done in a minute and I'll be sitting here by myself, feeling stupid. It's a revolving door around here. Derrick comes in, Derrick goes out. Wait until they come out and I'll tell him we're going to eat. I know you're hungry now."

Emerging loudly from the back room, Derrick was full of energy. His beady eyes danced in his head and his feet couldn't keep still. He startled everyone by copping a feel of Sheila's voluptuous chest without warning. All five feet six inches of Keith salivated in his tracks.

Sheila pulled away, gave Derrick the evil eye, and announced, "Nina and I are going out to eat."

In a surprise move Derrick responded, "Why don't we go with you? Keith and I could use some nourishment too."

"Uh . . . sure, if you like," Sheila said. "I'll drive."

Nina squeezed into the backseat of Derrick's car with Keith, who kept feeding her lines, hoping something would stick.

"Nina, I understand you're in law school. In my line of work I need to know lots of lawyers. Heh heh." Keith slapped Derrick on the shoulder to get an amen.

Sheila drove to the restaurant in stony silence. The men, oblivious to Sheila's mood, carried on like everything was fine.

At the restaurant, Keith approached the maître d' and asked, "Is there someplace I can take a piss?"

Derrick howled in amusement. Sheila rolled her eyes in disgust. Nina grabbed her wine, took several sips, and buried her face in the menu.

Upon returning to the dining room, Keith became an instant critic of the restaurant's decor. "How can anyone hang a moose head, tarnished bugles, old-assed pictures, and assorted junk from the ceiling and call it decorating?"

When no one answered, Keith increased the volume. "Is this called junkyard chic? I could make a killing cleaning out my grandmama's basement."

The waiter saved them from a more in-depth analysis by coming to take their order.

"I don't see fried chicken or fried fish on the menu," Keith complained to the flustered waiter. "What's the problem? Y'all don't get many soul brothers in here?"

"Sir, we pride ourselves on catering to the more health-conscious diner by minimizing the amount of oil and saturated fats in our selections," the waiter explained.

"I was just messin' with you, man. I don't want any food. Bring me a scotch on the rocks," Keith said.

"I have to apologize again, sir. We don't serve hard liquor, only beer and wine."

"Man, I need to hook you up with a friend of mine. He can get any kind of license you want." Flashing gold crowns proudly, Keith grinned at the waiter.

"Is there anything else you would like, sir?" the waiter asked.

"Get these ladies whatever they want. It's on me. Ain't these some fine sisters?"

Sheila placed her order before Keith could say another word. Nina ordered but wasn't sure she wanted to eat. Derrick and Keith drank their dinner, consisting of two bottles of white wine. Listening to Keith's never-ending tales about his property, his women, his this, and his that was almost as annoying as the slowness of the service.

Back at Sheila's apartment, Nina declined the invitation to come up. She could tell that Sheila was primed to lay a few choice words on Derrick.

"I'm going to drop Nina off. I'll be back in a minute," Sheila said.

"Which way is she going?" Keith asked.

Nina wanted to say whichever way you're not going, but she was polite. "I'm at the low end of Alcatraz."

"I can give you a lift. I'm going that way. You two lovebirds deserve some time alone. Sheila, it was a pleasure meeting you." Keith stepped forward and kissed the back of Sheila's hand.

"Ready to roll, mama?" he said to Nina, who suddenly felt trapped.

Making conversation wasn't a problem. Keith talked incessantly. By the time he pulled in front of the flat, Nina hadn't said more than two words. Across the street she spotted the Thunderbird. David was in it. She coudn't see his face, only the top of the red, black, and green knitted cap he wore to look fly. David's head leaned back against the seat, as if he were resting. His windows were fogged, streaming with rivulets from steady rain. Still, she could feel his prying eyes.

"Thanks for the ride, Keith. I gotta boogie," Nina said hurriedly.

"What's the rush? Can I get your number and other vital statistics? I enjoyed your company and I suspect you enjoyed mine."

"That's not possible, Keith. In fact, you should leave now."

"Why?" Keith persisted, leaning over to breathe on her.

"That's why." Nina nodded toward the T-Bird. David was opening the door to get out.

"Is that your man?"

"No. That's my husband." Nina lied to get rid of him.

"That's all you had to say, sweetheart." Keith zoomed away before Nina could close the car door completely.

"Did I run your boyfriend away?" David asked, swaggering toward her. "You didn't wait long before replacing me."

"The race is to the swift," Nina said, unlocking the door. She wouldn't give him the satisfaction of explaining Keith.

"Lita," Nina called out to see if her roommate was home. She tried again. "Man on the premises. She must not be here if she hasn't run out in her underwear."

"Who was that jive turkey who brought you home?"

"Are you speaking of Keith?" Nina said without blinking.

"Where do you know him from?"

"Possibly from the same place I know you. What difference does it make?"

"Don't do something stupid just to get back at me. If you needed a ride, all you had to do was call me."

"Why should I call you? You needed time to think, so I'm giving you time to think."

"Quit being stubborn. Let's go to my place so we can talk," David suggested.

"We can talk right here."

David backed her into a corner and tried to kiss her. She turned her head away.

"How much wine have you had?" he asked, pressing against her until she had no room to move.

"Enough. Now move, David."

"Like this?" Instead of moving, he unbuckled his belt and began lowering his pants. Estrellita strolled in to surprise them.

"Hi, guys . . . oops." Estrellita backed out the doorway and knocked, giving them a chance to regroup. Nina fled to her room. David walked in behind her and closed the door.

"I'm sure Estrellita has seen worse. Don't be embarrassed." David tried to comfort her.

"Estrellita's not the reason I'm embarrassed. I'm embarrassed by my own behavior. I swore I wouldn't let you come in here, whip out your dick, and get over on me."

"It's not like that between us. It's more than just a physical thing. . . . I love you, Nina."

She could tell from his expression, David had shocked himself. He looked like a baby going "uh-oh" after taking his first step.

"Now . . . I said it. Are you satisfied?" he asked.

Nina started smiling and couldn't stop. She grabbed him around the neck, hugging him so tight, they toppled over on the bed.

"How do you feel?" he asked after she calmed down.

"I loved you the first time I saw you."

"You fooled the hell out of me."

"I had to. You were such a sly guy. I couldn't make it that easy."

"You risked never seeing me again just to prove a point?"

"That's right. I want a man who's for real."

"Come here, tough stuff. I'll prove how real I am," David said, rolling on top. He put a rush on her emotions. When his hand squeezed her breast she stopped him.

Breathlessly he asked, "What's wrong now?"

"Is that the only reason you said it? To get sex?"

"No. I meant it. I love you, but I need you too."

Nina slipped in one final question. "Is the door locked?"

"Yes. Your roommate saw enough of me for one day." He thrilled her till she shook with pleasure. Their unabashed enjoyment drove Estrellita out into the rain.

Lightning illuminated moist bodies captured in silhouette against a barren wall. Nina watched as they came together—he in her, she in him. Movement slowed to imperceptible, except in spaces shared between them.

She dreaded the moment he would pull away. To keep him inside, that was what she wanted. Her muscles squeezed, the way he liked it. Ecstasy began again.

Too tranquil to cover their nakedness, they fell asleep as a single unit, warmed only by the fire between them.

The rain rallied through mid-January. As water engorged the earth, they tumbled deeper into a state of cocooning. David broke the first rule of bachelorhood: He kept her coming to his home each night.

"The house seems empty when you're not here," he told her when she asked if he wanted to be alone.

Harmony was disrupted periodically by visits from David's friends. Late one evening his best friend, Reggie, came unexpectedly. Without asking, Reggie turned up the volume on the stereo. David turned it down.

"Nina has to get up early."

"Nina, Nina, Nina. Got my man staying home."

David grinned. "You'd stay home too, if you had a good reason. Grab yourself a beer while I put on a shirt."

David sat on the edge of the bed, pulling his shirt down over his head.

"That was Reggie at the door."

"Should I get up?" she asked.

"No. Stay here and entertain me when I get back. We'll have a couple of beers. I won't be long." He kissed her sweetly and headed downstairs.

The conversation between Reggie and David was more a monologue than a discussion. David looked uninterested until the subject turned to Nina. He made the mistake of confiding in Reggie, who had no clue to what a "love jones" was.

"I've never felt this way about a woman. She does things to me I don't understand."

"Tell me about it. Is she freaky?"

"That's not what I'm talking about, Reggie. And if she was freaky, I wouldn't tell you. I'm trying to have a serious conversation and you're talking stupid."

"I hear where you comin' from, brother. I'm just saying go slow, don't move so fast. Women are wicked if they get the upper hand."

Reggie glanced toward the stairs and back at David. He left after guzzling one beer. David had played a central role in their partying, and Nina was spoiling things. She was always there messing up the game.

Sensitive to disrupting David's lifestyle, she scheduled nights out on the town with the girls. The whole time she'd be giggling and clowning. Behind her smile, Nina thought of David. At her place she'd resist the urge to call him. He'd call, pick her up, and bring her home.

They shared an intimacy so intoxicating, he let his guard down. Nina sailed right in. David let her read his manuscript, the diary of Izaak, a time-traveling hero. The pages, written in longhand, were stained and yellowing; the message she completely understood. Izaak searched for a place to be somebody and for a soulmate to share it with. Pitted against forces of oppression, he traveled valiantly through time and space. Nina hoped for a happy ending, but Izaak was still wandering as she devoured the final pages.

She read it all in one sitting, breaking only to stretch her limbs. Her lover's words were soothing, invigorating. He could make her laugh and cry in the same paragraph.

David's usual unflappable demeanor withered the moment he placed his work in her hands. He slipped out of the study—couldn't be there when she read—and puttered around the house.

Finally Nina said, "The story is beautiful. The hero sounds a lot like someone I know."

She critiqued him, gently and lovingly, giving him the impetus to go on. The weight of David's self-doubt lifted.

"You're really shy when it comes to your writing."

"Exposing emotion to another person is hard for me. Some things I want to keep inside."

"You carry yourself like someone totally open. But you're the most private person I know, trickling out bits of information. When I think I understand, you rewrite the page. It's never finished."

"I don't understand myself. I'm not sure I ever will. Are we still on for tonight?" David changed the subject. It was her birthday and he was taking her to dinner.

"Sure, why do you ask?"

"I didn't want to take anything for granted. I thought maybe Keith was taking you out."

"You're never going to let me live that down, are you? Don't try to wiggle out of taking me to dinner tonight."

"Who, me?" David asked innocently.

"You made the reservation, didn't you?"

"Yes, I made the reservation at Hoity Toity's."

"Quit calling it that. It won't kill you to take me to a decent restaurant. You didn't think we'd hang out at Sadie's Soul Kitchen on my birthday, did you?"

"What's wrong with Sadie's? I thought you liked the over-the-hill gang."

"No. Just the over-the-hill gang leader."

The Thunderbird floated over deep pockets of water as they crossed the bridge to Sausalito. They had ignored traveler's advisories for the sake of celebration. Halfway there, she knew David was right when he suggested dinner at home, a bottle of champagne, and dessert in bed.

The road winding up to the hillside restaurant was closed due to mudslides.

"Go ahead and say it. I told you so," Nina said.

"I can't be cruel on your birthday. Look at it this way— you're the cutest woman out in the rain tonight. Did you get a new dress?"

"This is the same dress I wore to Roland's fund-raiser. Of course, you were preoccupied that evening."

"Don't get into that. I was trying to pay you a compliment."

"I'm sorry. This is my fault. Coming out in this mess dressed like Cinderella. I should've called ahead to make sure they were open. Do you mind stopping by my place for a minute? Estrellita hasn't answered the phone in two days and I'm concerned."

A foot of mud oozed out to meet her as she opened the door to the basement flat. She stepped ankle deep into dirt and debris covering every inch of walking space. Nina waded through, shocked by the damage done by flooding.

Everything was wet, including the top of her bed. Water seeped up the sides of the bedspread and saturated through to the box spring. The couch was drenched from the floor to the top of the homemade cover. There was no place to sit down and cry.

In the kitchen Nina found Marshall the mouse, floating faceup with his head caught in a trap. A note from Estrellita was taped to the refrigerator door. Which one made her scream loudest, she wasn't certain.

David let her wait in the car while he assessed the extent of the damage and eliminated safety hazards. Then he gathered her things and carried them to the car.

"There's nothing we can do tonight. I'll bring a truck in the morning and clean up. Give me the key so I can lock the door."

"Wait. I have to go back in there. I need my books."

"I grabbed all the books I saw."

"I know, but I need to make sure I'm not leaving anything," Nina insisted.

Estrellita stated things succinctly in her note.

I'm overwhelmed by the flooding. I can't handle the cleanup alone. Didn't want to bother you with such problems. Don't worry, the flood is a good sign. By the way, I'm pregnant and won't be returning to school until next year. Call me at my mother's house. Sorry about the rent.

"Give me all the bad news at once," Nina muttered, wading into her bedroom. Her heel wedged between carpeting and padding that had separated to form a sticky trap.

Nina grabbed another jacket, blue velvet bell bottoms, and a fitted silk blouse. She would be well dressed among the homeless.

She averted her eyes as she walked past the kitchen. David had given Marshall a proper burial inside the only garbage can that hadn't floated away.

Inside the car she showed David the note as the magnitude of the problem hit her. "Maybe it'll look better in the morning," she said.

David couldn't lie. "You didn't want to stay here anyway," he said, trying to lighten her gloomy mood.

"Yeah, but it was nice having a home."

"I've been thinking, you should come live with me. We're together most of the time anyway, and we can stop carrying your clothes back and forth."

"I know you're feeling sorry for me, but I'm not as pitiful as I look. Thanks for the offer, but I don't want to force you into anything."

"I was thinking about it before this happened. As Estrellita put it, this is probably a good sign. Don't pretend you hadn't thought about us living together."

"Sure I thought about it, but only in the abstract. I know how, uh . . . I know how you are." Nina stumbled in describing her feelings.

"How am I, since you know so much?"

"You've lived alone for a long time and I don't want to cramp your style. I hear your buddies kidding you about me."

"They're not used to seeing me with the same woman for this long."

"Shall I take that as a compliment?" Nina asked.

He ignored her question. "You crept up on me. I never would've picked you up that day, if I'd known it would come to this."

"What!" Nina shrieked.

"Just kidding. Seriously, Nina, I'm not proposing marriage or anything that radical. I thought we could pull our teepees together and see what happens." David took her hand and held it. "You want to sleep in my teepee?"

"Yes, but . . ."

"Stop worrying. You worry too much. Come here and give me some sugar." David leaned over and kissed her.

Nina didn't know what she was feeling. She was either the happiest woman in the world or the shakiest. Everything had happened so quickly: finding her flat flooded, losing a roommate, finding a new roommate, all in one day.

There was a note tacked to the door when they arrived home. "Must be the day for notes," she quipped. Blue ink on the envelope blurred into the letters of David's name.

"Who's it from?" Nina asked.

He crushed the rain-soaked stationery in his hand and slipped it in his pocket before explaining. "From Reggie. He stopped by while we were out."

"I wasn't being nosy. I thought maybe Estrellita cruised by on her way out of town."

"Why don't you make us a snack while I unload the car?"

"Sure," Nina answered.

She watched from the kitchen window as he descended steep steps. David sat inside the car, slowly unfolded the note, and began reading. When the phone rang Nina jumped like a peeping Tom being discovered. She experienced the same uncertainty as the first time she answered David's phone. This was her home now. She had a right to answer.

Nina grabbed the receiver, said hello, and waited. A click

sounded on the other end. Annoyed at first, she accepted the fact that they needed time to adjust to their living arrangement. The anonymous caller, whoever it was, would get the picture soon enough. Nina was certain of that.

Chapter Nine

"I TOLD YOU she was a flake, didn't I?" Sheila said in response to the news of Estrellita's departure.

"Don't be so hard on her. Yes, she has a lot of problems, but there's good in her too," Nina said.

"So what are you going to do about a roommate?"

"Nothing," Nina answered flatly.

"Huh?" Sheila looked baffled.

"I moved in with David."

"What? The last time we talked about David, he was in the dog house. How did all this come about?"

Nina filled Sheila in on the details.

"No wonder you have such a forgiving attitude. Estrellita did you a favor," Sheila said.

"I guess. I'm having a few problems adjusting."

"Like what? Stepping over his funky drawers or smelling his bad breath when you wake up in the morning?"

"Shut up, Sheila. You're sick. Nothing about David is funky or smelly."

"Let's see if you feel that way a month from now."

"The problem I'm having is people calling the house all the time. They either hang up or have a bad attitude when I answer the phone."

"You know what to do about that. Tell those floozies to stay off your fucking phone. I had the same problem when Derrick and I got together."

"I don't want him to think I'm trying to take over. It's a thin line between respecting his privacy and demanding respect for me. He should be the one to square away his friends."

"He should be, but men are chickenshit when it comes to certain situations. One chick kept hounding Derrick six months after we started living together. I finally told Derrick if he didn't get rid of her, I would. We never heard from her again."

"What does that say about us as women?" Nina asked. "Is it that hard to find a man?"

The women looked at each other and said simultaneously, "Hell, yes."

When the laughter subsided, Sheila asked, "Do you have time for lunch?"

"Not today, girl. I have to run to headquarters. I've been slacking off."

"Need a ride?"

"No thanks. I have David's car."

"Ummmm . . . Aren't we thick as thieves."

Nina smiled, promising as she rushed off "I'll call you tonight."

Only a few volunteers were in Roland's campaign office; Nina wondered if the rain had dampened their enthusiasm. Even Austin, the diehard agitator, was absent.

"Nothing like a little excitement," Nina said.

"Don't come in here acting all peppy and shit. You might ruin the ambience."

"Well, excuse me for trying to bring a little sunshine into a tired situation. Where's Roland?"

"At home with the flu. Brenda's coming down to pick up his files so he can work on his speech for the Rotary Club meet n' greet. Can you man the phones while I grab a sandwich?"

"Sure, but only for a hot second. I need to finish my report."

With few interruptions, Nina breezed through the day with the efficiency of a woman supercharged by love.

Promptly at five o'clock she called it quits to pick up David. She was having trouble fitting a box of flyers in the T-Bird when Brenda drove up in a screaming yellow Porsche. Nina's eyes were drawn to Brenda's feet as she exited the Porsche. Brenda was the only woman wearing black patent leather stiletto heels in 1973.

"Hi, Brenda, how's it going?" Nina closed the T-Bird door and straightened up, smiling.

Brenda didn't waste time with "hello." "You think you're pretty slick, don't you?" she said.

Stunned by the rudeness of her greeting, Nina said, "What?"

"Don't pretend with me—playing little miss innocent and doing everything you can to steal my man."

"I don't know who's been lying to you, but I have a good idea. There's absolutely nothing to worry about. Roland and I have a strictly platonic, professional relationship."

"I don't give a damn about you and Roland. I'd be thrilled if you took him off my hands. It's David I want. I'll do whatever I have to do to get him," Brenda announced calmly.

Nina had the dazed look of a boxer recovering from a severe blow to the head. Maybe I didn't hear her right, she thought. She focused on Brenda's cherry-red lips. Brenda was on a roll now, talking and gesturing with wild animation. It was an unreal scenario, worsening by the second.

Nina's voice emerged from behind a wall of confusion. "You have something going on with David?"

"Do I have to write it in the sky? I'm doing you a favor by telling you. David will string you along and dump you like all the rest. I'm the only one who can satisfy him," Brenda boasted.

"You sound ridiculous. If David wants you so much, what's he doing with me?"

"You're young and cute—a temporary distraction."

"I don't think so, lady. You have a lot of nerve confronting me like this. If you have a bone to pick with David, speak to him directly. And don't bother calling the house and hanging up on me."

"I'll call him anytime I want."

"Not as long as I'm living there."

"*Living* there?"

"You got that right. I—am—liv-ing—with—Da-vid." Nina emphasized every syllable. "If you'll excuse me, I've had enough of your bullshit. Maybe I should discuss this with your husband. Get his opinion."

"You don't scare me. Roland knows about David. He's too chickenshit to react. It's easier to pretend nothing is happening. My husband will compromise anything, including me, for the sake of his political ambition. David is the only man I care about. I won't let him go."

"You're making a fool of yourself, Brenda."

"I'm not the only fool. It's not just me and you. David has other women. Can you handle that, sweetheart?"

"I'd better leave before I do something foolish."

Nina walked around Brenda and sat down in the driver's seat, trying hard to look composed. She jammed a key several times in the ignition before realizing that it was the wrong one. The Thunderbird eased away from the curb as Brenda talked to herself. Nina summoned all of her strength to resist throwing the car in reverse and backing up over the woman.

Cars whizzed past as she crept down the busy boulevard. She considered pulling over, but her exchange with Brenda had made her late. Nina tried hard to control the surging anger. Wait to hear his side of the story, she rationalized, then stepped on the gas with a vengeance. The engine growled and the Thunderbird shuddered at the intensity of her assault.

David was standing by the curb with his bag slung over his shoulder.

"Want me to drive? Looks like you had a rough day," he said.

She was quiet as he slid into the driver's seat.

When he leaned over to kiss her, Nina went rigid.

"What's wrong?" David asked.

"Brenda Hill is what's wrong."

"Uh . . . What does that mean?"

"David, if you have to whore around, could you do it with someone other than my boss's wife?" Nina's resolve to be cool flew out the window.

"Where did you hear that?"

"Cut the crap, David. I got it from the horse's mouth."

"Don't believe everything you hear. Brenda's upset because I told her I couldn't see her anymore."

Nina shouted, "Why were you seeing her in the first place? The woman is married. She has a child. How am I supposed to face Roland?"

"Look, Nina. I met Brenda before I knew you. I'm not seeing her now and that's all that should matter. I told you up front—I didn't come into this relationship with a clean slate."

"Yeah, but you didn't tell me Brenda Hill's name was written all over it."

"It was a mistake, one that I regret. What happened between me and Brenda was not a big deal."

"It sure is a big deal for Brenda."

"I can't help that. Brenda knew what she was getting into from jump street. She tried to turn it into more than it was. Don't let this come between us."

When David reached for her hand, Nina instantly recoiled. "Would you mind not touching me?"

She rode in silence, thinking thoughts that made her insides churn. She saw visions of David in bed with Brenda, doing things he had done with her. Nina wondered if she could handle it.

When was the last time he had slept with Brenda? Who were the others? She was afraid to ask.

Nina tucked inside the jealousy, trying to conceal how hurt she was. She rolled down the window for fresh air.

Insecurity blew in with the power of the wind. Brenda was probably more seductive, more slinky. Nina thought about the cotton T-shirts she sometimes wore to bed. She imagined Brenda in a red-hot silk negligee and tons of expensive perfume.

"If you want that slut, you're welcome to her. I can move out in nothing flat," Nina said, knowing she had nowhere to go.

"Baby, don't say that. Stay with me. I know you're upset, but take a minute to think. I swear I'm not interested in Brenda."

Nina sat in the study most of the night, pretending to read. David tried to butter her up with food and drinks that she refused to touch. She could barely stand the sight of him. Her heart ached when she imagined living without him.

Nina waited until the end of the next day to confront Roland. "You knew what was going on. Why didn't you tell me?"

"I distinctly recall being told to mind my own business."

"How could you stand by and watch the two of them make fools of us?"

"I wanted to spare you, Nina. I was tempted more than once to blurt it out, but I doubt you would've listened. I found out who she was seeing a few weeks before the fund-raiser. She'd been acting peculiar for some time, so I knew something was going on. I hired a private investigator to follow her. Brenda was with David the night you were arrested."

Nina's heart sank.

"I confronted Brenda the next evening. She showed no remorse. Told me that if I didn't like it, she'd be happy to give me a divorce. For the first time in fifteen years of marriage I wanted to hit her. It wasn't just the affair; her total lack of regard for my feelings just blew me away.

"My wife needs help. She's having a hard time accepting

that she's not a young girl anymore. Brenda frets over every line or hint of a wrinkle. The worst part is, she's convinced David is in love with her. I ran into David at Sadie's Soul Kitchen and warned him to leave my wife alone. He said, 'No problem,' turned around, and finished his drink. Does that sound like a man in love?"

Nina scowled in disgust.

"Brenda nearly had a coronary when David showed up at the fund-raiser with you."

"That explains why he was so reluctant to go."

"Brenda split the moment you guys arrived. Too much reality. I realize David is fast, flashy, and apparently a big hit with women. What I can't understand is why you cling to a man incapable of loving. He's going to hurt you, Nina."

"He already has."

"Then do something. Don't just sit around and wait for him to get tired of you."

"It's not that simple, Roland."

"Yes, it is."

"If it's so simple, why haven't you done something about your wife?"

"We have a child together. I seriously contemplated divorce, but it would be a death knell to my campaign."

"You let a campaign take priority over your personal life?"

"There's no such thing as a personal life in politics. Brenda's not the only one at fault. She's a woman who requires a lot of attention, a lot of reassuring. When we met at Grambling, Brenda was the prettiest thing I had ever seen. She could have had any man she wanted, but she chose me, not because of my charm or handsomeness, but because of my drive. Brenda knew I would move heaven and earth to make her happy. She never had any ambition of her own, just wanted to be taken care of."

"How could you marry someone like that?"

"That's not an altogether loathsome proposition, as long as I was getting something out of it too. She made me look good and I kept her looking good. I didn't realize how frustrating that would be for Brenda in the long run. I was too busy doing my own thing."

"This puts me in an awkward position as far as continuing with the campaign."

"I realize that, but there's not much time left before the election. If you leave, I'm dead. You're more than a campaign worker to me."

Nina was confused by his comment.

Roland fidgeted before explaining "You're the only one I can talk to. I used to love campaigning, almost as much as I love winning. But this has gotten vicious. I'm spending more time attacking the other candidates than setting forth my own program."

"Roland, you're not the problem. I can't tolerate your wife harassing me."

"I'll make sure she doesn't bug you. If there's a way to get her into therapy tactfully, I'll make it happen. I'm sorry you had to deal with this."

"It's not your fault. Sometimes I think I'm coming apart." Nina became pensive.

Roland walked behind her and began massaging her tight shoulder muscles. It surprised her at first. He had never touched her that way.

"Just relax. Let it all go," he said.

Her chin dropped to her chest as he skillfully plied her upper back. He pushed her hair up from her neck and pressed gently on either side. She was relaxing when she heard a noise outside Roland's office.

"What was that?" Nina jumped up.

"I don't know. I thought everyone had left."

Roland went to investigate with Nina following close behind him.

They found Austin standing at his desk, rifling through papers.

"Austin, you scared us," Nina said.

"Oh . . . Hope I didn't interrupt anything. I came back for files that I need to work on tonight."

"We didn't hear you come in. I thought I locked that door."

"It was open. I didn't have to use my key," Austin said, dangling a large key ring. "I found what I was looking for. See you tomorrow."

As Austin closed the door Roland said, "That dude gives me the creeps."

"Me too, but I'm more concerned about my own forgetfulness. See what stress is doing to me? I'm bugging out."

"No, you're not. Forgetting to lock a door is no big deal. Austin probably sneaked in here trying to catch us in the act. Don't worry about his tired butt. What you need to do is figure out your next move. Do you know what you want to do?"

"I have no idea."

"If you need money, I'd be happy to give you an advance on your salary."

"Thanks, but I don't think money can solve my problem."

"You have time for a drink? I need to talk to you about another matter."

"I have time, but I don't want to hear another word about David or your wife."

"No, this is an entirely different subject. I need you to visit the San Quentin client I was telling you about."

"When?"

"This week. Let's get out of here and I'll give you the details."

They drove to a cliffside restaurant in San Francisco.

As they pulled into the cobblestone parking lot, Nina protested, "I'm not properly dressed."

"If you were in rags, you'd be the most beautiful woman here."

"You could've given me a chance to change. I thought we were having a beer at the local greasy spoon."

"If I had told you where we were going, you would've said no. We're here so we might as well enjoy it."

The maître d' greeted Roland by name and escorted them

to an intimate corner booth. Roland insisted on ordering
dinner as well as drinks.

"I'm not really hungry, Roland."

"Nonsense. I can't have my ace wasting away to nothing. Eat something, Nina." Roland took her hand, which
was resting on top of the table. "Take it from an old fool
like me. This is not the end of the world. I hate seeing you
down. David doesn't know how lucky he is having a smart,
beautiful lady who loves him in spite of his foolishness. I'd
give anything to have a woman like you."

Heat emanating from his hand made her uncomfortable.
Afraid of what he might say next, Nina eased her hand
away and fixed her gaze upon the water. There was no mis-
taking it—Roland was raising the stakes in the game.

She could have nipped it in the bud before it transcended
the point of innuendo, but she didn't. It floated in the air
like moisture about to become rain.

Nina redirected the conversation to business. "Tell me
about this client in San Quentin."

"The case is on appeal. The brief has been filed, so
there's little legal work. Mainly, I need you to sit with him,
reassure him that we're working on the case. Prisoners like
to see pretty girls, but let me warn you, he'll fall in love instantly. Whatever you do, don't give him your address.
You'll get reams of love letters and perhaps an unexpected
visit in the unlikely event the conviction is overturned."

"Why do you say unlikely?"

"My client was serving the last year of an armed robbery
conviction when there was a prison riot, and a guard was
taken hostage. Kwaku was accused of murdering that
guard. He's on death row."

"You're not talking about Kwaku of the 1969 rebellion
fame."

"Yes. That's who you'll be visiting."

"This is exciting."

"It's actually more depressing than exciting at this point.
Armed guards will search you thoroughly as you enter and
leave the prison."

"Not a repeat of my strip-search episode, I hope."

"No. Nothing that invasive. For maximum security prisoners, the visiting area is a very narrow, claustrophobic compartment. You'll be locked in behind a heavy steel door. A thick, bulletproof glass divider will separate you from the prisoner. Don't be alarmed when they bring him in from the other side with chains around his wrists, waist, legs, and feet."

"Whew."

"It's quite shocking the first time you experience it. If you can get past the initial uneasiness, you'll find him an extremely interesting man to talk to. I'd suggest you tape-record some music. Kwaku loves music, and an hour is a long time to be locked in."

Once the business was exhausted, Nina focused on the food she was previously uninterested in. Roland had a drink and then another. It didn't seem to relax him. His hands trembled the entire time they were talking. It was what he didn't say that made her nervous every time she looked at him.

"Maybe this prison visit isn't a good idea," Roland said, "considering your brush with the law. I wasn't thinking when I suggested it."

"No. I'm okay with it. I have to do what lawyers do if I'm going to be a lawyer. Besides, my arrest wasn't the first time I've seen the inside of a jail. Not as a detainee, but visiting a former boyfriend."

"You're either extremely unlucky or have a penchant for choosing wild men. Which is it?"

"I thought we weren't talking about David any more tonight."

Roland chuckled. "You're right. Strike that question."

Roland watched as Nina climbed the stairs leading to David. For two hours in the restaurant he had made no further moves. He rested his head against the steering wheel as Nina turned the key in the door and stepped across the threshold. She was safely inside. There was no reason to wait. Roland put the car in gear and drove away.

Nina walked past David, who was sitting alone in the dark. The flickering fire cast somber shadows on his face. On the stereo her favorite love song was playing. Nina pretended not to notice.

She dropped her backpack on the floor, flicked on the light, and began reading the mail.

A week and a half had passed since she confronted him about Brenda. David had the look of a man brimming with pent-up sexual tension. She was feeling a wee bit tense herself, but forgiving him was getting harder each day. Nina had dug into an intractable position. She didn't know how to come out.

David broke the silence. "I waited all day for your call. How did you get home?"

"I hitchhiked."

"Nina, I told you to stop doing that."

"You told me a lot of things."

"Look, I admit I fucked up."

"Well stated," she remarked sarcastically.

"Stop treating what happened like a major incident. You're acting like an old lady."

"Oh, no. You have me confused with your other woman."

David laughed. "Okay. That was a good one. You get two points, but I don't want to keep score. I want to get back to where we were. I know I hurt you and I'm sorry. Let's not fight anymore."

He touched her hand. She pulled away.

"Don't do this," he pleaded.

She turned away to hide the tears. The hurt bubbled to the surface despite Nina's determination to be strong. David stood close behind her and placed his hands on her shoulders.

"I just want to talk to you, baby. Don't shut me out." He whispered words of apology over and over. She wanted to believe him, but the pain got in the way. She whimpered in protest as his touch became more intimate. His arms wrapped around her waist.

"I can't make it without you." David pulled her closer with each endearment. Pride made her wish for strength to pull away, but Nina needed to confirm that she was the one who thrilled him the most, the one who turned him on.

She let him lead her into the bedroom. Nina made love the way some men do: detached, observing, looking for signs of conquest. Her eyes were open as she hovered above him with no intention of coming. When David cried out her name, strong fingernails pressed deep into his chest. She wanted to love him. She wanted to hurt him. In the end forgiveness triumphed over the anger she struggled to hold on to.

Nina shuddered as David's warmth flowed deep inside her. The argument wasn't over, but the rage had emptied into a well of tranquility, where she left it.

When the phone rang a few seconds later, she almost anticipated it. She didn't expect Brenda to give up that easily. Nina snatched the receiver, asking gruffly of the caller, "Whadyou want?" After a five-second pause she was ready to slam down the receiver. Then she heard Sheila's voice faintly on the other end.

"Sheila, is that you?" Nina asked, conveniently resting her elbow under David's neck.

"Yes. It's me. I need your help. Derrick got busted. Can you come over?"

"Do you need money?"

"No. His father will take care of that. The bail is so high, we couldn't handle it if we wanted to. I just need a friend."

"I'll be there in half an hour. Be cool until I get there."

Nina unstraddled David before he could ask, "What was that about?"

"Sheila needs help."

"You're not going to jail again, are you?"

"I'm not planning on it, but in the unlikely event it should occur, find someplace to be other than Brenda Hill's bed."

"Damn. You know about that too. Nothing gets past you. Nina, I swear, Brenda showed up unexpectedly right after we talked that night. I refused to open the door. She started yelling and screaming, trying to wake up the whole neighborhood. I gave her a drink and calmly explained that she couldn't come here anymore. She went berserk. Started ranting, raving, and taking off her clothes . . ."

"And so you did the honorable thing and fucked her," Nina finished his sentence.

"No. I did not fuck her. A nude woman foaming at the mouth is not sexy. I let her stay until she calmed down, then sent her home. I didn't answer the phone that night because I thought it was Brenda."

Nina listened to his explanation and decided to think on it a little longer. "Just because we made love tonight doesn't mean everything is copasetic."

David kept quiet, taking no chance of starting the argument again.

"I need the keys to the car," Nina said, holding out her hand. "I may be late."

"What about us?"

"Us can keep until tomorrow. Us have probably had enough of us for a while," Nina suggested.

"Speak for yourself."

"I'll call you later."

David watched as Nina be-bopped down the stairs, jumped into the T-Bird, and took off. He glanced across the street toward the vehicle parked in the driveway of a vacant house. On a night lit only by an overcast new moon, the car and the driver were almost invisible. Once Nina was safely off on her mission, David closed the blinds and went upstairs to read.

"Girl, it was awful. I was sound asleep when I thought I heard an explosion. I grabbed my robe but didn't get a chance to put it on. The police had busted down the front door. I ran out, like a fool, in my nightgown. Derrick was three or four steps behind me. They made us lie down on the floor with our hands behind our heads while they ransacked the place. I thought they were going to shoot me until I figured out what they wanted. They were looking for drugs."

Nina listened in disbelief as Sheila recapped the horrifying incident. "Derrick had just gotten rid of his stash and was supposed to pick up another package last night. The package wasn't ready. That's the only thing that saved me."

"That's not what saved you. What saved you was a Higher Power. If you haven't said your prayers, now is a good time to start."

"You got that right. They were so busy looking for the big stuff, they never found the two joints I had in my purse."

"That's small potatoes."

"They found some other shit in Derrick's car, which they also had a warrant to search."

"There must be more to it. Why would they waste time busting a small-time reefer dealer?" Nina asked.

"They were looking for cocaine. Derrick started dealing coke heavily a few months ago. I begged him to quit, but he wouldn't listen to me."

"Sheila, I had no idea it had gotten that deep."

"It's a lot deeper than you think. He's not just selling it, he's using it. Derrick's wired up all the time, doesn't sleep, won't eat, and walks around like he's king of the hop. You see how skinny he is. Lost all his ass. He's gone too far this time, risking my life and my career. He's nothing like the man I met when we were roommates at Mills."

"I couldn't believe it when you introduced me to Derrick," Nina said. "He seemed so soft, so indulged. That boy took to herb like a duck to water. While we were having fun with it, Derrick turned it into a major business venture. Why do men deal in such extremes? You cain't tell 'em nothin'."

"I don't understand what Derrick was thinking when he started this shit. He certainly wasn't thinking about me," Sheila said.

"He wasn't thinking at all. It's a male thing. Men aren't happy unless some shit is in the game."

"Uh-oh. This doesn't sound like the same Nina who was full of love and peace a minute ago."

"I'm not the same Nina. I'm a hell of a lot smarter." Nina gave Sheila the lowdown on Brenda Hill.

"I don't know if it's worth it, Sheila."

"If what's worth it?"

"The changes we go through for men."

"Of course it's worth it, or we wouldn't do it."

"I don't know. A few days ago I was walking on clouds. Now every time I look at David I think about Brenda. She took what I thought was pure love and turned it into muck."

"That cloud stuff is good for a hot minute, then the real nitty gritty kicks in. Don't let her steal your happiness. I'm sorry I interrupted the reconciliation."

"No big deal. My head needed to catch up with my heart."

"So everything's back on track?"

"I wouldn't say all that. Let's just say the stew is simmering instead of boiling. If he screws up again, I'm outta there."

"That's what we all say, until it happens again. Then we find a reason to keep hanging on."

"David's almost old enough to be my father, a fact my own father pointed out to me. My parents are cool, at least for the time being. They're not happy about me 'shacking up' with a man. But I'm grown, so there's nothing they can do. I risked a lot to be with David, and I expect him to do the same for me."

"That's the right attitude. If you don't demand respect, they sure as hell won't give any."

"What about Derrick?" Nina asked.

"I don't know. It's easier to give advice than take it."

"I hear you, sister. I hear you."

Together they cleaned the ransacked apartment, piecing together fragments of Sheila's life.

Chapter Ten

A FEW HOURS later Nina called to say she was staying overnight with Sheila.

"I'll be home by seven."

"Don't mess me up, Nina. I have an interview at eight," David reminded her.

Nina woke up early enough but was distracted when Sheila decided to destroy the evidence overlooked by the police. They each lit a joint, smoked it, tossed the roaches in the toilet, and flushed. An hour later Nina and Sheila were sitting in the same spot, rehashing subjects thoroughly exhausted the night before. On her tenth attempt to get up off the couch, Nina made it. Now she was late, oblivious to David's request that she be on time.

David was sitting at the bottom of the steps, waiting with an attitude, when Nina pulled up at seven forty-five. She had the heat blasting and the windows rolled down. She looked like she'd been up to no good.

"Thanks for making me late," he said sarcastically.

"I'm sorry, David. I stayed up all night helping Sheila. The interview completely slipped my mind," she apologized, looking pitiful.

"Helping? You look like you've been partying. Are you going to school?"

"Not till later. I have to go by headquarters, but I think I'll take a nap first."

Nina watched as he drove away in a mad rush, looking more than a little miffed. As usual, she had left the gas tank on empty. She had a thing about stopping for gas.

Nina was glad to have the house to herself. She was ready to unwind from the stress of recent days. She turned on the water in the bathtub and poured in two drops of oil to maintain the silkiness of her skin. Then she checked the thermostat to ensure a pleasing room temperature when she emerged, if ever, from the tub. She was disappointed to find that David had already used the oversized, fluffy towel she favored to dry off with. Nina closed the door to trap the steam inside the bathroom. She drifted into another dimension where the only reality was the flow and caress of the water. Nina lingered in the realm of nothingness until her peace was shattered by the sound of movement downstairs.

She lunged from the tub in a single motion. Someone's in the house, she flashed, yanking open the door. David and Reggie looked up from the bottom of the steps. She stood frozen in the doorway, dripping wet, without a towel.

Embarrassed as hell, Nina slammed the door in their faces. Reggie, the creep, had caught her in her birthday suit. He wouldn't be cool enough to pretend nothing had happened. Reggie would rub it in, make a point of it. He was sleazy like that.

When she gathered the courage to join them, Nina sat as far away from Reggie as she could, which placed her between Janine and Debra, who were hanging with Reggie. David's interview had been cancelled. No one bothered telling him before he made the wasted trip to the office. On his way home he ran into Reggie, who promptly invited him to join his party.

"If you want to take the car, it's cool. Reggie can drop me off when we're ready to go," David offered.

"Nonsense. I wouldn't think of leaving without feeding these folks," Nina said, but was thinking, "I wouldn't think of leaving two old fools here with women wearing bloodred lipstick this early in the morning."

She escaped to the kitchen and found solace among the pots and pans that clanged her displeasure at having Reggie over for breakfast. The oven hadn't even gotten warm before Reggie popped in to chitchat.

"Looks like we surprised you this morning."

"Looks like you did," Nina answered, keeping her eyes glued to the bread she was buttering.

Reggie was quiet for a few seconds, beaming his X-ray eyes on her as she continued working.

"Can I help you with anything?" His husky frame occupied too much space. She could smell the blend of tobacco and liquor coming from his mouth.

Nina stopped what she was doing, folded her arms, and said, "No, Reggie. You can't help me with anything. Not one single thing."

David walked in and grabbed Nina around the waist. "I'm sorry we scared you."

"I'm not," Reggie interjected shamelessly.

"Man, you betta back up off my woman," David warned.

"Nina knows I'm kidding her. Don't you, Nina?" Reggie asked.

Nina didn't crack a smile.

"Go entertain your friends," David said. "I'll help Nina finish up in here."

Being a trooper, Nina fixed a breakfast consisting of cheese omelets, hash browns, toast, fruit, and juice. When Reggie complained that there was no meat on the menu, she wanted to choke him with an unripe banana.

Why David hung out with Reggie was a mystery. The man was a drag from the word go. At every opportunity he tried to ease up on Nina, touching her unnecessarily or saying things that offended her sensibilities as a woman. She was constantly on the brink of cursing him out.

When Janine, or maybe it was Debra, started jumping to the music from the stereo, Nina excused herself. She holed up in the study for more than an hour, then became curious when Reggie's loud voice subsided. She tiptoed down the steps toward the kitchen. The butt sisters giggled in the living room, reapplying their makeup. Their asses were perfectly round and voluptuous, giving their waistlines an exceptionally narrow appearance. Nina wondered if David was into that type. He didn't seem to discriminate. To him all of it was good.

David and Reggie lounged outside the kitchen door, smoking a joint. She could hear them talking.

"Man, we miss you over at Sadie's. The brothers been asking what it is. I told 'em that little love thang has you tied up nowadays," Reggie said.

"You calling me pussy-whipped?" she heard David ask.

"Naw, man. That's not how it came down." Reggie tried to change the subject, as he always did, when challenged.

"Come take a ride with me and the ladies. That's two wild chicks in there, David," Reggie tempted him.

David paused and answered, "I can't do it. Nina's upstairs and I'm not that bodacious. Even an old dog like me has scruples."

"See what I'm sayin', man. You lettin' a woman come between you and a good time."

"Lighten up, Reggie. Ain't nothing wrong with giving your woman a little respect. That's why you can't attract anything but wild women. You don't know how to act. You're on your own today, brother. I'll catch up with you later."

Nina turned on the kitchen faucet, pretending to wash dishes. She didn't know what to make of the conversation. At least he had passed on Reggie's offer, even though it was an equivocal no.

The phone rang as David was ushering out his guests.

"Who is it now?" she muttered to herself. "Grand Central Station," Nina answered.

"Hel-lo . . . uh, is David there?" the woman asked slowly on the other end.

Nina thrust the phone toward David, while making a face reflecting her annoyance.

David's face lit up when he recognized the voice on the other end. "Hey, pretty lady. How've you been? You won't believe this, but I had you on my mind all week. I was gonna call you from work, but I got delayed at home."

This jackass has a lot of nerve talking like that right in front of me, Nina thought.

"Oh, that was Nina who answered the phone. You remember I told you about her."

Nina waited for David to walk into the other room with the phone, which was his custom when women called. His end of the conversation consisted of a series of "uh-huhs" and "oh, yeahs." Having heard enough, she was ready to leave the kitchen when David handed her the phone. Nina looked confused.

"It's my mother," David said. "She wants to talk to you."

Feeling silly, Nina took the phone.

"Hi, sugar, this is David's mama. I was just trying to straighten him out. I've been telling him for the longest that he's too old to be running the streets. I'm glad he's found a nice girl."

"It's so good to hear from you, Mrs. Hamilton."

"Call me Sarah. Mrs. Hamilton sounds like an old person. I've been trying to get my son to come home for a visit. Maybe he'll bring you with him. We talk on the phone all the time, but it's been awhile since I saw him. David hates his hometown and I can't blame him. Ain't nothing changed around here but the highway signs."

"Why don't you visit us?"

David's ears perked up on hearing Nina's suggestion.

"You can't pay me to get on an airplane, and it's too far to take the bus," David's mother responded.

"I'll work on him then."

"You do that, Nina. Take care of my son. He's a handful. Let me say bye to him."

Nina handed the phone to David. After hanging up, he said, "Mama's all excited about you. I'm an only child and she's afraid I'm getting too old to give her grandkids."

"She may be right," Nina teased him.

"You're not funny." David grabbed her menacingly, then released the pressure into a gentle hug.

"Why do you hate going home?"

"I'm out of step with that place. I feel like a freak, everybody staring at me."

"That's not surprising. You go out of your way to look different."

"You like it."

"Yes, I do," Nina admitted.

A far-off look came over his face. "I don't talk about my family much. There's things I don't want to remember."

"It might help if you talked about it."

"My mother sent me to live with my aunt when I was sixteen. She was afraid I would kill my father or he would kill me."

Nina couldn't believe what she was hearing. She couldn't imagine David wanting to kill anyone, especially his father.

David continued. "My father was an unhappy man. He worked in the coal mines most of his life. He felt fate had dealt him a bad hand. He was right, but it didn't justify him hitting my mother. Mama worshiped him. The more she gave, the meaner he got. I took up for her when he went crazy, then he would turn on me.

"At sixteen I was taller and stronger than he was. His strength had been drained by years of backbreaking labor. The last time he jumped on her, I beat him until I couldn't breathe. The neighbors had to pull me off." David looked away with a kind of sadness Nina had never seen in him.

"Mama rushed me off to her sister in California. I begged her to come with me, but she wouldn't leave. I didn't know it at the time, but my father was dying of black lung disease. When he died, I refused to go home to the funeral. All I remember is the way he looked at me after we fought. He was crushed, humiliated. No words were exchanged between us. I never understood why Mama tolerated him or why he hated me so much."

"I'm sure he didn't hate you, baby. He probably hated himself."

"That's cool on an intellectual level. But as a child, I was terrorized by this man who was supposed to love me."

Nina took his hand, wishing she could erase the painful memories. The door to his past had opened a little wider. She wanted to barge in, but Nina knew he wasn't ready.

David leaned against her and placed his cheek next to hers. Nina held him close and caressed him. Two minutes into consoling him she could feel his nature rising.

"I think I'm getting in touch with my feelings," David said, half jokingly. "Let's go to bed."

Nina glanced at the clock. "I'm supposed to meet Roland at the office."

"Forget Roland. I need you."

Nina couldn't argue with that.

It began with little kisses that sent shivers through her body. His tongue parted her lips, played in her ear, and kept roving. Nina was mellow, needing nothing more. For David it was only the beginning.

After they made love she watched him sleeping. She wiped moisture from his forehead and smoothed baby-soft hair around his temples with her little finger. Then Nina curled up behind him and draped her arm across his chest. His breathing settled into a slow, even rhythm. They were as close as they could get without being inside each other.

Nina eased into a deep sleep that lasted throughout the morning. By noon she unglued herself and slipped into the study to call the office.

"Roland, I won't be in today. I have personal business to attend to."

"Is everything all right? David didn't have a problem with me bringing you home, did he?"

"No. Everything is fine. I'll give you a full report when I see you tomorrow."

"Listen. I hope I didn't offend you by what I said the other night at the restaurant."

"No. No. We were both feeling lonely and abused. I was wigging out, but I've got it together now."

"Okay. Call me if you run into unexpected turbulence."

After Nina hung up she tiptoed into the bedroom and

snuggled up to David. His back was to her, his eyes open, but she couldn't see them. Nina inched a little closer. David never made a sound.

Chapter Eleven

THE ALAMEDA COUNTY Press Club awards banquet was the premier event for local newspaper people. Women broke out glittery, sequined gowns and men stuffed themselves into too-tight tuxedos. Nina was thrilled when David received an award for his series of profiles on the mayoral candidates.

The series was thought provoking, although Nina thought the latest profile on Donna Dixon was overly generous. David glossed over the fact that Dixon had never held public office and, before declaring as a candidate, lambasted the establishment that she now sought to join. Dixon was portrayed as a modern-day Joan of Arc with unselfish love for her people. Forgotten were her ties to a group dubbed the Black Enforcers, reputed to extort payments from local businessmen. David deemphasized Dixon's failure to account for the principal sources of her campaign funding. The elaborate campaign waged by Dixon suggested resources far beyond what could be raised at neighborhood rallies. Other writers speculated that perhaps the "people's candidate" was a puppet controlled by White strings.

"Am I missing something or is 'revolutionary Democrat' an oxymoron?" Roland had chuckled when he read the Dixon article. He teased Nina, "You'd better watch your man, Nina. Sounds like Donna Dixon's giving him more than a free scoop."

"I take jabs regularly from other people. I shouldn't have to take it from you," Nina said.

Roland apologized quickly, admitting he was way out of

line. Nina was the rope in a muddy tug-of-war. No matter who won, she was destined to end up dirty.

David characterized Roland as a seasoned politician with the right credentials but "questionable depth of spirit." Nina had no idea what that meant, but resisted the urge to comment, adhering to their pact to keep political differences outside the house. The only saving grace was that Candidate McFarlane didn't fare much better.

At the banquet the editor-in-chief of the *Sentinel* seized the opportunity to rib her.

"I'm surprised you're still speaking to David after his uneven profiles of Donna Dixon and your candidate," Richard Grant commented.

"I can handle it. I respect David's opinion, even when he's wrong," Nina said.

"You couldn't persuade him to see things your way?" Grant asked, fingering his beard.

"I guess not. David insists he's neutral regarding the candidates. Apparently you read the articles the same way I did."

"There's no such thing as neutrality in journalism. The use of a phrase, selection of a word can make all the difference in the world. Roland Hill is lucky. He could've really taken a beating, if he didn't have you in his corner. Then again, the same can be said of David. Look at how he's progressed. Getting all kinds of recognition. You must've lit a fire under him."

David captured the evening's top honor, the coveted Vigilance Award for exposing corruption in the county's goods and services procurement process. At the podium the presenter said, "David Hamilton's reporting exemplifies dogged determination to uncover the truth. He sets a high standard of excellence for others to follow. His work will result in substantial savings to the county and will go a long way in eliminating favoritism in the bidding process."

David dragged Nina into the photographs of him receiving his awards. Beaming with pride, Nina kept saying, "I knew you could do it. I knew it."

In his acceptance speech he thanked her for being his anchor and a source of inspiration. Nina almost cried.

The ceremony dragged late into the night. Tedious speeches, rubbery chicken, and a bad band took their toll on Nina. When David invited her to the afterparty she declined, saying, "Go ahead and have a good time. I have to get up early."

Nina caught a ride home with one of his coworkers. She had made a conscious decision not to monitor David's activities. She had to trust him or exist in a constant state of doubt. No more arguing or asking where he was going. Nina mastered everything, except the worrying, which needed substantial work.

At three o'clock in the morning David wasn't home. When he called, funky music boomed and rowdy laughter roared in the background. "Baby, I'm too buzzed to drive right now. I didn't want you to worry."

"I'm okay. Sounds like a lively party."

"It was, but things are winding down. It's just the fellows sitting around talking shit." David hurried off the phone.

She turned on the television to keep her company, but turned it off quickly after seeing what was on. A chill suddenly descended while she sat reading a magazine. Nina looked around, trying to shake the cold feeling—someone was watching her. A fleeting sound, like the rustling of shrubbery, made her heart race erratically.

Nina tiptoed downstairs and peeked out the kitchen window. She turned on the light. Tall uneven hedges lining the perimeter of the property assumed monstrous proportions in her mind. She grabbed a butcher's knife from the drawer, just in case.

Nina turned off the light and looked again. Vibrant yellow eyes appeared out of the darkness. She gasped. It was the neighbor's bobtail cat, prowling in search of rodents. His back was arched, his hair stood on end. Nina could see the faintest outline of his pointy, bared teeth.

Withdrawing from the window, she patted her chest and

took a deep breath. Her heart continued to thump wildly. Nina thought about calling Sheila, then realized that was ridiculous since her friend lived on the other side of town.

She stationed herself in the bedroom. Anyone coming after her would have to enter through the bedroom door, unless it was a ghost, in which case, there was nothing she could do to stop it.

"Oh, hell, why did I have to think of that?" she said. Nina positioned the knife so that the handle was readily accessible. She took a couple of turns at grabbing it quickly before admitting that she was giving in to irrational fear. She turned on the television again, setting it at the lowest possible volume. Twenty minutes of mindless viewing eventually lulled her into a fitful sleep.

A buzzing sound intermingled with the crazy nightmare she was experiencing. She sat straight up in bed and saw the sign-off pattern on the television screen. Nina rose on wobbly legs and hit the off button, but the buzzing continued. Finally it dawned on her that someone was ringing the doorbell. She looked back at the clock. It was four-thirty in the morning. She couldn't imagine who it was unless David had forgotten his key. Nina started downstairs absently, then stopped in her tracks and went back for the knife.

"Who is it?" she asked, standing a safe distance from the door. She was reluctant to look through the peephole for fear of what might be out there. No one answered. She waited a minute, then parted the blinds. There was nothing, except lingering darkness and the predawn haze blanketing the sky.

Nina leaned against the wall, hyperventilating. For several minutes she was frozen in that position, clutching the knife. When her legs felt steadier, she grabbed a blanket from upstairs and sat tensely on the couch, counting the minutes before daybreak.

A dead bird lay on the welcome mat the next morning. Its neck was broken and its beak and eyes gaped open. Nina jumped back, covering her mouth to stifle the scream.

"This is sadistic," Nina said out loud after recovering

from the initial shock. She held her breath as she walked past the bird, trying not to look at it.

David pulled up as she was leaving.

"You need a ride?"

"No, thanks. I've got it covered. By the way, your friend left a present on the doorstep. I didn't have the heart to spoil the surprise."

David looked baffled, but Nina kept walking.

That night when they discussed the dead bird incident, David was sympathetic to Nina's distress.

"I should've stayed home last night," he said.

"It was your night to celebrate. We can't let her control our lives, but it's been bugging me all day. Maybe it was the cat and not Brenda who killed the bird. The cat was prowling around last night, but it certainly wasn't the cat who rang the doorbell."

"You saw her?"

"No. By the time I looked out she was gone. I'm not certain it was Brenda. But who else would pull a stunt like that?"

"I'll make sure she doesn't come back."

"Please don't talk to her. She's crazy."

"I won't, but I'll be ready if she tries it again."

David's comment frightened rather than reassured Nina. She didn't want him baited into a situation that could backfire in his face.

The house came alive under Nina's care and attention. There were plants in every room and color in spaces once barren. David drew the line on flowered curtains. They settled on bamboo shades.

One day when she was feeling particularly ambitious, she recruited him to cut back and fertilize the shrubbery. Since moving into the house he had let the foliage grow wild—"do it's own thing," as David called it.

She said, "A garden needs structure, like everything else in life. Plants form their own patterns, but with trimming and the proper feeding, the roots grow strong and the colors leap out in spring. I learned that from my mother, the master gardener."

He was having fun, although he wouldn't admit it. David raked as she rambled through the garden, clipping, shaping, and piling leaves for him to pick up.

"No resting on the job," she yelled when she caught him idle.

"I was checking out your backside when you bend over. It's a rare, entrancing sight."

Nina laughed and went back to working. The garden was beginning to take shape. The flowers reminded her of the Mills College tradition of "passing the candle," signifying a woman's engagement. A diamond ring tied delicately inside a bouquet of flowers beneath a burning candle was passed slowly around the dinner table. The drama intensified until the candle stopped in front of the lucky lady, who blew out the candle and slipped the ring on her finger.

At the time it seemed a hokey tradition, a cop-out to modern thinking. Nina never thought she'd want the candle passed to her. Then she fell in love with David, her wild yet fragile flower. Burgeoning desire for a deeper commitment remained her secret. David couldn't deal with forever. He had said so many times.

"Give me some slack, baby. Don't try to change who I am," was his refrain whenever she hinted she wanted more. Nina wondered if he knew, any better than she did, who he really was. She hoped he would change, but felt the probability of that happening was about as good as the odds of Sly Stone showing up on time for a concert.

Nina silenced the rumbling in her heart and carried on.

Rather than giving him an incentive, the awards chilled David's creativity. He developed a major case of writer's block. When Nina asked what was bugging him, he answered cryptically, "The pressure. There's too much pressure."

"Am I interfering?" she asked with concern.

"No, sweetheart. You inspire me," he insisted.

Getting David to sit still long enough to complete a project was a major challenge. She hid his stash to prevent "inspiration breaks" and took the phone off the hook when he was working. At first he balked when she cut off his distractions. Upon reflection, he thanked her for doing what needed to be done.

"I'm not worried about my job. I can do that with my eyes closed," he said. "What pisses me off, I was making progress on the novel and then it just stopped."

"Go back and do some cleanup work. If you don't feel creative, tighten up what you have. It'll happen again, once you relax."

Together they edited the completed portion of his manuscript and outlined a few ideas for an ending. Nina was stuck with the bulk of the typing. She didn't mind. She would do almost anything for him. Just when she felt they were making real progress, David tore up the new pages and tossed them into the fire. He was obsessed with searching for a perfect ending, unable to decide whether the hero would find his place in the universe or wander forever. At every stop in the hero's time travel there was a woman waiting to love him. Inevitably at the point of crisis the hero catapulted into a different time zone, leaving the woman and his pursuers behind. A happy ending was always just beyond the hero's reach.

"There's no such thing as a happy ending for a Black man," he said when she questioned him.

"Maybe not politically speaking, at least not in the present time. But there are other things. Your writing is unique because of its energy and excitement. But after all the hoopla, readers want their heroes to find satisfaction. Your hero, Izaak, has traveled through ancient African civilizations, hung out in medieval times, and jetted into a wild and wacky future. Don't you think it's time for the brother to settle down?"

"Why mess up the groove? He's got fire and he's got passion."

"Fire and passion have their place, but they burn out.

What comes next? What's beyond the fire? Answer that and you'll have the perfect ending."

"I knew I shouldn't talk to you about certain things," David said in a fit of agitation.

"Why, because it's hitting too close to home?" Nina asked.

"Certain aspects of the male personality you can't appreciate."

"Like what? Help me appreciate these inscrutable male things."

"Come over here. I'll show you an inscrutable male thing," David answered jokingly.

Nina wasn't amused. "You can't deal with anything serious." She got up and went downstairs for water. When she returned David was typing. She wondered if he had heard anything she said.

An uneasy silence pervaded the room as Nina watched him work. She was curled up in a chair, studying the back of his head. From a distance his hair looked formidable— large and looming in every direction. When she ran her fingers through it, it compressed like cotton candy, then sprang back like a sponge when released. She loved his hair and everything beneath it, except the quirkiness of his character that seemed destined to keep her at bay.

Without reason she felt like crying. Nina missed him, desperately, even though he was still there in the room.

She walked over and massaged the back of his neck. He read it as a sign of sexual interest. Wanting touching, not teasing, she resisted when he tried to pull her down. Their signals had crossed again.

David stood up and asked, "You want anything from downstairs?"

"No," she answered, and went back to reading.

Chapter Twelve

"LISTEN, YOU TWO. There's less than eight hours before tonight's debate and I need a consensus on this issue. I don't want to sound like I'm talking out of both sides of my mouth." Roland stuck his feet up on his desk and waited to be convinced.

Austin explained his position. "I think you should dodge the issue at all costs."

"How can he dodge one of the main issues in the campaign? Neighborhood police substations are on everyone's mind."

"Nina, give him a chance to finish," Roland insisted.

"If you support it, people in the community will feel betrayed. If you oppose it, you'll be viewed as weak on crime. The only safe approach is to say you're studying the issue, but haven't reached a decision," Austin said.

Nina could barely wait for Austin to finish.

"That would be political suicide," she stated firmly. "The last thing you need, Roland, is to come off sounding wishy-washy. So what if you turn off a few voters? You'll look ridiculous when the question comes up and you fail to take a stand. We know where McFarlane stands, we know where Donna Dixon stands. Don't be afraid to say where you stand. I think Austin is underestimating the Black community by assuming we don't want police presence. What we want is responsible, controlled, and representative police presence. The old lady who got her purse snatched doesn't give a damn about the teenager running around screaming 'Off the pig.' Sure, you'll take flack from the more militant

134

organizations, but they won't endorse you anyway. You know my reservations about the police, but it's time to get beyond our personal feelings and weigh each issue in the broader context."

"You sound like a politician," Roland commented, smiling his approval of Nina's approach.

Austin slammed his folder shut and hastened from the room.

There was no point engaging in an argument that he would surely lose. Roland gave his stamp of approval to almost anything Nina proposed. She had a private line to him that no one, including his campaign manager, could tap into.

"I did it again. Offended Austin," Nina said.

"I wouldn't worry too much about him," Roland answered, looking unconcerned.

"I could've said it nicer, but we can't afford to be in the 'no opinion' category again. It's killing us."

Nina was totally absorbed in campaigning. When she wasn't at headquarters, she was into her studies. Sheila stopped to chat during an infrequent foray through the library.

"Let's go up on the roof and fire one up," Sheila suggested.

"No, I can't. I have to finish this outline before the candidates' forum tonight.

"You're so serious nowadays," Sheila observed.

"I have to be serious to get anything done." Nina's eyes went back to the outline. When she looked up Sheila was still standing there, assessing her critically.

"What's up with you?" Nina asked.

"What's up with you is the question. You ain't got time for nobody but Roland. Maybe I need to talk. Maybe my shit is shaky." Tears were forming in Sheila's eyes.

"I didn't mean to cut you off," Nina apologized. "Let's take a walk. I can always come back to this."

Nina listened as Sheila unloaded weeks of pent-up frustration.

"I had no idea you were so down about Derrick. You looked like you were handling it well," Nina said.

"Even the ice princess melts every now and then."

"Have you had a chance to talk to Derrick, one on one?"

"Not really. His parents secluded him from his friends. They were the problem to begin with. Derrick never wanted to go to law school. He was a star athlete on the U.C.L.A. tennis team, could've turned pro. His parents convinced him that sports is not a respectable way to make money. They pooh-poohed his talent to the point that Derrick stopped believing in himself. You should've seen him in his heyday, Nina. In addition to having good technique, he was graceful and quick. He'll never be happy as a lawyer, especially working in his father's law firm."

"Do you think the drug bust will ruin his chances with the bar?"

"They'll figure a way to get him out of it. Derrick will never be his own man as long as Mommy and Daddy are pulling the strings."

"Do you want him back?"

"No. I miss him like crazy, but our relationship has run its course. I just want to feel good again."

"You will, Sheila."

Nina never got back to the outline. She had a hard time shaking the melancholy after wallowing in Sheila's problems. Sheila dropped Nina off at the auditorium after declining an invitation to attend the forum.

"I'll probably go home, wash my hair, listen to some records. I'll be okay," Sheila reassured her.

"Keep your head straight," Nina advised.

After a quick emotional adjustment, Nina bounded inside the auditorium where the debate was taking place.

She instantly spotted David huddled with Donna Dixon. Donna was "cheesing" so hard Nina wondered what could possibly be that interesting.

By the time David finished with Donna, Nina was preoccupied, too busy to talk.

"You coming home with me tonight?" David asked.

"We have a debriefing after the debate. I'll get home on my own."

"It would be nice to spend some time together. We seem to be going in different directions."

"So it seems, but there'll be plenty of time after the election. I'm sorry, sweetheart, but I have to set up. Your photographer is trying to get your attention."

Nina pecked him on the cheek and went back to what she was doing. She straightened Roland's tie, whispering last-minute instructions in his ear. David watched with folded arms and raised eyebrows.

Nina took a seat among the roomful of spectators and waited nervously as the candidates took their seats. A lot was riding on tonight's debate, the final showdown featuring all the candidates. The tension in the air could almost be felt.

T.J. sat next to Nina. She camouflaged her annoyance by smiling stiffly. The moderator opened the meeting.

Roland's opening statement was clear, concise, and touched upon all the major issues. Eloquently he stated, "City services are in a dismal condition, particularly public transportation. We have people fighting, smoking dope, and generally intimidating the people who need public transportation the most, our valued senior citizens." The applause was loud and sustained. Nina nodded, recognizing the tidbit she had fed him about the bus system. "Poverty and crime are serious issues facing our community. The only lasting solution is to put our young people to work instead of putting them in jail. It's cheaper to build and maintain industry than to build and maintain prisons." More applause. Nina made a mental note. In future speeches, this would be an appropriate point to address the issue of police brutality as a way of balancing out his anticrime stance. Roland went on to decry the condition of the public school system and pledged to work with the superintendent and the school board to "give our children a better future." Safe, sound, well said. Nina relaxed.

Next up was the front-runner, Michael McFarlane, who

rambled on about his close ties to the community—pure fabrication. When the audience applauded, Nina suspected he had "plants" among them, since no one had the slightest idea what he was talking about.

Donna Dixon was equally cryptic in her message, but her dynamic speaking style made her a crowd favorite. T.J. hooted and howled his approval. Then Dixon took a shot at Roland. "Let me know the next time you ride a city bus, Mr. Hill. That would surely be a sight."

Dixon crammed everything from socialized medicine to reexamining corporate tax breaks into a five-minute presentation. McFarlane, a big-business advocate, could barely control himself.

Each candidate was allowed two minutes to answer a set of questions asked by the moderator. In a nonresponsive answer McFarlane pointed out, "Miss Dixon's comments regarding tax incentives demonstrate why people unfamiliar with business or government should not hold public office. If we create an unfriendly atmosphere for business, they'll move somewhere else. We need them more than they need us."

Donna Dixon answered indignantly, "Don't question my qualifications, Mr. McFarlane. Your experience has dulled your sensitivity to the people rather than sharpening your ability to lead."

McFarlane countered, "You're not a serious candidate."

Fuming, Dixon looked ready to strangle him. Roland stayed out of that fray.

By the end of the structured portion of the forum, Nina was satisfied with Roland's performance. He managed to get in a few licks without taking any major blows.

The moderator solicited questions from the floor. T.J. launched into a long statement preceding a question directed, naturally, to Roland. Roland did an excellent job of summarizing and answering what he believed to be the question. His previous run-in with T.J. had prepared him well.

"My final question for you, Candidate Hill . . ." T.J. persisted.

"I'm sorry, but in fairness to the rest of the audience, I have to limit each person to one question." The moderator cut him off.

"I don't mind responding to a follow-up question, assuming it's brief," Roland said.

"Is it true that you're romantically involved with a member of your campaign staff?" T.J.'s question stunned the audience.

Roland's eye twitched furiously. He was hyperventilating so hard, he couldn't get words to come out.

Nina restrained herself from slapping T.J., but the words flowed freely. "That's it! You're way out of line."

"Hey, you can't blame a fellow for asking a legitimate question."

"That's the lowest form of slander. You're a fool and you're invading Mr. Hill's privacy," Nina said.

"Public figures have limited rights to privacy. Besides, truth is an absolute defense."

Nina took two steps toward T.J., unsure as to her next course of action.

"Everyone settle down. Take a seat," the moderator urged.

David grabbed Nina before she was forced to decide between letting it all hang out in public and allowing the snake, T.J., to slither quietly into his hole.

"Sit down or deal with me," David warned T.J.

"I got no problem with you, brother man. We're on the same side. I don't know why the sister is so upset. The question was directed to the candidate." T.J. scanned the audience to see if his question had the desired effect.

After repeated attempts to restore order, the moderator convinced everyone to take their seats. T.J. wisely moved to the back of the auditorium. Nina was livid, trembling with anger, but managed to stay in her seat. The debate was reduced to a meaningless exercise. Everyone remained focused on T.J.'s wild allegation, which effectively neutralized Roland's previously sterling performance.

David came up to Nina and said, "Maybe you should come home with me."

"No. I can't. If I run away now, they'll think it's true. I'll see you later," she responded, and hurried to catch up with her group, which was reassembling at headquarters.

"What the hell is happening?" Roland pressed his supporters the minute they gathered behind closed doors. No one spoke. Austin was busy biting his fingernails, gnawing with the intensity of a dog coveting a fresh bone.

"It's hard enough getting mentally psyched for these events, but having to deal with vicious gossip on top of that is unacceptable. Am I coming from left field or is someone undermining my campaign? Where is this stuff coming from?" Roland pounded the desk to emphasize his point.

The room fell quiet. Finally, the conspiracy of silence was broken by a brave, somewhat naive volunteer. "Roland, the rumors started circulating last week."

"Who started it?"

"I don't know," the young man answered, obviously sorry he had spoken up in the first place.

"When these rumors started, why didn't one of you tell me instead of waiting for it to surface at a public meeting. Where's your loyalty?" Roland threw his hands up in despair.

Everyone squirmed and looked at their feet, except Nina, who knew that she was the unnamed object of the rumors. Although no one would come out and say it, they blamed her for all of Roland's problems.

Austin seized the opportunity to wade into murky water. "Roland, you've been so involved with giving speeches that you've obviously forgotten how important appearances are."

"Are you suggesting I've done something improper?"

"No, but a lot of other people are," Austin quipped.

"Anybody can start a rumor. What's the matter with you? I shouldn't have to explain myself to my own staff."

"Yes, you do, when the only person you listen to is Nina." Austin had stopped pussyfooting around. Once the cat was out of the bag, they all chimed in their discontent. It was apparent that the focus was more on Nina's favored status with Roland than on winning the campaign. Nina listened in resigned silence as the staffers enumerated a long list of complaints.

Roland adjourned the meeting at midnight, after agreeing to be more open to their concerns through the remainder of the campaign. Everyone was exhausted, but no one more so than Nina, who had suffered the greatest abuse.

"You need a ride home?" Roland asked as the group began to disassemble.

"No, thanks. It wouldn't be a good idea under the circumstances."

"Nonsense. I won't let a bunch of gossipmongers control me. We need to talk anyway. Grab your stuff and let's go," he insisted.

As they entered the freeway, Roland asked, "What did you think of the debate—that is, before your law school buddy blasted me?"

"You were splendid. Anyone who came with an open mind had to pick you as the winner. Of course, a lot of folks were already committed."

"That's the problem with that format." Roland paused, then said, "Nina, I want to apologize for all the bullshit you've put up with. From my crazed wife to that jealous bunch down at headquarters. And that little bastard Austin had a lot of nerve challenging me in public."

"I brought some of it on myself."

"How so?" Roland asked.

"Austin thinks I pushed him out of his spot."

"He needed to be pushed out. With the lousy job he's doing, he's headed for the unemployment line. You know I wanted to get rid of him, but you insisted on letting him ride it out. He ought to be thankful rather than resentful."

"We also need to talk about the other problem." Nina paused to figure out how to say it. "We've been playing a dangerous game, Roland. I was flattered by your attention and I needed a friend to talk to. Now it's affecting the campaign, which is the last thing I wanted."

"It hasn't been a game for me. The only thing I regret is that the rumors aren't true." Roland fell quiet. "I don't care what people say. I like being with you."

"It's not right, Roland. No matter what David and Brenda did, it doesn't justify walking wide-eyed into an impossible situation. I respect you as an employer and I love you as a friend. Let's keep it at that. You don't need scandal."

"You're right, but I'm sick of doing the right thing." Roland exhaled loudly, gripping the steering wheel tighter. "Maybe it's the pressure of the campaign. I'm surrounded by these people, supposedly working on my behalf. I've never felt lonelier in my life. Everybody's looking over my shoulder, second-guessing me. I need to be supported, to be appreciated. Not just as a candidate, but as a man."

"I wish I could make it easier for you, but I can't. I love David."

The conversation ceased until the car stopped in front of the house.

"Would it be better if I left the campaign?" Nina asked.

"It would kill me if you left. Promise you won't desert me. I don't want you to be uncomfortable, but I need you to get through this campaign. I was wrong telling you how I feel. I can't control my feelings, but I can control my actions. Can you forgive my stupidity?"

"It's all forgotten," Nina assured him.

Roland leaned over and kissed her on the cheek.

David watched as Nina climbed out of the car. It surprised her to see him standing in the window with the blinds completely open.

He went on the offense the second she opened the door.

"You've got a lot of nerve hugging and kissing that sucker right in front of the house."

"Oh, please. I was not hugging and kissing him. He kissed me on the cheek. That was all."

"You're not fooling me, Nina. All this bullshit about work and the campaign is a bunch of crap. At least be honest about it."

"Don't try to label me, David. If I wanted Roland, I'd be considerate enough to leave first, which is more than I can say for some people."

"I'm not the one on trial. You think you know so much about Roland. You don't know anything. I've seen the man operate in the street. He's not the quiet family man you think he is."

"You're talking out of jealousy."

"I'm speaking from firsthand knowledge. I may not have degrees like you and Roland, but I'm not stupid."

"You're sure acting stupid."

Her words pierced his heart. David glared at her, then stomped out of the room.

She hadn't done anything wrong, except for choosing her words poorly. There was no reason to apologize, but she couldn't forget his look of a wounded child. Why am I always the one making amends when he's the one being unreasonable? she wondered. Nina considered taking a hard-line stance, then decided to call a truce.

"David, I'm sorry," she said as she entered the study. "I didn't mean to imply that you're in any way stupid."

"Okay, fine," he answered without looking up.

"Then look at me if it's fine."

David raised his eyes reluctantly. There remained a residue of anger that needed to be resolved.

"We can't keep snipping at each other."

"I'm trying to figure out what's goin' on. I can tell by the way that muthafucka looks at you—he wants to get in your drawers. It pissed me off hearing that shit in public."

"I'm not doing anything with Roland. I don't want anyone but you. . . . You have this ridiculous double standard. It's okay for me to be publicly humiliated, but your ego is sacred. I can't accept that. If you were doing right by me, you wouldn't be worried about Roland."

He heard what she said but sidestepped the issue. "I

don't understand your thinking. You let him bring you home after what came down at the meeting. It's a form of insanity."

"Brenda doesn't have a lock on insanity."

"What do you want from me? I apologized for my mistake, but you keep throwing it in my face. It's like you want me to do wrong, or maybe you're looking for an excuse to do wrong yourself."

David waited for Nina's usual quick comeback. She slumped in a chair as if the wind were knocked out of her sails.

"I'm sorry, baby, I didn't mean to jump on you. Are you all right? I was hyped when you came in."

"It's not you. It's what happened after the debate." Nina went on to describe the debriefing.

"Don't let that bother you. Austin Greene is nothing but a chump, riding on other people's coattails. It's time for him to be revealed for the no-talent fraud that he is."

"Now don't get started. I shouldn't have told you about the meeting."

"Why? I thought I was more than just your boyfriend."

"You are, but I'm in an awkward position trying to protect Roland's campaign and share my thoughts with you."

"I'll be glad when it's over so we can go back to being friends. I miss my friend."

"I miss you too. I'm sorry if I upset you," Nina said.

"All is forgiven."

"I think I'll go to bed. I'm whipped. You coming?"

"I'll be up in a minute. . . . And, Nina," David added as she started up the stairs. "Tell Roland to keep his lips to himself."

Chapter Thirteen

DAVID YELLED FROM downstairs, "Nina, what's taking so long? Reggie's outside blowing like a madman."

Nina pulled the sharp metal prongs of the hair pick through her afro, while staring blankly into the mirror. "I'll be down in a second," she yelled back. Her mind was preoccupied with the whereabouts of her birth control pills. She always kept them right there in the medicine chest. Better hurry up, though, before Reggie had a heart attack. The thought of hanging out all day with Reggie was less than appealing.

She had no choice since the T-Bird was in the shop being repainted. Someone had maliciously dug a deep scratch in the door of the car. David was incensed. They were messing with his prized possession. Nina talked him out of naming Brenda as a suspect when he filed the police report. While there was no physical evidence connecting Brenda to the crime, Nina started keeping a log of the incidents.

"David, did you see my birth control pills? They're not in the cabinet."

"Yeah, I took a couple to give us a little extra protection," David kidded.

"We'll see how funny it is when you cain't git none," Nina answered, pressing her index finger into his chest. "Did you get the picnic basket?"

"Everything's in the car, except you. Now bring your fine self on before we miss the whole concert."

David held open the front door to Reggie's super-fly

Cadillac. The pimpmobile, as Nina called it, sported a diamond in the back window and deep-set chrome rims that dazzled the eye when in motion. According to Nina, Reggie used the car to attract women and used David to keep them interested. Reggie's rap left everything to be desired.

"No. I'll ride in the back." Nina plopped down on the plush red velvet interior. Before they could hit the highway, Reggie turned up the volume on the radio so loud that the back speakers reverberated. Nina tried to conceal her irritation.

"Turn that down, man. You'll blast Nina out of here," David protested.

"That was obviously his intent," Nina muttered too low to be heard. She looked straight ahead, past Reggie's mutton-chop sideburns.

"I thought you were setting me up with one of your girlfriends," Reggie said to Nina.

"My friends were busy today," Nina lied, knowing she hadn't tried.

"It's their loss," Reggie answered. "How many young, successful, handsome businessmen do you know?"

At least he was right about being successful. Reggie had built a fledgling carpentry business into a lucrative enterprise employing more than twenty men. He worked hard at least twelve hours a day, played for ten, and slept for two.

"There aren't many men like you, Reggie," Nina answered, tongue in cheek.

They parked almost a mile away from the stadium, the site of the all-day jazz concert. Reggie didn't want anyone parking too close to his car.

"We missed the first two acts," David said, grabbing Nina's hand and whisking her inside to find a spot. It was high noon under unrelenting California sun, "earthquake weather," as Nina's mother referred to it. Nina could tell from the fogged-out look on their faces that most of the audience had started partying before the first note was played.

Nina had spread a handmade quilt over parched grass and arranged refreshments by the time Reggie, huffing and puffing, caught up with them. Sweat streamed down his high yellow face, which had turned a strange hue of crimson. Purple veins popped out of his neck.

"Damn. I feel like I ran the hundred-yard dash five times," Reggie complained.

"It's hot like a mutha out here. We tried to find something in the shade, but the early birds beat us to it. Is that Mike from the *Sentinel* over there?" David asked.

"Yeah, that's him," he answered his own question. "I'll be back in a second." He was off and running.

"You want something to drink, Reggie? Might cool you off."

"Sure. Pass one of those beers."

"Maybe you should start with something nonalcoholic. Alcohol makes you hot."

"I'm already hot," Reggie responded.

Nina ignored the tacky pun, poured lemonade, and passed it before he could argue.

He took two gulps and put a steady bead on her. "Despite what you think, Nina, I like you a lot."

"Oh, is that right?" she answered without changing expression.

"Our relationship was strained at first, but now I understand completely why my man is so into you. You're intelligent, attractive, and possess certain domestic skills that a lot of women nowadays don't have."

"Was that a compliment?"

"Yes. It was. Being a good homemaker is not a negative, contrary to popular opinion. I admit I was a little upset when you came on the scene."

"Why were you upset?"

"You don't realize how much you changed things. We used to meet almost every night after work down at Sadie's. The party would move on from there, usually to my place or David's. I can't stop by in the middle of the night anymore or convince David to stay out until daybreak."

"I'm sorry I ruined your party, but there's a time and

place for everything. David does what he wants to do. You know that."

"I'm not criticizing you. I think the change is good—in most respects. But don't try to change him too much. The man's a magnet. David will do anything for anybody. People love him because he knows how to bring them up, put them at ease. A lot of times you read him the riot act when he's trying to be a friend to me."

"What? Like helping you chase women."

"That's not all I'm about. Sometimes we sit up bullshittin' all night, just me and D. Brothers need to do that. He's crazy about you, but a man needs freedom. Put him in a gilded cage and he'll fly away. . . . So much for my unsolicited advice." Reggie stood up before Nina could respond. "Let me see what those fools are lying about over there." He walked away.

Nina thought about what Reggie had said. Was he trying to frighten or reassure her? She couldn't figure it out.

Reggie approached David and Mike, who were deep in discussion. Mike paused long enough to clasp hands with Reggie and then returned to pressing his point.

"Man, you can't bypass a story like that. Fifty percent of good journalism is timing. That's some sensational shit, a candidate accused of sleeping with his assistant."

"Even if it's not true?" David asked.

"How do you know it's not true? And why do you care? All you had to do was include the word 'alleged' several times in the column and the paper would be in the clear."

"I know it's not true because the person he's supposed to be sleeping with is my woman."

"Oops! You should've said that up front, brother, instead of letting me put my foot in my mouth."

"I wanted your unbiased opinion. The editor jumped all over me for not running the story. I've earned my reputation, but there's limits to how low even I will go. In all good conscience I can say that I've never written a story I didn't believe was true."

"Yeah, man, but if he finds out why you killed the story, he'll nail your black ass to the cross."

"He already knows. I told him."

"What! Who is this woman that's got you putting your job on the line? This doesn't sound like the David Hamilton I know."

David wasn't about to reveal Nina's identity to Mike, the snoop. Reggie did it for him.

"That's her, standing over there in the hiphuggers and white top." Reggie pointed toward Nina, clapping appreciatively for the set that was ending. Low-slung jeans hung just below her belly button. Her T-shirt was knotted under braless breasts, exposing a long expanse of narrow midriff. Sunlight struck her chestnut hair, shimmering with streaks of gold. At that instant she caught David's eye and smiled the sweetest smile he had ever seen. Mike was in a trance.

"Close your mouth," David warned Mike, staring in awe at the bronzed beauty. Her skin was perfect, a deep golden honey spread with a finely bristled brush.

"I take back everything I said. Fuck the story. That's worth losing a job over," Mike said. "You gonna introduce me, man?"

"Hell, no. You standing here with a hard-on in the middle of the stadium. Stay right where you are. I'll catch you later."

Mike ignored David, following him like an eager puppy to where Nina was standing. Reluctantly David introduced him to Nina. After two minutes of Mike's drooling David reminded Mike that his date was looking for him.

The sun descended behind rolling hills under a lingering cloud of incense and herb. David slept soundly through the middle acts. His head rested on Nina.

The voice of Pharoah Sanders warbling "The Creator" rejuvenated him. He sat up and pulled Nina into his lap, cradling her in his arms. Warm lips kissed the back of her neck as she gripped the underside of David's strong thighs. Nina was on fire, but she grabbed his hand when it touched her swollen nipple.

An intruder in the midst of their happiness, Reggie got up to circulate.

They left before the final act played out. Exhausted and saturated with music, they decided to beat the stoned-out crowd to the freeway. Nina drove since Reggie had consumed a full bottle of Rhine wine.

"Did you find your pills?" David asked, anticipating being alone with her.

Nina shook her head and looked into the backseat where Reggie was supposedly sleeping. Reggie looked out of it, but she suspected he was listening to every word.

Lying on the welcome mat when they arrived home were two empty packets of birth control pills. Every tiny pink pill had been removed from the circular containers. The front door was wide open.

"Oh, no." Nina held her head in her hands. "She's in the house."

"Stay here while I check it out."

"No, David, don't go in there."

"I've got to. It's my house."

"Be careful."

Nina held her breath as David entered.

Within ten seconds panic struck. Nina called out, "David, are you okay?"

No answer. She stepped inside, calling out again, "David, where are you?"

When he appeared at the top of the stairs, Nina breathed again.

"Everything's okay. No one's here." David came down to hold her. "You all right? She's trying to scare us."

"She's doing a damn good job."

"Let me turn the lights on, then I'll call the locksmith."

"How did she get in? You didn't give her the key to the house, did you?"

"Of course not. The only woman with a key to this house is you. We should call the cops."

"Let's think about this first. Is anything missing?"

"Not that I noticed, but I haven't had a chance to check."

"Do you really want the police prowling through the property?"

"Come on and say it, Nina. You don't want Roland's wife implicated in a break-in."

"Do you?"

David didn't say anything. He found a flashlight and started searching the house, inside and out. Nina was his shadow, too spooked to be alone.

It was an hour before the locksmith showed up and rekeyed all the locks. When he left David took out his tool kit and nailed the windows shut. Now they were completely shut in, safe until they ventured outside. Nina scowled as she remembered what Reggie said about the caged bird.

David had unleashed the fury of a wild woman he thought he could control. If there was any humor in the situation, it was watching David squirm every time the phone rang or someone knocked unexpectedly. Nina tried hard not to blame him for Brenda's madness, but she couldn't help feeling that he had brought this on himself.

Despite appearing outwardly cool, the continuing harassment had shaken Nina badly. She considered calling the police, but what would she say? "My boss's wife is out to get me because my boyfriend stopped sleeping with her?" She would sound as crazy as Brenda. On an even deeper level she had an inbred mistrust of police, stemming not only from her arrest but from years of watching them operate in the Black community.

Nina was too nervous to sleep, but David insisted she get some rest. "I'll stay up and keep an eye on things."

"What are we going to do, baby? You can't stay awake forever."

"I'm an old hand at this late-night stuff. Go to sleep and let me figure it out." David added, "I love you," as she slipped beneath the covers.

Now she knew he was worried.

David waited until Nina had left for the day before entering Roland's campaign office.

Roland looked up from his desk to see his least favorite person standing in the doorway.

"You heard enough gossip at the debate to fill your little column. Surely you don't expect an exclusive interview," Roland said.

"I'm not here for an interview. I don't deal with gossip, just the facts. We need to talk about Brenda."

"The last time I tried to talk to you about my wife, you were abrupt to the point of rudeness."

"You're right. I didn't handle the situation well. When you asked me to leave Brenda alone, I had already left her alone. The problem is getting her to leave me and Nina alone. Do you mind if I close the door?"

"Go ahead. Not that it matters. Everyone knows more about my business than I do."

"Look, Roland. I was wrong to get involved with your wife. I would change things if I could, but it's too late for that. All I can say is I'm sorry. I can't tolerate what she's doing to Nina."

"I know Brenda's a nuisance, but Nina seems to be doing okay."

"She's not okay. She doesn't tell you half of what's goin' on because she doesn't want to upset you. Brenda calls the house continuously and hangs up. She left a dead bird on my doorstep. So many messages have been scrawled on the car window, I stopped counting. She scratched my car. Yesterday someone broke in the house while we were gone. Nina was scared to death."

"How do you know it was Brenda?"

"The only thing missing was Nina's birth control pills. The empty packets were left on the welcome mat. Sounds like the work of a jealous woman to me."

"In your case there could be any number of jealous women."

"You're so self-righteous. You were in the same streets that I was in. The only difference between me and you is that I'm straight up with my shit. Pretending to be this holier-than-thou politician doesn't give you the right to judge me. I came here to get help in stopping Brenda. If you don't cooperate, I'll go to the police myself. I've tried to convince Nina to get a restraining order. She refuses. She's trying to protect you from negative publicity."

"Nina doesn't have to protect me."

"Why'd you give her the song and dance about how the publicity would damage the campaign and hurt your son?"

"That's a fact. I didn't try to persuade her one way or the other."

"You're more interested in protecting yourself than protecting Nina or anyone else, for that matter. Preying on her sympathy to get what you want. You're the latest cause. Once Nina's dedicated, there's no changing her mind."

"Is that why she puts up with you?"

"That's none of your business. Or is it? Let's make it plain. Are you using Nina to get back at me?"

"I don't give a damn about you, or Brenda either, for that matter. My wife and I lost touch before you came on the scene. Your cheap little affair was an untimely embarrassment. I could have done without it. Unfortunately, Nina loves you and there's nothing I can say or do to change her mind."

"Then back off. Why were you kissing her?"

"So that's what this is about. Casanova's concerned about me moving in on his territory. I don't owe you any explanation. You weren't concerned about territory when your big feet were trespassing all over mine."

"I didn't come here to argue. I'm trying hard to be civil, but you're making it tough."

"You created this problem, now you want to dump it in my lap," Roland responded.

"Wait a minute. I've accepted my share of responsibility, but don't sit there and suggest I created this monster. Brenda's problems didn't start with me."

"What do you want me to do?"

"Whatever you have to do to make her leave us alone."

"Anything else?" Roland asked.

"No."

"I trust this conversation won't make tomorrow's headlines."

"This is a private matter, unrelated to your campaign. In case you haven't noticed, I didn't report the allegations made at the debate."

"Was that your feeble attempt to protect Nina?"

"Somebody has to protect her. You sure as hell won't."

Chapter Fourteen

NINA WAS FURIOUS when David told her about his visit to Roland.

"You asked me not to talk to Brenda or the police. What other choice did I have? If Roland can't stop her, we're getting a restraining order."

Whatever Roland said to Brenda seemed to work. Brenda was quiet, which was almost as scary as knowing what she was up to.

Two weeks without incident lulled Nina into false security. She could leave the house without wondering what was on the other side of the door.

Then a typewritten note stuffed in her mailbox at the office made the danger more ominous than ever.

"Leave David or he'll be writing your obituary," the note read.

Nina stuffed the note in her backpack and scanned the office quickly. Austin was at his desk, typing feverishly. He must have felt her eyes upon him. He looked up, smirked, and continued typing.

Nina lifted her eyes to heaven and said, "One psycho at a time, Lord. One at a time."

Austin fueled Brenda's anger, she suspected. He was always listening and loitering around her work area.

If Nina wasn't stressed, she could've pitied Brenda, locked in fanatical obsession, allowing a man to rule her heart and her mind.

Nina decided against mentioning the note to Roland. He was having enough trouble with preelection jitters. If David found out, he'd head straight for the cops. The break-in had been the final straw for him. "Brenda can't be tripping in and out of this house. Who knows what she'll do next?"

Nina had a class within the hour. She headed for campus, still undecided about what to do.

"Is that you?" Nina called out to T.J., trying to sneak by in the law school corridor. T.J. was wearing a Brooks Brothers suit straight off the rack. He looked ridiculous in the stiff suit with his three-inch afro and a beard that needed trimming.

"Yeah, it's me."

"What's happenin' wit da clothes? You're not your usual dashikied self," Nina said sarcastically.

"Oh ... Uh ... I have a job interview?"

"Say whuuut?" Nina pressed him.

"I have an interview with Simpson, Hatcher and Leland."

"That's a large White firm, T.J. Were you aware of that?"

"Yes, I'm aware of that," T.J. answered softly. He glanced around furtively to see if anyone was looking.

"You were the one who insisted that the Black man must not join institutions that enslave us. So why are you, a Black man, interviewing with that firm?"

"It's kind of involved, you see. My father is a judge in Philly and he set up this interview for me. I'm doing it out of respect for the old man."

"That's a lame excuse. It's all right for you to do it out of respect, but it's wrong when someone else does it for any reason." Nina jammed him.

"Cool down, Nina. Don't embarrass me," he pleaded.

"Why not? You embarrass everybody else. You're a fake, using heavy-handed tactics to crush people like Roland and Estrellita. You've got everything and everybody figured out, except yourself. When we disagreed in the past, I always respected you as a man of conscience. That shit you pulled the other night was low-down, dirty, and nasty."

"My information came from a reliable source."

"What reliable source?"

"You know I can't divulge that."

"Then I'll have to divulge that you're interviewing with Simpson, Hatcher and Leland. The brothers and sisters will get a kick out of that."

"Okay, okay. I got the information from your campaign manager. Austin Greene hipped me to what was happenin'."

"Did it ever occur to you that Austin has his own reasons for telling lies?"

"Why would I care about his reasons? If it helps my candidate, I use it. Since we're in the information-trading business, let me drop another tidbit on you. I hear your boy Austin is on the take from the McFarlane camp."

"Don't try to play me. This is serious. Where'd you hear that?"

"I already gave up more than you bargained for. If you want to sweeten the pot a little . . ." T.J. said, looking at Nina devilishly.

"You want a knee to the nuts?" Nina stared him down.

"All right. Let's just say I'd bet my stash on the information. There's nothing you can do at this stage in the game. Election day is right around the corner, and Donna Dixon is sitting pretty."

"How do you figure that?"

"Defectors from Roland Hill's camp will come over to Donna Dixon."

"That's real smart thinking, T.J.," Nina said. "Defectors, if any, will go to McFarlane, not Dixon. Let me do the math for you. By taking votes away from Roland, you increase the chance that McFarlane will win a majority in the primary. If he gets a majority, by one vote, no runoff is required."

"Roland should have thought about that before putting his name on the ballot."

"He did. That's why he asked Donna to stay out of the race. She can't win, she's just a spoiler." Nina stopped to catch her breath. "Getting back to the issue at hand. I'm not surprised about Austin, but I'm surprised you would stoop so low to imply that Roland and I were having an affair."

"I didn't use your name."

"You might as well have. Everybody caught the drift."

"It's nothing personal. All about winning. You know, like Malcolm said, 'by any means necessary.' "

"Malcolm also said, 'as long as it's intelligently directed and designed to get results.' Your candidate gains nothing from this. The only person you're helping is McFarlane."

"Perhaps my technique was faulty. I get a little out there sometimes, but I'm basically a decent guy," T.J. said, deluding himself.

"By 'out there' you must mean selfish. You brothers are so selfish. . . ."

"Don't stereotype. Are we still talking about me, or do you have something else on your mind?" T.J. asked astutely.

Nina took a deep breath before answering. "What you do is none of my business. What I do should be none of yours. Good luck in your interview."

Roland had to be told about Austin. She called him from a pay phone in the basement. "Roland, I need to talk to you."

"Shoot."

"Not on the phone. In person."

"What did my wife do this time?"

"It's not about Brenda."

"This sounds enticing. Should I break out the champagne?"

"You won't feel like celebrating when you hear what I have to say. Meet me at Peppy's on University, in, say, twenty minutes."

"I'll be there."

Coffee and pastry were waiting on the table by the time Roland arrived. She figured he might need sustenance.

"I can't believe that son of a bitch did this. I never trusted that freckle-faced bastard in the first place," he said when Nina revealed what she had learned.

Surprised by Roland's language, Nina said, "I didn't know you had that in you."

"I didn't either until just now."

"That's why I didn't tell you in the office."

"Good thing. I might've kicked his ass on the spot."

"Stay focused. It'll work out." Nina reached across the table to calm his shaking hand.

"What do we do now?" Nina asked.

"Fire his butt!"

"Let's think this through. T.J.'s not the most reliable person in the world. There's a chance he might be lying."

"I don't think so. Everything adds up to sabotage. Mishandled press releases, screwed-up account books, mailers getting misplaced between Austin's hands and the post office. Remember how you found the invitations conveniently stashed behind the filing cabinet? If you hadn't followed up with phone calls, we might never have known it. I'm sure Austin was looking forward to an empty ballroom and a stack of unpaid bills. How blind could I have been?"

"Don't beat yourself up." Nina moved closer to Roland in the booth and rubbed his back.

"I can think of a better target. Let me go deal with him." Roland rose from his seat.

"Wait. Maybe there's a better option than firing him. What about placing him on administrative leave? It could deflect some of the fallout in the office."

"No. I'm firing him. That turncoat will squeal like a pig anyway. I want him totally and completely out of my sight."

"Do you want me to go with you?"

"I can handle this myself. It's probably better that you not be there."

When Austin exited Roland's office, his back was stiff as a board.

"Where is she?" Austin asked, cleaning out his desk.

"Where is who?" Roland responded.

"Our dear Miss Nina, the prime architect of this hatchet job."

The office froze. Everyone knew what was going on but tried to steer clear of the fallout.

"It's time you stopped blaming Nina for your shortcomings. You've got nobody to blame but yourself. Now leave before I tell everybody what a weasel you truly are."

In his parting speech Austin said, "You'll be hearing from me. Tell Nina I'll deal with her later."

Roland shook his head. "It would be just like him to try to sue me. Why is everybody standing around? There's a lot of work to do. We have to clean up Austin's mess."

Roland waited until he cooled down before making the formal announcement.

"You're all aware by now that Austin Greene has been relieved of his duties as campaign manager. I won't go into specifics, but I will say that his removal is based on general mismanagement and dereliction of duties. Considering the short time until the election, no formal replacement will be announced. We'll continue to operate as usual. I've asked Linda to assume responsibility for publicity and press relations. Since this matter is media-sensitive, refer all questions to Linda."

They had been on the road almost an hour before David emerged from his pensive mood. "The first time I saw you I thought you were the finest woman on earth," he said. "But it was more than your looks that kept my interest. You had a natural sweetness beneath your bold exterior. Your inner and outer beauty captured my heart. Now I see you changing, Nina, growing cynical, moving away from me."

"Was it sweetness or naïveté, David, that you found so attractive?"

"See what I'm saying? Everything is a contest. We can't talk anymore."

Her comment had sounded harsher than intended. "I'm sorry. I shouldn't be defensive, but I feel like I'm under siege."

"I'm not the enemy, Nina. I don't want to see you hurt."

Nina was quiet, confused by where the conversation was going.

"Reggie said he saw you yesterday with Roland, sitting in a booth at Peppy's Diner. You were so focused on every word Roland was saying, you never noticed Reggie looking at you. He said your brown eyes sparkled with excitement. You took Roland's hand and reassured him, rubbed his back, and smiled tenderly. I could picture the scene Reggie was describing. You used to be that way with me."

"David . . ."

"Don't talk. Shhh." He pressed one finger against her lips. "Let me finish. I haven't always lived up to your expectations. I've loved you as best I can. The pressure is deep, trying to please you and stay true to myself. I turned my life upside down for you, Nina, and now you're doggin' me with another man."

"It's not true."

"I don't want it to be. Since I met you I haven't been with another woman. Nobody can please me the way you do. I know I'm losing you, Nina."

"I thought I was losing you."

They cruised the road to Bodega Bay talking, sharing fears and unexpressed doubt.

"If you were lost in the ocean," Nina asked, "who would you want with you? Me or Reggie? Would Reggie share his last drop of water with you? You have to believe me, David, no matter what Reggie told you. I closed my ears to gossip and trusted you."

David's fingers laced inside her slender fingers. He raised her hand and kissed it tenderly. Nina rested her head lazily on his shoulder, counting giant eucalyptus trees passing overhead. The winding road and aroma from the trees made her dizzy. He stopped twice to let her catch her breath. At a quaint country store they found motion sickness tablets. Nina gulped down two, leaning against David for comfort.

David had scrambled to rent a weekend cottage when Nina said she needed to get away. They dropped everything and drove away from the city to a place where they could be alone.

Nina ran ahead of him on the beach and waved for him to come to her. David kept his distance, wrote a love song in his head. He was hale fire. She was delicate wind that could fan his flame or smother him out of existence.

"I don't want to go back," she said when he caught up with her.

"Do you mean that?"

"Sort of."

"I knew it. You're hooked on the action. I kidnap you to get your attention and I still can't pull the plug."

"You wouldn't if you could."

"Maybe not. I'm glad you're doing your thing, but sometimes I want you all to myself. We used to spend hours alone doing nothing. Well, not quite nothing."

"I thought you wanted me to be independent."

"I do, but don't exclude me. Let's go inside."

"Sounds good to me."

They lay face to face talking and caressing.

"Where have you been?" David asked.

"Right here."

"Uh-uh. I've been looking for you," he said, inching his way between her legs.

David loved her like a man afraid of losing his woman. She was satisfied quickly, but he went deeper and made her come again.

She stole a catnap; he started growing and filling her inside. He loved her until he knew she was his woman and the fear inside him died.

David stopped at a newsstand on the way home. Nina was sound asleep.

"Nina, wake up. Look at this headline. Roland fired Austin Greene. It's all over the *Tribune*. They got the scoop on me—again."

Nina yawned loudly. "What did you say?"

"You know exactly what I said. You talked me into leaving town so I'd miss the news about Austin's firing. 'I need to get away, David,' you whined, then whisked me off to no-man's land to keep me occupied. You knew about this, didn't you?"

"Of course I did, but it wasn't something I could share with you."

"You have a strange way of deciding what to share and what not to share."

"There was no way I could tell you what was coming down without betraying Roland. We discussed this before. Our business and personal lives are separate."

"Your business is your life. You don't have time for me. All you think about is Roland and the campaign."

"I won't talk while you're irrational."

"Irrational? You haven't seen irrational. My job is a joke to you. You think I enjoy wading around in people's garbage? I don't, but for the time being it pays the bills. Your priorities are screwed up, Nina. Think about supporting me for a change instead of looking out for Roland."

David slammed the car door and started the engine. It was no use trying to talk to him. His jaw was tight and his teeth were clenched. He looked straight ahead and didn't say a word, all the way to Oakland.

Chapter Fifteen

NINA ASSUMED HE'D get over the incident, but her "disloyalty" had inflicted a serious wound. David took on the attitude of an aggrieved victim. She suspected his hurt was connected more to her relationship with Roland than to the Austin Greene story, which wasn't earth-shattering news.

"Can we get beyond this, David? I've gone out of my way to apologize. Forgiveness is a two-way street."

"I know."

"Do you want me to leave?"

"No," he said, then turned his back on her. The freeze was on, especially in the bedroom.

Nina questioned whether subconsciously she had betrayed him. The answer kept coming back no, but it did nothing to improve their relationship. She had to carry on without waiting for David's forgiveness. Get through the election and graduate. That was the simple strategy.

Estrellita appeared unexpectedly, bearing gifts to atone for the disappearing act. Nina touched Estrellita's swollen belly and felt the miracle of life move inside.

Insensitively David warned, "Don't get any ideas."

"That's mighty presumptuous of you," Nina said, looking him up, down, and out of her face.

The news update began before Nina and Estrellita hit the couch.

"Derrick is out on bail, living with his parents pending trial. They treated Sheila like the culprit, claiming she led their Black Prince astray. Can you get to that?" Nina asked.

"Sheila had some rough moments, but my girl moved on

to the next phase. Next to my mama, she's the toughest sister I know. She should teach a course on how to love 'em and leave 'em. I could use some pointers."

"Speaking of which, how's things going?" Estrellita motioned toward the bedroom where David had retreated after a respectable interval.

"It's, uh . . . going. That's all I can say." Nina raised her eyebrows, signaling a necessary delay in discussion.

"Girl, tell me all about your job interviews."

"I started late, but I'm on the case now. The hardest part was psyching myself up. I have a mental block against job hunting. My latest encounter with T.J., which I'll tell you about later, reminded me that I had to get off my butt. According to my estimate, I'll be working for the next ten years to pay back Uncle Sam. That's assuming I find a job. What happened to the lady lawyer who cops a glamorous position right out of law school?"

"She moved to Mars."

"The interviews haven't been too bad, except for one. This asshole senior partner from a no-name firm in San Francisco asked what my father did for a living. I asked him what that had to do with anything.

"My father worked all his life doing manual labor. He was forced to retire due to work-related injuries. He's a proud man. He'd rather work than sit home and bug my mother. I couldn't let this nerd belittle him. I looked at the interviewer, stood up, and walked out."

"It's a shame we have to put up with that shit."

"Welcome to the real world. It's fun being a student, old enough to do anything and young enough to shun full-time employment. Grown-up work sounds like a drag."

"I wouldn't mind trading places with you." Estrellita looked down at her fat belly. She put her hand in the center and gave it the pregnant-woman rub.

"Everything okay with the baby?" Nina asked.

"The baby's fine. It's the baby's father I can't deal with. He ran like a coward when he found out I was pregnant. I'll have to take him to court to get child support. Since he's still in school, it'll be like dipping into an empty well. I feel like the world is rushing toward me, full speed, without brakes."

Nina tried to think of something comforting to say but came up short.

"We'll manage though. My mother's been really supportive, which shocked the hell out of me."

Nina leaned forward, lowered her voice, and said, "This job crisis is minor compared to my personal life. I can't continue indefinitely this 'loose' living arrangement. Somewhere along the line my parents' 'antiquated' values started creeping up on me."

When David came down the stairs, Nina didn't budge.

"I'm going out," David announced, standing in the doorway.

"Bye," she answered, instantly resuming her conversation. He closed the door and kept stepping. The impasse deepened.

After a brief silence Estrellita asked, "Nina, will you be the baby's godmother?"

Nina cried as she accepted humbly. "This is as close as I'll get to motherhood."

"Don't say that. There'll be a house full of little Davids running around before you know it," Estrellita reassured her.

"Not likely," Nina said.

"David's not as bad as you think. He takes care of you, he's handsome, and he's employed. I'd take any one of those three. You're too hard on him, Nina. Compared to the fool I'm dealing with, David's a saint. You know you love that man. So work with it."

"I love him, but he's driving me crazy. There's no comfort in love that makes you compromise yourself. David's content to keep things the way they are. He's scared to death of commitment—runs when his freedom is threatened and clings when I pull away. The man is master of the yo-yo syndrome."

Estrellita laughed. "Girl, you're insane. But you need to

lighten up. You jumped all over David when he made the comment about my pregnancy. He was just kidding."

"You think I overreacted?"

"Just a tad. David's a decent man. He trips out every now and then, but they all do. If he was the kind of man you could keep under your thumb, you wouldn't want him. It's rough out here. Don't throw him back too fast."

"I'm not ready to give up, but it's getting deep. All we do is argue. It started out with me not trusting him. Now he doesn't trust me. He's thinks I'm fooling around with Roland."

"What's the skinny on Roland?"

Nina described the situation with Brenda, the campaign rumors, and the impasse with David.

"Reggie must specialize in killing other people's high. You have to be careful though. Men don't handle infidelity well. When they screw up they expect us to roll over and live with it. We get caught and it's a federal offense."

"I haven't done anything wrong. Maybe a little flirting."

"Give David's ego time to heal. It'll all be forgotten when the election is over."

"I hope so. You didn't come here to listen to my problems. Let's have some fun."

"Old whale body can't drink and can't smoke because of the baby. Don't let me hold you back. I can enjoy it vicariously."

"That's not what I was talking about. I've gotten to the point that I don't enjoy it myself. After the shit that came down with Derrick and being spied on by a madwoman, I had to cool out. I need all my brain cells to deal with David Hamilton. What about a triple treat? We could hit Baskin-Robbins and eat ourselves silly. I can taste the hot fudge and caramel. Let me grab my shoes."

They were steady yakking when the lights went out in the ice cream parlor. They waddled out of Baskin-Robbins and headed home. Estrellita decided not to come up when she dropped Nina off.

"You and your man need some time alone," Estrellita insisted.

"Why? So I can kill him without witnesses?" Nina laughed. "The car's not here. I guess he's still brooding."

"Can you blame him after the cool send-off you gave him? Do me a favor. When he gets home, find a way to make it right. You could be sleeping alone, like me, with a fat belly."

Nina nodded. "Take care of yourself. Call me as soon as the baby comes, or even sooner, if you need me." She knew Estrellita would need her. More amazingly, she believed her godchild would have a good mother.

Nina ran upstairs and straightened up the bedroom. She changed the sheets, put on new pajamas and perfume, then waited for David to come home.

David seized upon Estrellita's visit as a chance to hang out at Sadie's Soul Kitchen.

The usual contingent of regulars was seated at the counter, sopping gravy running freely from homemade mashed potatoes. The energy level in the room shot up when their local celebrity, David Hamilton, made the scene. The fringed vest he wore over a pointed-collar print shirt shimmied each time he took a step.

"Hey, man. What it is?" David slapped five with a husky-voiced brother wearing a too-tight leather jacket. A Pall Mall cigarette balanced between the man's deep-brown tobacco-stained lips.

David kept meeting and greeting as he cruised through the dining area to the back room. He stopped at the bar, shrouded by a heavy cloud of smoke. Sadie, the grand matriarch of the establishment, exited the kitchen to give him a hug. At seventy, Sadie still enjoyed the attention of the relatively young men who gathered almost ritualistically to eat the same fried food, fraternize with the same people, and tell the same lies they'd been telling since Sadie's opened.

"Where you been, sweetheart? I thought you'd put me down," Sadie said, looking up at him.

"No way, baby. Just a brief hiatus. You knew I'd come around to check on my girl." David kissed Sadie's wrinkled forehead before she moved on to the front room. He was home again, in his element.

"My main man. What's happenin', brother?" Reggie greeted David enthusiastically. He ordered another cognac from the bartender and set it down in front of his friend.

"I'm surprised to see you here tonight. I thought you'd be home banging out the story."

"What story?" David asked.

"You didn't hear? A process server strolled in an hour ago and served Roland Hill with divorce papers. Every brother in the joint went on alert when the man blew in. He walked straight to Roland's table and dropped the bomb on him. I felt kinda sorry for the brother. This is the first time I got a scoop before you. You losin' your touch, David."

David bolted from the bar stool.

"Where you goin'?" Reggie asked.

"I have to get home. . . . On second thought, you live closer than I do. Can I use your typewriter?"

"No problem. Do I sense trouble in paradise?"

"Nina's on a rampage. You know how women get sometimes. I don't need her looking over my shoulders."

"Let's go," Reggie said. "What if I line up a couple of babes to help us unwind when you finish working?"

"Man, all you think about is pussy," David said. "I'm not into partying right now."

"Okay, okay," Reggie agreed reluctantly, pushing his skullcap back to reveal a half-moon bald spot. "I can make a few phone calls . . . just to get things rolling."

David was too preoccupied to answer him.

Reggie tossed a bill on the counter and trotted to catch up with his friend, running fast into the wind.

* * *

Nina rose with the dawn and hit the bricks before weariness from the night spent alone could weigh her down. She wanted to be in the wind when David came home full of excuses why he didn't call. She would get angry and lash out, he would apologize, swear he was sorry, then turn around and do the same thing again.

Professor Collins walked into the classroom, empty except for Nina, who was sitting and waiting for the lecture to begin.

"Are you all right, Miss Lewis? I don't believe I've ever seen you here this early."

"I'm fine, Professor Collins. Just excellent, in fact," Nina answered.

"The essay on your last exam was also excellent. I like what I've been seeing," he complimented her.

"Thank you for noticing."

Nina moved through the morning like an efficiency expert, intent on getting to headquarters as early as possible.

With only a few days before the election, the last thing she needed to deal with was David's foolishness. He built wide emotional rivers; she was tired of trying to cross. Despite her worries, Nina kept pretending she had it all under control.

"This place looks like the morgue. What's the scoop?" Nina said loudly as she walked into the office. "And you look like the dearly departed," she said to Roland, who was sitting in the outer office in what appeared to be a stupor. His coloring had changed from deep, rich cocoa to an ashy, gray pallor emulating death. Roland's proud shoulders sank beneath his burden.

Nina shuddered as the worst possible scenario scanned through her brain. The silence escalated her fear to unbearable proportions. This has something to do with David. I know I wished him dead last night, but I wanted to be the one to kill him, she thought.

Someone shoved an article containing David's picture and byline into her hand. Nina sat down and read while the rest of the staff studied her face for reaction. There was no way to hide her shock and disappointment. David's article announced that Brenda Hill had filed for divorce from Roland. He didn't stop there. He suggested that a man who cannot handle the home front is unfit to run the city.

The second paragraph read, "Roland Hill sacrificed his home life in his quest to become mayor. Attorney Hill, you're wearing too many hats, none of which seems to fit you well."

"Thanks to your boyfriend, we could be finished. Did you give him an inside tip?" someone accused before Nina finished reading.

"I didn't know anything about this. Roland, you don't think—" Nina said.

"Everybody slow down," Roland demanded. "Nina had nothing to do with this. I was served with divorce papers in a very public place frequented by a certain journalist, whom we will not discuss at this time. My wife is having major personal problems, which, unfortunately, she's trying to resolve in a public manner. I appreciate everyone's concern, but this is my life, my career. I'd like to see it through with some degree of dignity. Infighting is counterproductive. We have a few days to go, so let's get on with it." Roland rose to his feet like a weary cowboy ready for the final roundup. He asked Nina to come into his office.

Nina opened her mouth to speak, but Roland cut her off. "Don't apologize for him, Nina. I've never known David to do anything this mean-spirited. Fucking my wife was bad but not surprising. This type of character assassination is an all-time low, even for him."

Nina was speechless, unable to defend or understand what motivated David to write the article. He scavenged enough trivial gossip to fill the lines he was required to produce each week. To twist the knife in Roland, whom he had already wounded, was merciless.

"Roland, I'm sorry. I have to get out of here. It's too much to handle right now. I'll call you when I get my head straight."

Nina was too upset to react to snide comments overheard

as she hurried from the office. It was a contest to see who could pick her bones clean first.

She leaned on the buzzer at Sheila's, rousing the next-door neighbor before the midday nap queen made her way to the door. Sheila's hair was completely flat on one side, giving her face the appearance of a squashed tomato. She opened one eye and recognized Nina, who was talking too fast for a mind submerged in sleep.

"Do you still need a roommate?" Nina asked.

"Yes. Why the sudden change?"

"I'll fill you in while we ride." Nina handed Sheila her purse and sandals and literally pushed her friend out the door.

"I can't believe he wrote that," Sheila commented after hearing about David's article.

"Believe it. I don't see his car. I guess he's still out on last night's binge. Let's get in and out before he comes home," Nina suggested as they pulled up in front of the house.

"Can everything fit in the car?"

"Sure, I don't have that much stuff. Mainly my clothes."

Nina pulled clothes from hangers and handed them to Sheila. The bulkiest item, a muskrat coat purchased from a secondhand store, she wore while she packed. Books and school supplies were tossed into a cardboard box too large for one person to carry. Nina slipped on the stairs, almost taking Sheila down with her. The box wouldn't fit, so they dumped everything in the trunk.

"What about my plants?" Nina asked. "David won't take care of them. They'll die."

"I don't think they'll fit. We'll have to come back later."

"There is no later. What we can't carry, I sacrifice."

"Anything else?" Sheila asked, huffing and puffing from the challenging climb.

"My albums. I have to get my records." Nina attacked the stairs, two at a time. Her adrenaline was pumping.

"Check the bathroom and study to see if I left anything,"

Nina told Sheila. "I'll sort through these albums while you do that. Then we can haul ass."

They moved quickly through the house, fanning out to gather her belongings. There was no time to reflect on the meaning of her actions. Flipping through the albums made the memories move a little closer. They tugged at her heart-strings as records she associated with David were pulled from the pile. When Nina felt herself tearing up, she accelerated her work, determined not to swim in sentiment that could bring her down.

She had to leave today or accept his bewildering brand of love. A volcano of sadness was about to erupt. Nina put a lid on it, grabbed as many albums as she could carry, and headed out.

David was standing in the open doorway, looking perplexed. He asked casually, "Baby, what's goin' on?"

Nina blew past him without saying a word and proceeded to the car to dump her last load. Sheila soon followed with an armful of goodies.

"Let me grab my purse and give him his key. I'll be right down."

"Do you need backup?" Sheila asked.

"No, I'm fine," Nina answered with steely conviction.

David was sitting on the couch when she reentered, obviously recovering from last night's adventure. His normally luminous eyes were bloodshot and the stubble on his face made him look old.

"Come talk to me, Nina." He patted the space on the couch beside him. Nina kept standing, looking at him coldly.

"I know you're pissed off because I stayed out without calling, but I got so involved with this article that I lost track of time. Why don't you bring your stuff back inside? I'll help, soon as I get my head straight."

"You don't get it, do you, David? I don't give a damn about you staying out. I'm through worrying about a man who doesn't respect me or himself."

"I respect you, baby. I had a few drinks after I finished

working, so I slept at Reggie's. You were so evil when I left last night, I didn't think you cared."

"Save it, David. You respect me so much that you wrote a low-class—no, correction—*no*-class article about a decent man that I've been busting my ass to get elected. You didn't think about Roland, you didn't think about his family, you didn't think about me."

"Now wait, Nina. I'm a journalist. What I wrote was the truth. It's my business to report newsworthy items."

"How does a divorce action filed by a deranged wife qualify as a newsworthy item?"

"I didn't create the story, just reported it."

"Like hell you didn't. You don't think your fuck-a-thon with Brenda Hill had anything to do with this divorce? She did this to get attention, and you helped by giving her headlines."

"If I didn't report it, someone else would."

"This is one time you should have let someone else take the lead. The lowest blow of all was your suggestion that Roland is unfit to be mayor. Who made you the judge of fitness? You went way beyond objectivity."

"You can't see straight when it comes to Roland."

"Was the article directed at Roland or me?"

"That's ridiculous."

"Is it, David? Here's the key to your house," she said, struggling to get the key off her ring.

"I can't believe you're leaving because of the article."

"It's not just the article and you know it. We're miserable. We don't belong together."

"You don't mean that. Nobody can love you the way I can."

"That's sex, David, not love. . . . You've been running since we got together. You don't know how to be happy."

David looked at her with puppy-soft eyes intended to break down her defenses.

Nina threw the key on the couch and walked out.

Her footsteps faded as she walked away. A car door

slammed. An engine started. David didn't get up to look outside.

"She'll be calling me within an hour to come pick her up," David said. He glanced around the house, suddenly large and empty, and noticed the plants blooming in the windowsill. "See, she left the plants so she'd have an excuse to come back," he said, still talking to himself.

Too agitated to sit still any longer, he got up to shower and shave. David rested his hands on the porcelain basin and dropped his head to think. He needed a minute to digest what was happening. In the mirror he saw a man frozen in confusion. The mechanics of everyday existence eluded him. He couldn't shower, he couldn't shave, he couldn't decide if he was coming or going. Walking to the bedroom was a major feat.

"That woman must have put a whammy on me." David laughed, then collapsed atop the bed. A coat hanger tossed in her haste to get out stuck him in the back, propelling him to his feet. David cried out from the pain and cursed her for leaving. He ranted for a full minute before returning her pointed weapon to the closet. Her clothes had hung there less than six months, neatly pressed and well organized. He had teased her about her penchant for order. In a matter of minutes order vanished from his life.

Sheila's phone number was scribbled on a note pad buried somewhere in the study. After a frantic search he found the number and dialed it. No answer.

"Answer the damn phone," he hollered at the ringing receiver before slamming it down forcefully. His phone rang almost immediately. He leaned back and said smugly, "Hello."

David's face fell when he heard Reggie on the other end of the line.

"Man, the tongues are waggin' about your article. I know you're stopping by Sadie's to celebrate."

"I don't feel like celebrating. Gimme a rain check."

"What's this rain check shit? You're on fire, man. Let it burn," Reggie insisted loudly.

David was quiet.

"Oh, I see, the little lady got you doin' penance again?"

"The little lady has left."

"Take it easy, brother. Look at it this way. It might not be so bad. You can stop pretending to be a homebody. That domestic shit ain't your style. Hold on a minute. I gotta catch this dude before he leaves."

"I'll check you later," David said, hanging up. He closed the blinds in case Reggie decided to drop by.

David sprawled across the bed and shut his eyes. Bubbles of light exploded wildly beneath tired eyelids. His eyes popped open. He stared at the pattern in the ceiling, searching for space where misery could not find him.

Finally exhaustion conquered his restless energy. David dozed throughout the chilly May evening, then awakened foggy and disoriented. His feet, weighted down by boots he had slept in for hours, were numb, disassociated from the rest of his body. His face bore a set, pained expression. David ran his tongue across his lips and tasted the sour resin from the madness he had created. Nina was gone.

Chapter Sixteen

NINA GROANED AND turned over in slow motion. She wiped the crust from her eyes and squinted at the popcorn ceiling. The crick in her neck from sleeping on Sheila's hard, lumpy couch was a painful reminder.

Nina glanced around the living room of the third place called home in less than nine months. It was time to kick-start her brain into action. She would arrange to get her bed out of storage, but first she needed to check in with Roland. Her discomfort was probably minor compared to what he must be feeling.

She reached stiffly for the phone and made her call. "Hi. Let me speak to Roland."

"He's not in," someone answered.

"Do you know what time he's coming in?"

"Who is this?"

"Nina."

"He may not be coming in today. I'm sure you can understand. Is there a message?"

"No. I'll check his law office. Thanks," Nina said, and hung up.

She left a message at the law office, rolled off the couch, and jumped in the shower. When she emerged, Sheila was struggling to face the morning.

"Where you headed so early?" Sheila asked.

"Nowhere. I wanted to feel clean."

"Ready to celebrate your freedom?"

"Celebrate? I'm barely breathing. I know I did the right thing, but it hurts."

"It will for a while. . . . So, what's up with you today?"

"I'll probably sit around and watch the soaps. Anything to keep from thinking. Sanford said he'd help get my bed out of storage, but that may not happen until tomorrow."

"How's Roland?"

"I don't know. I haven't been able to get in touch with him."

"Well, hang in there. It'll take three months to get David completely out of your system."

"Three months? You've got it down to a science."

"Exactly. The first month is for healing. Month two is for scouting but not committing. By the third month, put on your high-heel sneakers and break out. It's too bad we're not at the same point in the cycle. We could do some serious damage."

"I'll pass for now."

Nina fixed dinner by scraping together the few edibles in Sheila's refrigerator. By the time Sheila got home, Nina's eyes were puffy from crying. Sheila pretended not to notice.

They watched television until Nina couldn't stand it anymore. *Sanford & Son* was a rerun. She'd puke if Cher flipped her hair again.

"I'm throwing a few things in the washer. My clothes didn't fare too well in the trunk. You have anything that needs washing?" Nina asked.

"No. I did that yesterday."

"Where's the key?"

"There's no key. The laundry room is open. Use the washer farthest from the door. The other one breaks down if you look at it hard."

Nina gathered her clothes, grabbed the Tide and an oversized bottle of Clorox.

"If Roland calls, tell him I'll be back in five minutes. You know what to say if you-know-who calls."

"David knows I'm lying every time I say you're not here. I hate being in the middle."

"You'll have to hate it a little while longer. I don't want

to see his face or hear his voice," Nina said, closing the door behind her.

Frayed, dingy hallway carpeting looked funkier than ever. Everything looked gray and kind of dull since yesterday. Cement stairs led down to the garage where the laundry room was located. One good thing about not having a car, she wouldn't have to spend much time in the dimly lit garage.

Nina shoved the clothes in quickly, added detergent, and waited for the bleach light to come on. Out of habit, she looked over her right shoulder, checking for nothing in particular.

A door closed in the distance, possibly a car parked above on street level. Nina stepped to the door of the laundry room and looked toward the ramp entrance to the garage. Darkness had already fallen. The Bay was blanketed by the shadow of night. Evening brought with it a deeper loneliness. She wondered what David was doing. The thought of him made her anger rise. Nina pursed her lips and blinked back tears that she refused to let fall.

She checked the machine again. The light was yellow, not quite ready for the bleach. "Let's go, let's go," she said to the machine. Patience was at an all-time low. They could at least put pictures on the wall or get some magazines, she was thinking when the lights went out in the laundry room. A grinding sound followed by a gurgle made her heart leap. It was the machine, taking its last gasp before dying.

From what she could see, the garage was pitch black too. Clutching the bleach, she blindly inched her way toward the door. Halfway there she heard footsteps moving in her direction. Maybe someone was coming to fix the problem.

"Who's there?" Nina called out, but received no answer.

She stood still, backed up against a machine, and waited. A hot, prickly feeling invaded her body. Sweat saturated her armpits as she tried not to breathe too loudly. The footsteps stopped, then started again, this time more slowly. She listened as they lingered near the door.

Nina clutched the Clorox bottle tighter. A presence within arm's reach rustled. She reared back and swung the bottle with all her might. The assailant groaned and hit the floor. Nina's foot brushed the fallen body as she ran screaming out the door, up the ramp, and into the street.

A man skidded to avoid hitting her with his bicycle. Not so skillful was the driver of a car following close behind. Before the driver knew it, she was right in front of him. He hit the brakes, but it was too late. Nina was hurled into the air like a long-limbed rag doll.

The driver bolted from his car screaming "I didn't see her. I didn't see her."

The cyclist rushed into the street, grabbed the driver, and shook him. "Calm down. We need your help. Call an ambulance. I'll stay with her."

Kneeling, the cyclist told Nina, "Hold on, lady. Someone's gone for help." He put his hand in front of her nose and mouth. He couldn't tell if she was breathing.

The driver returned minutes later. "I called an ambulance and the police. What do I do now?" he asked in desperation. The driver looked down at Nina, who lay there totally still, and began falling apart again.

A yellow Porsche hovered in the intersection, gunned its engine, and zoomed in the opposite direction.

Sheila heard commotion outside but didn't pay it much attention. Something was always happening on her street. When sirens stopped outside the apartment, Sheila went to the window. There was a police car, an ambulance, and someone lying in the street.

Sheila's wail echoed through the building and into the street where she found Nina, lying facedown, on pavement.

When the phone rang David hesitated before answering. Reggie had called too many times and Nina was still holding out.

"Hello," he answered finally.

"David, this is Sheila, Nina's friend."

"I know who you are. You've been giving me the run-around since yesterday. Did Nina put you up to this? Put her on the phone. We don't need a go-between."

"This is not a social call. I have bad news."

David shifted the phone to the other ear, waiting for the punch line.

"Nina's been in an accident."

"Don't play with me, Sheila. This isn't funny."

"I'm serious. She was hit by a car outside the apartment."

"What?"

"I don't know what happened. She went downstairs to do laundry. The next thing I knew, there was an ambulance and police car outside. It happened so fast. . . ."

"How, how bad . . ." David could barely ask the question.

"I don't know. They took her to Kaiser on Broadway. I'm on my way over there."

David dropped the phone, grabbed his keys, and ran out of the house.

The hospital was a maze. Distraught, David could barely remember her name. When he found out where she was, no one would tell him her condition.

"Are you her husband, sir?" the nurse asked.

"No. I'm her boyfriend." Under the circumstances, "boyfriend" sounded silly. He watched helplessly as people in white clothes strode by purposefully around him.

"They're doing everything they can," the nurse reassured him. "The doctor hasn't finished examining her, but as soon as he does, I'll give you an update. Meanwhile, you could help the folks in admissions by providing information on her next of kin."

The term "next of kin" sent David into orbit. Until that point he hadn't acknowledged the possibility that Nina could die. David cried until his body shook.

"Please, sir, settle down. Take a seat over here." The

nurse ushered him to a chair in the waiting room and brought him a glass of water. "Will you be all right?"

"Yes. Did anyone call her parents?" David asked.

"Now we're getting somewhere."

He couldn't tell them if she had health insurance or if she was allergic to any medicine. Once David gave what information he could, he was left alone with his fears.

"Is there anyone I can call to sit with you?" the nurse asked, sensing the depth of his despair.

"No. There's no one. No one but Nina."

Sheila came running down the corridor. Breathlessly she asked, "How is she?"

"I don't know yet. They haven't told me anything," David answered. "If I hadn't upset her, she'd be safe at home with me."

"Don't start blaming yourself. Nina will be all right," Sheila consoled him.

"The last time I saw her we argued. I thought I'd have a chance to make it up to her."

"No matter what happened, Nina still loves you. That doesn't change in a matter of hours. We have to be upbeat. Send out positive energy," Sheila said, putting her arm around his shoulder. "I'm starting to sound like Estrellita."

Sheila sat down and waited with David for the longest hour. He would sit for a few seconds, jump up, and start pacing. David was inconsolable.

Finally Nina's parents joined them.

"Mr. and Mrs. Lewis," David greeted them, but didn't know where to start.

"David, where's my baby?" Nina's mother asked. Her father was too frightened to speak.

David pointed to the door. "The doctor's still in there. I'll tell the nurse you're here."

The doctor came out before David returned.

"Mr. and Mrs. Lewis."

"Yes." Nina's mother grabbed her husband's hand for support.

David walked over to where they were standing. The doctor's expression was not revealing.

"The physical injuries are not as bad as they first appeared. I suspected lung injury because her breathing was shallow when they brought her in, but it's stabilized. She has broken ribs, a sprained wrist, but no apparent injury to the spinal column. I've ordered complete X rays and lab work to make sure we haven't missed anything. Once that comes back, we'll have a fuller picture. She has abrasions on her face, arms, and lower body. They should heal in time. We'll keep her under observation to make sure there are no complications. She's suffered a good deal of trauma. Don't be alarmed when you see her. All things considered, she's an extremely lucky woman. Limit your visit to a couple of minutes."

"What about me? I want to see her." David said.

"Are you immediate family?"

David was tempted to lie but decided not to in the presence of Nina's parents. "No."

"I'm sorry, but immediate family only is allowed in intensive care. Come back in the morning. She wouldn't know you were here anyway."

The doctor reminded Nina's parents, "Keep your visit short."

"Thank God," Mrs. Lewis said, breathing a sigh of relief. "And thank you too, Doctor. We're very grateful."

David and Sheila stood alone in the corridor while the Lewises went in to see Nina.

"Can I get you anything?" Sheila asked.

"No. I'm all right. I want to hang around for a while."

"I understand. I need to check on the apartment. I probably left the door wide open."

"I'll call you with an update."

"Do you have the number?" Sheila asked.

"Do I have the number?" David repeated.

"That was a dumb question. Call me soon. Thanks."

David waited until the Nina's parents went downstairs for coffee, then sneaked inside to see her. He moved slowly to her bedside. Massive swelling had set in and the bruising was pronounced. Nina looked as if her soul had slipped into someone else's body. He reached out to touch her, to tell her that he was there.

"No visitors are allowed in here." The nurse on duty busted him.

"I'm leaving." With his head low David left the room. Nina's parents came back from the cafeteria.

David apologized for his intrusion. "I'm sorry, but I had to see her. Listen . . . uh, I know you don't approve of us living together, but I love your daughter. I'm probably not the kind of man you had in mind for Nina."

"We never interfere in our daughter's personal life," Mrs. Lewis responded.

"I know and I appreciate that. It's the old school versus the new wave." The Lewises stared at him blankly. "Instead of coming to you and telling you our intentions, we moved in together like it was no big deal. I should have taken the time to talk to you. I didn't want you to think I was trying to use her. I've made mistakes—too many mistakes—but I never wanted to hurt her."

"I believe you, David," Mrs. Lewis said. "You look exhausted. Why don't you go home and get some rest. Her father and I will be here."

"I can't leave. I want to be here when she wakes up. I have to tell her that I love her, that I'll do anything to get her back."

"What do you mean?" Mrs. Lewis asked.

"Nina walked out on me yesterday. She was at Sheila's when this happened."

"Does Sheila know what happened?"

"Not really. She said Nina went downstairs to do laundry and somehow got hit by a car. What was she doing outside? It doesn't make any sense."

"We'll have to wait until she wakes up," Mrs. Lewis said.

"I can't stand waiting," David said.

Mr. Lewis spoke up for the first time. "There are times

when life will test your faith. Nina is strong. Our faith must be strong."

"You're right," David admitted. "I'll give you a break. I'll be in the waiting room. Call me if anything changes."

David took a seat on an orange plastic couch, cracked in several places. He looked around for something to read but found nothing except books about motherhood and home-making. He tossed a quarter in a coin-operated vending machine. Coffee tasting like licorice with sorghum syrup trickled out.

The elevator door opened as he tossed the paper cup in the plastic-lined garbage can. Out stepped an enthusiastic young reporter from the *Sentinel*. David left the waiting room and approached him.

"Say, man, you're not covering the story on the babe who took a stroll in traffic?"

David couldn't believe the insensitivity of this rookie. "The babe you're referring to is a friend of mine."

"I didn't know that. Which room is she in?"

"Listen up," David said, backing the reporter up against the wall. "She's in intensive care in very bad condition. If you mess with her or her family, you will never write again. Understood?"

"Lighten up, bro. I'm just doin' my job."

David escorted the reporter by the arm back to the elevator. "Don't even think about coming back. I'll be here all night."

"The boss won't like this."

"Tell the boss to kiss my black ass," David answered.

Two uniformed police officers were standing over him when David awakened the next morning.

"What happened? Is Nina okay?" David asked, sitting up on the orange couch.

"Are you David Hamilton?" one officer asked.

"Yes. Where's Nina?"

"She's awake. Her parents are in with her. Miss Lewis

mentioned you might be able to verify some of the incidents involving Brenda Hill," the policeman said.

"What does Brenda have to do with this?"

"We're not sure, but we're checking out a few leads.
Miss Lewis said she's been harassed by Mrs. Hill. Is that
correct?"

"Yes."

"What kind of car does Brenda Hill drive?"

"A yellow Porsche," David answered.

The officers looked at each other knowingly.

"We need to ask you a few questions. Can you come
down to the station?"

"Yes, but I want to see Nina first."

"No visitors allowed." The nurse spoke from behind the
counter as David headed for Nina's room. It was a different
nurse, but with the same attitude as the one from the night
before.

"I won't leave until I see her," David insisted.

"Ma'am, could you let him in for two minutes so we can
complete our business?" the policeman asked.

"All right, but just for a minute after her parents come
out," the nurse acquiesced. "This is the last time I'm bend-
ing the rules."

When Nina's parents came out, her mother touched David's hand and smiled.

David entered the room apprehensively. Nina's eyes were
closed as he spoke softly to her.

"Remember the time I got stung by bees?" David said.
"You look like my twin."

Nina felt the laughter build inside, reach her face, and
die on her lips. A tiny cough was what came out. She was
too sore to laugh, but she did open her eyes.

"David," she said hoarsely.

He knelt beside the bed and smoothed the cover with his
finger. Every inch of her body was swollen, too tender to
touch.

David struggled to get his words out. "You scared the

mess out of me. Did you tell them I was a bad guy? I have to sneak or bribe my way in every time."

"Don't worry about me. It's not as bad as it looks. They've got me so numbed out I can hardly feel the pain."

"The police want me to make a statement. What did you tell them?" David asked.

"Everything." Nina recounted the ordeal in the laundry room.

"I knew Brenda was crazy, but I never thought she'd come after you like that."

"Neither did I. I think she's trying to kill me. I told the police about the break-in, the threats, the phone calls, and the note. . . ."

"What note?"

"It doesn't matter. Brenda put me through hell." A tear squeezed from the corner of her black eye.

David took a tissue and dabbed away the moisture. The nurse stuck her head in the door.

"I think they're throwing me out again. I'll come back later," he said.

"No. Please don't come back. I don't want to see you. What happened to me doesn't change what happened between us."

"It changes everything. When I thought I might lose you, I couldn't take it."

"David, listen to me. This is not about what you want."

"Nina, please . . ."

"I'm serious. I don't want to see you again. You remind me of Brenda and everything I want to forget."

"Okay. I won't upset you. But if anybody treats you badly or you're feeling down and need company, you know where I am. I'll be waiting."

At the police station, David detailed the incidents he was aware of and found out about a few Nina never mentioned.

"Why didn't you report these incidents before?" the officer taking his statement asked.

"Nina works for Brenda's husband, Roland Hill. He's a candidate for mayor. Nina was trying to protect Roland."

"Where were you on the night of the incident?"

"What?"

"I'm sorry, but I have to ask these questions."

"You'd better think of something else to ask, bad as I'm feeling."

"I'm not suggesting anything, just doing my job. You said Miss Lewis walked out on you. I have to consider all the possibilities."

David took a deep breath to calm himself, then answered the question. "I was at home. Nina's girlfriend Sheila phoned me right after it happened."

"How far do you live from Sheila?"

"Twenty, twenty-five minutes."

"How did the animosity between Mrs. Hill and Miss Lewis get started?"

"It started with me. I had an affair with Brenda before I met Nina. Brenda couldn't accept rejection. In a way, this whole thing is my fault. It all comes back to me."

David signed and dated the statement, then asked, "What happens now?"

"We'll finish our investigation and submit the information to the district attorney's office. If they file charges, you may be called as a witness."

David left the police station in a daze. He had trouble finding his car, which he had parked without thinking. He drove a few blocks, then pulled over and turned off the engine. Lost on his own stomping ground, David had nowhere to go.

Chapter Seventeen

THE TRUMPET OF defeat sounded early for Roland Hill, who spent more time comforting downtrodden supporters than hoping for a miracle on election night. By ten o'clock they shed all pretense of a victory celebration and began dismantling the vestiges of the doomed campaign.

To Nina, Roland was a hero, maintaining the facade of the optimistic candidate until the final ballot was cast. He had risen from the ashes of scandal and kept his message flowing, even though many were unreceptive to what he had to say.

Nina lay in her hospital bed, feeling that this must be her time for losing. A second-place finish was their reward for a brutal campaign that left in its wake a broken love affair, a shattered marriage, and many empty lives. McFarlane garnered 52 percent of the vote, avoiding any need for a runoff. Donna Dixon placed third with less than 10 percent. Nina's prediction had come true. The Black vote was hopelessly splintered. Roland's defectors rolled en masse into McFarlane's camp.

The band called it a night, the streamers came down, the balloons deflated.

The next morning Roland visited Nina in the hospital. They made a point of not talking about his wife.

"We have nothing to be ashamed of," Roland reassured Nina, who was feeling lower than she had after her close call. "We gave it our best shot."

"I can't believe how upbeat you are, considering the circumstances."

"I wouldn't call it upbeat. I'm decompressing after a long, exhausting haul. No one knows better than you how much I wanted to win this race. I guess it just wasn't my time. My son needs me more than ever and my law practice could use some attention. What about you? What are you going to do now that it's over?"

"Take it a day at a time. Can you believe they made me take finals in the hospital? The doctor said I'll be able to attend graduation. I'm not sure I want to, looking like this."

"Don't complain. You look a thousand percent better than you did a few days ago. You're always beautiful to me."

"Thanks. I needed that."

"I take it you decided to pass on my offer to work with the firm full time."

"Roland, you know I can't do that. Too much has happened."

"I understand, but remember, the offer remains open, if you ever change your mind."

"That means a lot to me. I accepted a position with the NAACP Legal Defense Fund. I'll be leaving for Atlanta as soon as I'm able."

"Do me a favor and take David with you." Roland laughed.

"That won't be possible." Nina looked away and sighed. "David calls every day. He's sweet, apologetic, and begging me to come home. Says he wants to take care of me. I keep telling him to let it go. I can't go back to that." Nina gazed at the morning sky and swallowed hard.

"I'm sorry. I know how you feel about him, but it's for the best. I hate to see you unhappy."

"I'm not unhappy. I have my whole life ahead of me and nobody's stalking me." Nina laughed nervously. "Maybe one day, given enough time, you can forgive David for what he did."

"Maybe," Roland answered, unconvinced. "Did you know we talked about the article?"

"No. What did he say?"

"He called it an error in judgment. I figured you put him up to it."

"I had nothing to do with it, but I'm glad to see he's finally taking responsibility for his actions. Take care of yourself, Roland," Nina said, embracing him. "You've been better than a friend to me. I'll never forget it. Tell Matthew I haven't forgotten about our baseball game. It's sad how important things get lost in the shuffle. Don't let Matthew get lost, whatever happens."

"Is this a bad time?" Sheila asked, opening the door to Nina's parents' home.

"No. You might as well be in on this."

Sheila braced herself. "What now?"

"The D.A. refuses to file charges against Brenda."

"What the fuck are they doing? Oh, I'm sorry Mrs. Lewis." Sheila forgot Nina's mother was present.

Mrs. Lewis popped up. "Can I get you girls something to drink?"

"Thanks, Mom. Anything is fine."

"I can't believe this," Sheila said, outraged.

"Believe it. I knew something was wrong when two weeks passed without action. I called the investigating officer again this morning. He said the D.A. declined to file due to insufficient evidence. Here I was pushing for attempted murder and got nothing. Absolutely nothing. I was so upset, I called the D.A.'s office myself."

"What did they say?"

"Everything I didn't want to hear. No battery occurred in the laundry room. I can't identify the assailant. He said it was questionable whether the laundry room incident could be considered the cause of the car accident. Since I didn't report the prior incidents, there's inadequate circumstantial evidence to support charges. It seems my effort to protect Roland boomeranged in my face."

"What about the witnesses?"

"The windows on the Porsche were blacked out. They couldn't identify the driver or say with certainty that it was

Brenda's car. No fingerprints could be lifted from the note I saved. I could kick myself for being so stupid."

"Don't say that. You were trying to do the right thing."

"Look what it got me. Three days in the hospital and a crushing election defeat. What about my pain, my suffering? What about me?" Nina started crying, then tried to get a grip. "I shouldn't be laying this shit on you, but I'm so mad I could scream."

"I understand completely. This was totally unexpected. Last thing I heard Brenda didn't have a lawyer."

"Roland broke down and hired one for her. She's still his wife."

"Bump that. After all you did for him, he should've let that fish get fried."

Nina tilted her head back, running her hand over her furrowed brow. "I'm getting out of here not a minute too soon."

"You still leaving next week?"

"Yes, barring any new catastrophes."

"Oh, I almost forgot what I came to tell you."

"I hope it's good."

"Cedric proposed to me."

"Proposed? You've ônly known him, what—four weeks."

"He's leaving for New York to finish his residency and he wants me to go with him."

"You're going?"

"I think so, but only if I decide to marry him."

"Pardon me for asking a dumb question, but do you love him?"

"He loves me, he has a plan for our future, and he'll be making megabucks in no time."

"I don't know, Sheila. It seems so sudden."

"You have to strike when the fire is hot. I look at it this way. This is about as good as it gets," Sheila said. "I don't want to get stuck in a dead-end government job, waiting for Mr. Right to bail me out."

"Maybe you're right. Just be careful."

"You know my motto."

Nina chimed in, "If the shoe doesn't fit, throw it out."

A sea of black mortarboards lined the lawn of the law school as Dean Wilbur welcomed the graduating class of 1973. Scattered protests appeared on homemade signs, on the back of T-shirts, and on leaflets distributed among the graduating class and their families. The overriding mood was one of peace and relief. The graduates had endured trial by fire and emerged intact, if not entirely sane. As Dean Wilbur had predicted at freshman initiation, their ranks were severely reduced by graduation day. Nina thought about Estrellita and Derrick, then counted her many blessings.

She scanned the faces in the audience until she found her mother and father, seated in front of tall hedges bordering the courtyard. Their intense pride was reflected on their faces.

First came the speeches that no one really listened to as they pondered, individually, the rest of their lives. The roll call began. Nina rose to her feet and waited until her name was called. She crossed the stage in a blur of memories that carried her back in time to her childhood, past the hardship, and into the realization that she had taken an important step. Reaching out, she accepted the degree of Juris Doctor that held far greater meaning than she would have expected. Through her efforts, Nina had moved up from the back of the bus.

As she was leaving the stage Nina spotted David, wearing a wide-brimmed hat and a wildly colored shirt that resembled the flag of a developing nation. Nina smiled and took her seat among the graduates until the final name was called. She needed to close this chapter in her life, which had been suspended since the day she left him.

David pushed his way through the crowd of wellwishers and handed her an oddly shaped present.

"You didn't have to do this," Nina said, holding the gift in her free hand.

"I wanted to. Hope I didn't ruin your graduation by showing up. I figured it was the only way to see you. We haven't talked since you left the hospital. When I call your parents' house, they say you're asleep or not available. I miss you, Nina. There's no joy in my life without you."

"This isn't a good time to talk. My folks are here and I want to enjoy the day."

"Will you have dinner with me?"

"I can't. My mother prepared a big dinner celebration."

"Am I invited?"

"No, David. It's a family thing."

He looked hurt. "I'll leave you alone, if you promise to call me tonight."

Nina looked up and saw her parents approaching. "Okay, I'll call you," she agreed under pressure.

"Hello, Mr. and Mrs. Lewis," David greeted them.

They acknowledged him politely and waited for Nina to take the lead. Nina handed the diploma and gift to her mother.

"Thanks for the gift, David. We have to get out of here before the turkey gets cold. I'll talk to you soon." Nina hooked arms with her parents and walked away, leaving David standing alone in the courtyard.

Nina hadn't told her parents why she had moved away from David's. She never mentioned the article or their disagreement over the election.

An artificial perkiness at dinner masked the pain she was hiding. Nina praised food she barely tasted. Graduation gifts were opened with excess fanfare. She washed dishes with a fervor her parents had never seen before.

When her mother asked if she was going to open David's present, Nina shook her head and said, "Maybe later."

As night fell, her parents wondered why Nina was lingering. She usually jumped at the first opportunity to escape the small Bay Area town. Nina pulled out old scrapbooks and reminisced until her exhausted parents excused themselves and went to bed. The rest of the family had left hours earlier.

Alone, with no further distractions, Nina stared at the gift from David. It spoke to her in silent whispers. She removed the wrapping and held a picture of the two of them in happier times.

The picture was encased in a hand-carved frame she had admired on Telegraph Avenue in early spring. The street vendor whittled a wooden figurine while she examined his wares displayed on black velvet. She browsed but kept coming back to the same picture frame. David was impatient to get to the park, so they left quickly without buying anything.

Nina pressed the gift against her bosom and remembered the sensations of that day: the comfort of his hand holding hers protectively, the urgency of their touching as they drove to Brione Park. She knew their love would last forever, beyond tomorrow and beyond the fire.

He challenged her to climb the hill overlooking the park. She beat him to the top and stood laughing until he arrived, huffing and puffing, at the peak. He took his shirt off to make a pallet, too short for their long torsos. When he tried to pull her down, she resisted.

"No one else is crazy enough to come up here," David reassured her.

"Yeah, but there might be bugs on the ground, or even snakes," Nina protested.

"I got your snake." David laughed, covering her with his body.

Afterward, they sat for an hour, gazing at the lush valley below them.

"When I'm a big-time writer, I'll build a house right there in the center of the valley," David fantasized.

"You can't build a house on public property," Nina reminded him.

"Minor detail. You can do anything you want, if you have enough money."

Nina rested her head on his shoulder and wondered how she fit into his plans, which were always amorphous where she was concerned.

The sound of tires squealing in the street snapped Nina out of her reverie. Her fingers traced the intricate carving of the picture frame. She couldn't believe David remembered how much she admired it. Nina contemplated calling to thank him but dismissed the notion quickly. He would plead with her to come to him. Nina knew she would go. The madness would start all over, unless she stopped it, while she still had control.

Nina wiped a smudge from the glass covering the photograph, then gently placed it inside the crumpled wrapping. She retired to her stuffy little bedroom and lay down, fully clothed, on the twin bed she had slept in throughout high school. She closed her eyes and imagined his warm lips and sensitive hands covering every inch of her body. Nina was healing from the wounds she had suffered, but she wondered if the pain gripping at her heart would ever ease.

Time crept by slowly. She kept moving, making illusory progress. In reality, she was locked in orbit around the rapture, which she had forfeited for the sake of her dignity.

Chapter Eighteen

Atlanta 1976

ESTRELLITA STEPPED OFF the airplane ready to take Atlanta by storm.

"You look great," Nina said, hugging her.

"No, you look great. I'm fighting off ten pounds stuck to my butt since I had the baby."

"I know you've got a million pictures, but I'll give you a chance to unpack. I can't believe you're here after three years of lying about coming to Atlanta."

"It's not easy when you have a child. My whole life is planned around Carmen. This is first time I've been away from her. I miss my baby already, but I needed a break. My mother took time off to baby-sit."

"How is your mother?"

"Great. I didn't think she'd like being a grandma, but she's loving every minute. Speaking of love, guess who I ran into in Berkeley?"

"Who?"

"David."

"David who?"

"Don't give me that. You know you're dying to hear this. I was in the Bay Area two weeks ago and decided to stop at the co-op. Who should be standing in the produce section but David Hamilton himself. The man is getting finer by the minute. You'd better be glad I'm your friend."

"Is he chasing women again?"

"No. He was rather subdued. He asked about the baby

and even wanted to see a picture. I told him I'd moved to L.A., then asked what was happening on the party scene. He didn't know. Said he doesn't hang out anymore. Brenda must've cured him of one-night stands."

The women laughed until they cried.

"Of course he asked how you were doing. Did you like Atlanta and so forth."

"And . . ." Nina pressed for more detail.

"You know I rubbed it in. I told him you were having a wonderful time," Estrellita said, waving her hand with flourish.

"I wish I was having a wonderful time."

"You're still dating Nathan, aren't you?"

"Yes, but it ain't goin' nowhere. Nathan is too intense. He had love on the brain after two dates. Nathan calls so often I had to tell him to pace himself."

"I don't understand you. I'd give anything to have a man love me too much."

"Not if it's the wrong man."

"Your problem is, you still have the David Hamilton bug. Talk to me Nina. You know I know."

"I haven't seen David in years," Nina said, trying to look nonchalant.

"So . . . David still carries a torch for you. Maybe I'm a hopeless romantic, but if someone loved me half that much, I'd swallow my pride and call him up."

"I can't."

"Why?"

"You know what he did to me."

"You mean what he did to *Roland*. That was years ago, and it wasn't all that bad. David told the truth."

"The truth? I thought you liked Roland."

"I did, but he had his faults. You were so gung-ho about the campaign, nobody could talk to you, including me."

"You should've pulled my coattail."

"I tried, but you wouldn't listen. You're such an idealist, Nina. Real people have problems. They don't always do what we expect of them. Did you read David's books like I told you?"

"No."

"I figured as much, so I brought my copies. I hear he's working on something different, a novel."

Nina smiled and said nothing.

"What are you smiling about?" Estrellita asked.

"Oh, nothing. I'm happy David got published. That's what he always wanted."

Nina told the truth. She was happy for him, but sad she hadn't been there when it happened. David was stronger than she thought. Maybe he was getting his act together.

"I'm surprised he never contacted you."

"He tried. The last time was a few months ago. I was working on a high-profile case for the firm. David saw my picture in a magazine and called the office. I never called him back."

"What are you afraid of, Nina?"

"I'm not afraid. Just cautious. So, what shall we do tonight?" Nina abruptly changed the subject.

"Anything involving men and mellow music."

"You haven't changed a bit."

"That's the point. Stay steady, stay strong," Estrellita joked, doing a muscle man pose.

They went to a nightclub where Estrellita charmed the men with a fake Latino accent, donning the persona of a diplomat's daughter on the wild.

"You oughta be ashamed of yourself. You speak less Spanish than I do," Nina whispered.

"Don't bust me now, I'm on a roll," Estrellita said, shimmying her way to the dance floor.

Nina thought the ploy hysterical. The brothers ate it up like catfish.

Estrellita headed back to L.A. in victory, vowing to return to complete her conquest.

Nina picked up the books she'd ignored for three days. David's first book was a series of essays entitled *Images of*

Our Fathers: Stepping Outside the Shadow. The second essay began:

My father never touched me, except to punish or push me aside. By the time I was five I heard him say "Get out of my way, nappy-headed nigger," so many times that I thought "nigger" was my middle name. Convincing myself that it didn't matter was my way of coping with his rejection.

The crawl space underneath the house became my refuge. I ran there when tears threatened to fall. No one could see me cry. I was a man. I didn't need him.

A hole in the porch let through a ray of sunlight, allowing me to write and draw pictures of my feelings.

Every move I made was calculated to show my dissimilarity to the stranger living in my mother's house. Whenever people commented on how much we looked alike, I cringed and vehemently denied it. But in the privacy of my room I mimicked his gestures, including his violent, unpredictable rage.

I didn't know my father well enough to hate him. When he died, initially I felt relief. The threat had been lifted; I fantasized he never existed. Lurking around every corner was fear that he might reappear. I was dogged by the weight of his shadow.

One day a shattered mirror reflected his image back on me. No longer could I discount the parallels between his life and mine. I had always prided myself on being a righteous man, but the suffering I caused was sometimes greater than any pain inflicted by my father. A crippled emotional holdout, afraid of being hurt any more than he already had been—that was my father, that was me.

Reaching out with the hands of a child, I whispered words of conciliation to his restless spirit. I will never know him, at least not on this earth. But I found the key to knowing and loving myself. Forgiving my father freed me to step outside his shadow.

* * *

When she finished the books, Nina immediately called Estrellita.

"Girl, I was so tired after you left I couldn't do anything but sit down and read. Thanks again for David's books. I needed to read them."

"Does that mean you'll get in touch with him?"

"No. It means I understand him a little better. I understand why we could never get together. David told me about his father, but I didn't realize how much he affected him."

"I'm an expert on the daddy blues. You were lucky to grow up with a mother and a father who loved you and loved each other. I'm trying to work out my neuroses to keep from burdening Carmen. It's a bitch, avoiding the sins of our mothers and fathers. Now that I have Carmen my mother and I are closer than ever. I guess it took being a mother to understand. The choices aren't always easy. All these years I blamed my mother for running my father away. She did the right thing. He didn't want us, but I couldn't accept that.

"When you told me about David's father, I felt a sense of simpatico. Maybe you jumped the gun cutting him off completely."

"I wouldn't go that far."

"At least you took the first step."

"I feel better. Now I can get on with my life."

"Don't be too sure."

While talking to a colleague in the lobby of a suburban hotel, Nina felt an arm encircle her from behind. She turned to see a man she hadn't seen since leaving the Bay Area.

"Nina Lewis. You're more gorgeous than ever. Shall I hug you or spank you for staying away so long?" Roland Hill stood back and surveyed her.

Nina was speechless, groping for words.

"This is too much. I thought I was coming down for a

boring meeting and here you are. Where have you been and why haven't you called me?" Roland asked.

"It's a long story, Roland. After everything that came down, I had to get away completely. I thought about you a lot. It's good to see you." Nina hugged him loosely.

"Excuse me, Cynthia. This is Roland Hill, a friend from the Bay Area. Do you mind if I take a rain check on lunch? I haven't seen this man in ages."

Cynthia excused herself.

"Have you been home lately?" Roland asked, taking a seat in the hotel atrium.

"No. I would've called you if I had. My folks come down regularly. I really haven't had a reason to go back. I'll be visiting southern California soon. I'm thinking about moving back to the West Coast."

"Fantastic. Is the NAACP sending you?"

"No. I left there after a year and started working downtown with one of the largest firms in the city."

"If you don't mind my asking, why are you leaving?"

"It's hard to explain. I'm like a fish out of water. Maybe I'm homesick."

"Atlanta is your home."

"It's my birthplace, but my closest relatives are on the West Coast. When I get lonely I drive to my old house and sit outside. The house is dilapidated, the streets are narrow, and the neighborhood is run-down. Everything seems so much smaller. Houses that used to look like castles have shrunk. Sometimes I think I'm shrinking too. I don't know what I'm looking for, but it's not here. The city is dynamic, people are friendly, and the opportunities are endless. The problem isn't Atlanta. The problem is me." Nina sighed. "Anyway, I'm talking with a firm out in Laguna. They need someone to handle civil litigation, and that's all I've been doing for two years."

"I hope you get the offer."

"I got the offer. They're waiting for my answer."

"Quit procrastinating."

"I will. I want to make the right move this time."

"The right move is working with me. I'll be patient as long as you're moving in the right direction. So what's your time frame?"

"I'll give my answer this week and the move should happen within the month."

"Good. I know you've been avoiding the Bay Area because of what happened. Hopefully that will change."

"I'm sure it will. I needed time away from that scene. How's your family?"

"Matthew is excellent. He's grown so much you wouldn't know him. He's losing his baby fat and starting to look like"—Roland hesitated before continuing—"like his mother. I apologize for bringing up bad subjects."

"It's okay, Roland. I can deal with it."

"Brenda and I are divorced, but she sees Matthew regularly. She has a job. Can you believe it? And her own apartment. Brenda had a complete nervous breakdown. She's still in therapy, which helped tremendously. I don't think you have to worry about her anymore."

"I'm not worried about Brenda. I know what to do the next time I run into her: Kick ass and talk later."

Roland and Nina laughed.

Nina looked down at her watch. "I've got an appointment in fifteen minutes. Why don't we get together for dinner tonight?"

"Great. I'm sick of room service."

"I'll make reservations and pick you up at seven."

Promptly at seven Nina arrived at the hotel. She phoned Roland from the lobby.

"I'm in the lobby. Meet me downstairs."

"Come on up. I just got out of the shower."

"The reservation is for seven-thirty at the L-Bow Room. We need to hurry."

"Come up for a minute. You can look at pictures of Matthew while I finish dressing. I have a suite. You won't be in the way."

"All right," she agreed reluctantly. "I'll be right up."

"I'm in room six-fifteen."

Nina entered an elevator covered with reflective metal on three walls and the ceiling. She looked straight ahead at gold-tinted doors, closing slowly enough to give her time to reconsider. An eerie sound, like the groan of a wounded animal, invaded the close compartment as the elevator ascended.

Long, deserted corridors created an aura of mystery. Nina was nervous and couldn't understand why. Several times she glanced over her left shoulder. Except for a room service tray left outside a door, there was no sign of guests in the sprawling hotel. Roland, wearing a bathrobe and nothing on his feet, opened the door as her knock reverberated through the hallway.

Nina smiled and stepped inside, exclaiming, "These rooms are huge. I had no idea the hotel was this nice. They usually put all the money in the lobby."

Roland stood near the closed door with his hands jammed into the robe pockets. The way he looked at her gave her the jitters. She hoped she hadn't made a mistake by coming to his room.

"Would you like a drink?" he asked after an awkward moment of silence.

"Oh, no, thanks. I'll wait till we get to the restaurant. Now get a move on. The place is so popular, they may give away our table."

"You're not taking me to a crowded meat market where we can barely hear ourselves?" Roland asked.

"Oh, no. It's called the L-Bow Room because it's shaped like the letter L. It's actually an intimate setting."

"I'll be ready in two minutes. The pictures are on the dresser," Roland said, closing the bathroom door.

Matthew had grown tall and angular. Nina hardly recognized him. Gone were the gap-toothed smile and round, pudgy face. He was a male version of Brenda with Roland's deep-set eyes.

* * *

Roland's hand touched her waist as he guided her to their table in the restaurant.

Nina inquired about his law practice as soon as they were seated. He gave a two-minute discourse on how his staff and client base had expanded.

Roland moved on to other subjects clumsily. "You're so beautiful, I can't take my eyes off you. Now that we're both unattached . . ."

Nina preempted what was coming next. "Roland, I intend to stay unattached for a while. I don't do well with romance. Either I'm miserable or making someone else miserable."

"Just because you had a bad experience, that's no reason to give up. Look at me. I keep trying, even though I get nothing but rejection from you." Roland laughed to lighten the mood.

"You're one of the nicest men I know."

"Nice. I don't want to be nice. I want to be naughty and unpredictable—the kind of man you love."

Nina laughed with him. "That's not true, it's . . . it's . . ."

"See, you can't articulate what it is. . . . It's been hard, Nina. My wife divorced me. You left and never looked back. None of us got what we wanted."

"I know," Nina said softly, fighting back tears.

Roland handed her his handkerchief. "I see I'm doing a great job of cheering you up."

"You've been wonderful. I needed a good cry. I try to keep the past in perspective. Seeing you, talking about old times, brought everything back. Let's order before the wine goes to my head."

Over a delicious, leisurely dinner they revisited the highlights and low points of the campaign.

"Do you ever think about running again?"

"No. I'd have to give up too much money to become a public servant. I'm where I want to be. Where I *should* be. I don't miss living my life under a microscope."

"One of the reasons I never contacted you was that I felt partly responsible for David's article."

"That's ridiculous. Did you put the pen in his hand and tell him what to write?"

"No, but his opposition to you grew as my involvement in the campaign broadened. I don't think he was conscious of what was happening."

"That's probably true. Man is by nature possessive. He doesn't want anybody pissing on his pole."

"That's a crude way to put it."

"It's crude, but I think it's accurate. David had a hard time not being the center of your universe while the campaign was in full swing. His article was a factor but certainly not the sole reason for the loss. Austin Greene and my wife deserve some of the credit. . . . Is David still important to you, Nina?" Roland asked before taking the last bite of his entree.

"No, no. I needed to get that off my shoulders. It's been bugging me a long time."

"What about dessert? That cheesecake looked mighty good."

"No, thanks. You have some, though."

"You mean you don't want a waistline like mine?" Roland leaned back, pinching several inches around the midsection.

During dessert Roland caught Nina yawning. "Is that a sign of tiredness or disinterest?" he asked.

"I've been up since five this morning and tomorrow morning will be a repeat."

"That's too bad. I thought we'd do the club scene after dinner."

"Let's postpone that until I get back to California."

Inside the hotel lobby Roland asked, "Come up for one last drink?"

"No way. I'm so tired I might fall asleep."

"That wouldn't bother me," Roland said.

"I know, but it would bother me."

When Roland walked Nina to her car, he reneged on his agreement to treat her as a friend. Nina could feel the tension in his body. His fingers pressed uncomfortably into her arms. He kissed her lips instead of her cheek.

A large bus carrying a rowdy group of conventioneers pulled in front of them and stopped. The passengers unloaded in a slow, disorganized fashion. Nina seized the opportunity to pull away. She got in the car quickly.

"Call me the minute you get to California," he insisted.

"I will, I will," she promised, and sped off into the night.

Roland lumbered toward the hotel lobby, turning once to look at the space where Nina's car had been. When one of the revelers accidentally bumped into him, Roland pushed the man, unnecessarily hard.

"Gee, buddy, I'm sorry I touched you," the drunken man apologized.

"I'm not your buddy," Roland snapped, and headed upstairs.

Chapter Nineteen

Laguna Beach 1977

TANGLED CLUMPS OF seaweed discouraged Nina from walking near the edge of the ocean. Exercising was a prerequisite this morning. Her neck was tight and her shoulders stiff from nagging, free-floating anxiety. Tomorrow's weather forecast called for strong Santa Ana winds that would swirl the sand and ruffle the waves.

Nina trudged slowly past the empty lifeguard tower, unable to summon the energy to break into a trot. A lone surfer bobbed against the blue-on-aqua horizon. He floated freely with nothing to hold on to.

The morning walk, usually invigorating, ended with Nina feeling fatigued.

Laguna Beach was indescribably beautiful, but for Nina it was an unreal world. Houses perched on hillsides resembled puppets suspended on strings. From early spring until long past summer deeply tanned teens, sporting mops of sun-bleached hair, dominated the beach and sidewalks.

Nina noticed a car parked in the driveway of her hillside bungalow. She made ready to do battle before realizing it was Estrellita's sky-blue Volkswagen, the latest in a long line of similar vehicles.

"Where's Carmen?" Nina asked, opening the door.

"With her father and his prissy wife," Estrellita answered.

"You should be glad she's spending time with her dad. That's what you want, isn't it?"

"I guess so. Just because he's paying ten cents in child support doesn't entitle him to all the privileges of fatherhood."

Nina corrected her. "Yes, it does."

"Who asked you anyway? That's not what I came to talk about. David is appearing today at a bookstore in Laguna. He's doing a book signing in L.A. tomorrow. Why don't you get in touch with him?"

"That would be cruel and unusual punishment. I've managed quite well without David Hamilton. I'm not about to make a fool of myself—again."

"You call no current love life managing quite well? Face it, Nina, you're holed up in Orange County with the intent of avoiding life. You're a gorgeous, intelligent woman. When we go out, men fall all over themselves looking at you, but you give them no play. What's the deal?" Estrellita threw her hands up in the air.

"I'm tired of trying."

"I can't blame you for that. It's not as much fun as it used to be. But David's not a blind date. He shared an important part of your life. You're just going through the motions, girl. Get in the groove."

"Quit fantasizing, Estrellita. That part of my life is over. David probably has so many women chasing him, he hasn't noticed I'm gone."

"Your problem, Miss Perfect, is that you're judging the man improperly. A Black man cannot be gauged by the standards of an oppressive society."

"What the fuck does that mean?"

"Things were different in Berzerkley. Free love, free sex, free drugs, free everything. You were trying to corral David while he was finding his wings."

"You sound like an apologist for the male species."

"I *am* an apologist. My problem has always been that I love men too much. I'm not trying to get in your business, but . . ."

"Uh-oh. Here it comes."

". . . you need release. You need someone with sparkle to bring out the best in you."

"Sparkle, yes. M-80, no." Nina walked out on the balcony overlooking the ocean. "Come look at my bougainvillea. I planted them less than a year ago and they're growing like crazy."

"How can you talk about plants at a time like this?"

"Flowers are always a good topic of conversation, especially when you want to change the subject."

"You're a stubborn woman, Nina Lewis. If I can't convince you to see him, at least read his latest book, *Beyond the Fire*. I left it on your desk. I swear, Nina, it's an open love letter to you. I also left the business card for my astrologer. She could do you a lot of good."

"Take your hocus pocus and your book away from here."

"Your mouth says no but your eyes say yes. I know you, girl. You'll be flipping through those pages the minute I split."

"You're not leaving, are you? I picked up a loaf of French bread from the bakery. I was planning to make breakfast."

"I have to pass. I've done my mission of mercy, the rest is up to you. I'm meeting a friend, a *man* friend," Estrellita emphasized, "in San Diego, for brunch and whatever else is on the menu."

"I can't compete with that. Call me when you get back."

"I will. Oh, I forgot to ask. Did you see that fool T.J. in this month's *Ebony*?"

"No. What's he in for this time?"

"Mr. State Assemblyman is now forming the Coalition for People of Color. Is that a hoot, or what?"

"We should tell him we recorded all his blustering from his law school days, especially the anticoalition rhetoric. It would scare him to death. Save that issue for me. I need a good laugh. Did I tell you I got a letter from Sheila?"

"No. What's Madam Society up to now?"

"Trying to decide between Europe and South America for vacation."

"That's what happens when you have too much money and no substance in your life."

"You're jealous because Sheila landed the big fish and we're out here without a pole."

"If that's what you call the big fish, I'll eat beef and I'm a vegetarian." Estrellita bugged her eyes and started toward the door.

"Drive carefully and don't speed," Nina warned as her friend bounded down the steep driveway. Estrellita let the top down on the Bug and slapped on movie star sunglasses. Her hair, which she now wore long and straight, flapped in the wind as she took off at a dangerous rate of speed.

Nina fiddled in the kitchen trying to pull together a meal she wasn't interested in eating. She decided to shower first and save the food for later. As she passed the desk on the way to the shower, she stopped and opened the book, under the guise of examining the business card.

Hypnotic eyes, darker than midnight after the storm, stared back from the jacket cover. Even on paper, he could still move her. David's hand rested beneath the cleft in his kissable chin. He wasn't wearing a ring. The bio said nothing about a wife or children. Nina smiled, then chided herself for caring.

Estrellita was right about one thing—she had been hiding out behind the Orange Curtain, Estrellita's nickname for the politically conservative county where Nina settled after leaving Atlanta. Being in Orange County minimized the chances of meeting men who might be interested in her. Blacks made up less than 1 percent of the population.

Laguna Beach at the tip of Orange County was picture perfect, straight out of *National Geographic.* After Oakland and Atlanta, it was like living in a foreign country. The sounds were different, the people less engaging. Nina was socially and politically disconnected.

Hibernating in a state of perpetual funk was what she was doing. She had almost convinced herself that she didn't need a man. In the hour before daybreak, the space between night and morn, however, Nina yearned to feel the fire again.

She stepped into the shower, still thoughtful. Why did David come here? It was easier not knowing. Seeing his photo resurrected feelings she hoped had died.

Her back arched to feel water pulsating against her nipples. This was as close as she had come to excitement in a long time. Nina closed her eyes and imagined David's fingers, kneading her tense muscles, then slipping inside.

She dried off and slipped into a cotton nightgown that felt comforting against moistened skin. Nina adjusted obsessively a mound of fluffy pillows, then she began to read.

Several miles down the Pacific Coast Highway, Estrellita reversed direction and headed inland. The article in the *Times* had mentioned the hotel where David was interviewed. There was a chance he might be staying there.

She checked her watch, wavered a few seconds, then drove full speed ahead toward the hotel.

At the front desk Estrellita tried to charm the desk clerk.

"Good morning. You look good enough to be in the movies. Do you work here or own the place?"

The young man blushed, too embarrassed to answer.

"I'm here to interview David Hamilton, but I've forgotten his room number. Can you get that for me?"

"Sorry, ma'am. We can't give out that information."

"Well, buzz his room and tell him I'm down here."

"Your name please."

"Miss Brown. Estrellita Brown," she said with an air of importance.

As the desk clerk picked up the phone to dial, Estrellita leaned over the counter.

"Oh, sorry," she apologized sheepishly when he caught her snooping.

"Mr. Hamilton, I'm sorry if I awakened you. There's a young lady here to see you. Estrellita Brown."

During a long pause Estrellita grew jittery. David might

not recognize her name or, even worse, might shine her on intentionally.

"Very well," the clerk said, and hung up.

"Ms. Brown, Mr. Hamilton will meet you in the lobby in ten minutes."

The moon had traded places with the sun by the time Nina was close to finishing *Beyond the Fire*. Her eyes were tired and her stomach was empty, but she read on with fervent interest.

It was substantially the same manuscript she had helped him edit, but with a new ending that completely surprised her. Either David had softened considerably or he had hired a ghostwriter to do the ending. While the hero retained his edge, he settled down instead of seeking new horizons.

She resisted drawing comparisons between her and the heroine, but the similarities were unmistakable. The heroine was politically active, forever championing causes. Even the physical description was identical, down to the fierce mane of natural hair.

Nina read the next to last chapter, put the book down, and walked out on the balcony. It was hot, really hot for Laguna. A faint ocean breeze did nothing to cool the moistness between her legs. She walked back inside, turned on the air conditioner, and started reading again.

When the doorbell rang sometime after midnight, Nina sat straight up in bed. She had fallen asleep. The book was on the bed beside her, still open to the last page.

Nina wasn't expecting anyone. She moved too quickly, making her head spin as she teetered to the door. Looking through the peephole, she was surprised to see Estrellita.

Before Nina could invite her in, Estrellita handed her an envelope and walked away, explaining, "You may never speak to me again, but I did it because I want you to be happy."

Nina closed the door, sat down in the living room, and read a letter from David.

* * *

Nina:

I'm sure you thought I had given up by now. The unanswered phone calls and letters were disheartening, but I remain eternally hopeful. If the choice were mine, I'd deliver this message in person. Estrellita wanted you to decide.

My heart aches every time I think about you. Precious memories refuse to fade. I miss you as much as the day you left. When you gave me my freedom I didn't want it. Being with you was what made me whole.

Believe it or not, I've cleaned up my act substantially. I'm not perfect, but I'm a lot different from the man you knew. I gave up all the shit that kept me from taking care of business. It's amazing how much more I can accomplish with a clear head. My writing career is moving in a positive direction. I want to share the excitement with you, but my joy is trapped in blind spaces. I need your vision to see it through.

I don't blame you for leaving. Loving you was easy. You gave me all the sweet reasons. I gave you heartache in return.

My love was a selfish love, placing limits on the depth of my emotion. Rather than focusing on what love had done for me, I worried about what it took away. The truth is, you frightened me, made me feel things I wanted to suppress: my humanness, vulnerability, dependence on someone else. I wanted to love you, but not too much. I succumbed to rumors and innuendo, withheld what I demanded—trust and complete devotion.

Tell me what's in your heart, Nina. If pride is in the way, call me and I'll come to you.

This is the last time I'll bug you. A fool in love has to know when to stop. Please give me the courtesy of an answer, even if you break my heart.

David

Enclosed was a card bearing the hotel's address and number. David's home phone number was written below it.

Nina laid the card on the nightstand and walked out on the balcony. The wind swirled in gusts of untamed energy. She hurried inside and lay down on the bed, to think.

Twenty

THE LIMOUSINE SAILED against the gale force of the Santa Anas, rippling the waves of the frothy Pacific. The driver had balked when his passenger suggested the Pacific Coast Highway route. David insisted upon trailing the ocean of loneliness, apparently without end.

He had waited until the last second before leaving. The phone was quiet. No one knocked at the door. As a final gesture, David called Estrellita.

"Did you give her the letter?" he asked.

"Yes. She didn't call?"

"No."

"Want me to try her?" Estrellita asked.

"No. You've done enough. I'm heading out now."

"I'm sorry it didn't work out."

"I'm sorry too. Thanks."

The car crept, like a stalking feline, down the final city blocks and rested in front of the bookstore bustling with energy. A long line of previously patient fans broke rank, rushing forward to greet the author. Concealed behind dark windows, David organized his thoughts.

"L.A.—ninth city on a ten-city tour. San Francisco next and then home." David reminded himself where he was going. It was too late to worry about where he had been.

Pollution blew in with the Santa Anas.

"My allergies are kickin'," David complained to the limo driver. He blew hard into a cotton handkerchief, triggering a ringing in his ears. "It feels like dirt particles floating in the air."

"That's exactly what it is. Pollution ain't nothing but a fancy word for dirt. You need to postpone this?" the driver asked.

"No. This is my lifeline. I can write a million books, but if nobody reads them, I'm exiled to oblivion."

He stepped out of the limo and waded into a sea of expectant fans, hyped to hear him read excerpts and answer questions. They were lively, maybe too lively, for the bluesy mood that forced him out of bed before daybreak. *Beyond the Fire* had debuted on the *New York Times* bestseller list in the number-three position, outshining his previous nonfiction titles.

Relaxed and open during the reading, David stiffened when asked about his private life.

"Like your character Izaak in *Beyond the Fire*, have you met your soulmate? If not, I'm available," a statuesque woman in a hot pink dress clinging tenaciously to her body stood up and tossed the first of many passes that would fly that afternoon.

"It's those kind of questions that keep me from having a soulmate," David joked. "Does anyone else have a question? Relating to the book, that is?" He emphasized the last part.

"Yeah, man. I been workin' on this story for about a year and, ahh, it's just not comin' together. How long does it take to write a book?" an aspiring young writer asked.

"There's no single answer to that question. Don't be discouraged by the length of time it takes to complete a project. You'll know when it's finished. My first book was drafted in six months. The second took a year. It took seven years to complete *Beyond the Fire*, my first novel. I guess I had to distance myself before I could tell the story."

"So it's not pure fiction. You *have* met your soulmate," the woman in the hot pink dress persisted.

"Nothing gets past you. You sure you're not with the FBI?" The audience laughed, and David changed the subject. "I've got about an hour to finish signing. Thank you all for coming. I'll check you next time."

A flash of hot pink radiated at the end of the line. David pretended not to notice her bouncing around like a kid who has to go potty. She leaned over the table, exposing her ample bosom and subjecting David to a blast of flowery perfume that sent his sinuses into meltdown.

David looked up, trying to avoid taking a deep breath. "Well, there she is. My number-one fan. To whom shall I address this?"

"To Celia. With all your love or whatever you have to spare."

David's eyes stayed glued to the page he was signing. "There you go, Celia," he said, sliding the book toward her. "Thanks for coming." Immediately he began gathering his notes. Celia didn't budge.

"A friend of mine is having a birthday party at the hottest club in town. Free drinks, free food, free entertainment. Care to join me?" Celia's hand slid down the side of her dress and rested on the back side of her hip. Her come-and-get-it pose left little to the imagination.

"That's really sweet of you, but I've got a plane to catch in less than an hour. Maybe next time."

"Here's my card," she said, flashing a business card the same radiant color as her dress. "Call me when you're back in town. I'll give you something to write about." Celia winked as the limo driver walked in. He stopped to observe Celia's departure, orchestrated to leave a lasting impression. The smell of perfume lingered long after she left the room.

The driver shook his head and said, "Damn. Maybe I should write a book. You hooking up with that?"

"Naw, man. That's too frisky for me. Here, see what you can do with it." David handed the woman's card to the driver. "I'll be ready in a second. I want to thank the store manager."

Chapter Twenty-one

NINA PULLED INTO the parking lot behind the bookstore fifteen minutes after the signing was scheduled to end. A series of unexpected events had delayed her. Her neighbor dropped in with a sad story that couldn't keep. His boyfriend had moved out and he was searching for the strength to carry on.

"Don't do anything until I get back," Nina advised, pushing him out the door while he was holding a half-full can of beer.

Construction on the freeway created bumper-to-bumper traffic, unusual for a Saturday morning. Nina took the wrong exit in Los Angeles and landed in unfamiliar territory. She navigated streets congested with people and traffic that seemed in no hurry. Vendors stood on every corner selling bundles of fruit and wilting flowers. A beggar pressed his nose against her car window. She cursed in annoyance, then guiltily rolled down the window and handed him a dollar before speeding off.

Nina checked her makeup in the mirror and blotted her nose, chin, and forehead. The shine on her face persisted despite her best efforts to eradicate it. Fighting back a full-scale anxiety attack, she forced her feet out of the car.

Satisfied fans drifted into the parking lot, clutching copies of *Beyond the Fire*. Nina entered the bookstore through the back door. A handful of customers milled around inside. There was no sign of David. She didn't know whether to be upset or relieved. At least the pressure was off. A store employee explained that the book signing, excellent by all accounts, had ended minutes before she arrived.

"That's too bad. I drove all the way from Orange County."

"Why don't you browse a bit? We have an excellent selection of Black literature. Also, the shops across the street carry merchandise difficult to find in Orange County," the employee offered as consolation.

David sat quietly in the backseat of the limo, waiting for the driver to come up with the aspirin he desperately needed. The blue velvet upholstery took on a funereal appearance, closing in on him from all angles. He had made it through the signing, but his head was pounding.

"Man, that's okay if you can't find them. I can pick some up at the airport. Let me check my briefcase one last time. I could've sworn I packed aspirin before I left." He removed the paper contents of his briefcase, then searched the side pockets to no avail. Repacking his bag, he said, "No luck. Let's get outta here."

David stretched out in the backseat and closed his eyes.

Nina eyeballed the long black limousine parked three doors up from the bookstore display window. Blacked-out passenger windows made it impossible to see inside.

At the front of the limo she made eye contact with the driver. Turning on his engine, he ran his radar over her. Nina looked fresher than a snow cone in the desert. The beige linen dress skimmed her body like fine silk. Against her long neck hung a pearl and diamond choker.

"Now, that's a woman with class," the driver said to himself.

While the driver gawked the green light turned to amber. He braked on a dime, jarring David and his head.

David's eyes and mouth shot open. "What the hel—" he was saying when he spotted her, walking past him, like a welcome apparition. Her sexy stride commanded the air around her. The smog lifted as she walked back into his dream.

David flung open the door, jumped out in traffic, and called out to her, "Somebody's in a hurry. Need a lift?"

Nina turned toward the voice, lovingly familiar. People stared at the man yelling in the middle of the street. He ran to her, oblivious to traffic. Nina was planted. How do you greet a man you haven't seen for four years? Uncertainty dissolved the minute he touched her, as if the intimacy they shared had never been broken.

When he gave her room, she said, "You stole that title."

"I know. You stole more than that from me. I can't believe you're here."

"I can't believe it either."

"Were you inside? Why didn't you say something?"

"I came late, but I understand you were excellent. Congratulations."

"Why'd you put me on hold for so long? I thought I'd never see you again."

"We needed time."

"I had more time than I could handle."

"I needed something you couldn't give."

"Did you find what you needed?"

"I guess I didn't."

"Can you find what you need with me? I want you so much, Nina. Let me love you the right way." His rap was strong, like the arms enfolding her. They kissed hard, the way young lovers do when love is new and the world around them invisible.

In a daze she asked, "Are we still in first gear?"

"I can't help speeding. I've been without you too long," David said, pressing her to him. Nina breathed against his body, glad to be home.

"Let's go somewhere and talk. What about that restaurant?" David signaled to the driver that he needed ten minutes. The driver pointed to his watch. David looked unconcerned.

Inside the restaurant Nina focused on an unwanted cup of coffee. It was hard to know where to begin. "How's your mother?"

"Better than ever. We talk all the time. I see her at least once a year and write her often.

"When you split I went on a binge, trying to forget you. Every morning I woke up with a stake wedged inside my head. I took a leave of absence and flew home to Virginia. For almost three months I stayed with my mother."

"I can't believe you spent three months in Virginia."

"It was pretty incredible, but I needed the time to deal with myself. We spent hours discussing subjects we'd been avoiding. I was drained, mentally and physically. She wouldn't let me give up. Mama kept me believing. She was more than a mother, she became my friend. We had a great time together, but it made her nervous when I was checking out her boyfriend."

"Your mother's dating?"

"This old fogy keeps creeping around her doorstep. I've got his number though."

"Listen to you, treating your mother like a kid."

"Somebody has to keep an eye on her. I spent all my time fixing up the house and trying to convince her to move to California. Of course, she wouldn't go for it.

"Before I left I had to take care of one thing. I visited my father's grave.

"The 'Colored Folks' cemetery was at the end of a dirt road overgrown with bushes and uncut trees. The closer I came, the more I dreaded my journey. I walked past gravesites covered with weeds, almost totally obscured.

"Frightened birds and squirrels scampered when I invaded. At the far end of the cemetery I saw three prominent, upright tombstones. My father was buried under a tree next to his parents. I'll never forget the wording of his epitaph: In loving memory of Horace Hamilton, devoted father and beloved husband. Mama must've known something I didn't. Either that or she created a myth of the man she wanted him to be."

"That had to be rough," Nina said.

"It was impossible. I knelt down on his grave and cried so hard I thought the earth was moving. Maybe it was.

"The family burial plot had been meticulously cared for. My mother pulled weeds and kept the markers clean all these years. She's getting old. One day I'll have that responsibility.

"My father wasn't much older than I am when he died. Mama gave me a picture of him to bring back with me. It's weird. We look like twins. Am I boring you . . . ?"

"Oh, no, this is good. You told me more about your family in the last five minutes than you did the entire time we were together."

"I couldn't talk about my family then. I couldn't talk about my feelings. You were right when you said I was running. I wanted you, but I didn't know what to do.

"When I got back from Virginia, I started writing like crazy. Writing saved me. If I was frustrated, I pretended you were there telling me to sit down and concentrate."

When their laughter ended David's mood turned suddenly somber. "A year ago I faced another challenge. My friend Reggie died of a heart attack. He was forty-three."

"I'm sorry to hear that. You two were so close."

"It messed me up, even though we had stopped hanging out together. Reggie was on the fast track. His doctor warned him to slow down, but Reggie thought he was invincible. His death made me realize, I don't want to go out like that—alone and with nothing to show for my life."

"You have a lot to be proud of."

"I want you to be proud of me."

"I've always been proud of you, David, except . . ."

"Except when I was using my poison pen."

"You apologized and I forgave you. I was too stubborn to let go of the anger."

"Everything that happened seems trivial now. You were good for me, Nina. I should've never let you go. Why didn't you answer my letters?"

"I wasn't ready."

"Did you read them?"

"Only the one Estrellita delivered." She couldn't confess

that every word he wrote stayed with her, haunted her memory, and dominated her dreams.

"It's not important," he said, looking dejected. "Did I tell you? I quit the job at the *Sentinel*. I'm teaching a course in creative writing at the junior college. The pay is lousy, but the students keep me moving. With a few dollars rolling in from royalties I feel like a real writer now."

David reached for her hand and said, "I need you, Nina."

"I need you too, but a lot has changed since we were together."

"Must've been all good. You look better than ever."

"It wasn't all good, but I learned a lot. I know what I want in a relationship."

"I guess we have a lot to talk about. The limo's across the street," David said.

"I don't do limos. I'm parked behind the bookstore."

"You mean you didn't hitchhike?"

He made her laugh the way he used to, resurrecting one sweet reason why she had loved him, and still might.

"Since when did you start riding around in limos?"

"My agent rented it to congratulate me on the book. Everywhere else it was taxis, rental cars, and subways. We can squeeze in one more hour and come back for your car. I want to pick up where we left off."

"No, David. You've got to do better than that. I'm not up for games or foolishness. I'll drive," Nina insisted.

"I should've known that was coming. Let me take care of the driver. Don't move." David took a few steps and raced back to kiss her.

Nina assured him, "I'm not going anywhere."

She watched as he leaned inside the limo. Nina wanted to stay steady, but she was totally into him now. There was a risk in giving in too quickly. He had the same lips, sly smile, and easy charm. He also had what Nina wanted, what she had come for: David had the fire.

Something about him was different. An easy calm replaced the restless look in his eyes. The energy was there, but it seemed more focused. Could David Hamilton be mellowing in his prime?

David carried a bag and briefcase as he came back smiling. Gone were the headache, allergic sniffles, and furrowed brow.

In the parking lot Nina asked, "What time is your flight?"

"I probably missed it."

"I thought you were on your way to San Francisco."

"I have to be there by noon tomorrow. I can leave at ten in the morning and arrive in plenty of time. You trying to get rid of me?"

"No. I didn't want to interfere with your schedule."

"My schedule is your schedule. Where are we headed?"

"To my place. It's about an hour from here."

"I don't mind, as long as you keep me entertained."

Nina turned the key in the door of her black XKE convertible.

"Whoa, baby. I see you're not doing too badly," he said.

"It's those pennies I saved living with you."

Settling in for the ride, David vowed their love would be sweeter. Nina's directive to take it slow was forgotten before they hit the open highway.

The journey to Laguna was a long one. It really djdn't matter. This time, Nina was in the driver's seat.

Chapter Twenty-two

"I DON'T UNDERSTAND why we have to rent a car," Nina said as the flight ended at the San Francisco airport. "Where's the T-Bird?"

"In storage. I gave it a much-needed rest. I'll put it in service, if you want to drive it."

"I do. I missed it almost as much as I missed you."

"Very funny," he said, tweaking her nose. "We'll need transportation after the signing."

"For what?"

"Quit being so nosy," David insisted. "Grab the bags while I get the car."

"I don't want to lug those heavy things," Nina complained.

"You brought more clothes for two days than I packed for a month. I'll get the bags and you get the car."

"No. On second thought, I'll get the bags," Nina said.

"Take this and get a skycap," he said, handing her dollar bills.

Nina had trouble deciding anything. It was so intense. David was all over her from the time they left the bookstore. She loved it, but drew the line when he tried to take a bath with her the next morning.

"Go make breakfast while I soak." She shooed him away. He wouldn't take no for an answer when she insisted she was too busy to leave town. It took major persuasion to convince her to fly back with him.

"I'll miss my signing if you don't come with me," David pleaded, pulling her against him.

"See what you make me do. I have to lie to get away from work, then scramble to find someone to cover my cases. Two days only. No more."

David agreed with his fingers crossed.

For a while they were lost in the hills of San Francisco. Nina worried that the rental car might not make it. It struggled and strained until they reached a blind peak. The view from the other side took her breath away. A panoramic snapshot of the ocean lay before them. The fog had lifted, unveiling a crystal-blue sky. David pulled over and stopped the car.

Nina sighed. "It's beautiful."

"Everything is beautiful. I'm so happy, I'm delirious," David said.

"All right, delirious. You're late."

The signing, scheduled for two hours, seemed to take forever. They were tired from being up all night. David was distracted by Nina's presence. Everyone could see from the way he looked at her that Nina was the center of his perfect world. Contentment showed when he smiled in her direction. His gaze settled lovingly upon her face.

"I'll take a walk while you finish," Nina suggested.

"Where are you going?" David asked her, leaving a line of people waiting.

"Down the street. There's plenty to keep you busy. I need to stretch my legs."

"Don't get lost and don't go too far." David stood up, held her hands and kissed her, unabashedly displaying affection.

"Yes, Daddy," Nina teased him, and headed into the streets of San Francisco.

It was amazing. She knew little about the city, even though she had lived in the Bay Area for years. Nina decided to change that. The city was fascinating, and now with David. . . . And now with David what? Nina had no idea where this was going, but she knew she was going with it.

She hopped a cable car down to Market Street and

strolled through department stores. On the sidewalk there was a woman selling handmade leather goods. Nina lost track of time trying to select a belt for David. When she returned to the bookstore fifteen minutes late, David looked worried.

"Where have you been?" he asked, then breathed a sigh of relief. "I thought you'd been mugged."

"Who would mug a lady looking this happy? I'm sorry I worried you. Since we're here, can we stop at the Wharf?"

"Can we do that some other time? I'm ready to get out of here."

"I can wait, but I wish you'd explain our mysterious destination."

"I'm not telling."

They drove across the Bay Bridge, past Oakland, past Berkeley, and continued down Interstate 80.

"This is getting too strange. At first, I thought you were anxious to get me home and take advantage of me. You're acting weird, David. What's going on?"

"Some people know how to spoil a surprise. We're headed to your parents' house in Vallejo."

"My parents' house? I love my folks and all, but I saw them two weeks ago. I thought we'd spend our time alone."

"We will. We'll only stop for a second. I need to do one thing."

"And what is that?" Nina asked.

"In fifteen minutes you'll see."

Nina hoped her parents wouldn't pass out when she drove up with David. They had survived her shacking up, breaking up, and now she was showing up with David again. She had planned to break the news gradually once she figured out what was happening herself.

Nina's mother peeked out the window as they pulled into the driveway. Mrs. Lewis was amazingly calm when David opened the screen door. Only the tremor in her voice as she said, "Hello, David. Haven't seen you in a while," betrayed her coolness.

"Hello, Mrs. Lewis. Is your husband home?"

Oh, shit, he's pushing his luck, Nina thought. I don't know if Daddy's up to this. I'm not sure I am.

"Yes, he's back in the bedroom. I'll get him," Mrs. Lewis answered.

Nina's father appeared with his reading glasses perched on his nose. He looked rather suspicious.

"Could we sit down?" David asked.

"Oh, sure, sure. With all the excitement, I forgot my manners," Mrs. Lewis said. Everybody sat down except Nina, who stood by the door in case she needed to "get hat."

"I want to do things right this time," David began. "You know the history of me and Nina. We've had our ups and downs, but we're back together." David's voice quivered, sounding very serious.

"I want to marry your daughter and I've come to ask for your blessing."

Nina leaned against the wall, trying to absorb the shock.

"Well, son," Mr. Lewis said, resting his pipe in a large ashtray.

Nina couldn't believe he was calling David "son." Was there a conspiracy afoot?

"We're surprised by the suddenness of this announcement, but if that's what you want, you have my blessing. What do you think, Ellen?" Mr. Lewis turned to Nina's mother.

"I want them to be happy. They need to take their time. Other than that, I don't see any problem with it."

Nina wondered if anybody was interested in her opinion. Her mother was first to detect Nina's discomfort.

"You okay with this, Nina?" her mother asked, perplexed by Nina's sour expression.

"Hmmmm . . . this is the first I'm hearing of it. David and I need to talk."

"About what? I thought this was what you wanted," David said.

"Well, it may be, but I'm not ready to decide right this second."

David's humiliation turned quickly to outrage. "Oh, I see. I'm a plaything to you."

"You've got it all wrong," Nina said.

"No. I've finally got it right. Some men are to marry and others are to fool around with. I forgot—you like lawyers, men in three-piece suits."

"Could you leave us alone for a minute?" Nina asked of her parents.

"That won't be necessary," David announced, popping out of his seat. "I'm leaving. Folks, I apologize for interrupting you. I promise not to do it again."

David left without saying good-bye. The screen door creaked in the wind before closing.

Nina ran after him. "David, wait. You're not being fair. It's been less than two days since we got back together. Give me a minute to adjust."

"Listen, Nina. I waited a long time for you to come back. All I had was hope. I want to be your husband, not your boyfriend. If that's not what you want, quit wasting my time."

David hopped in the car and turned the ignition. When Nina tried to talk to him, he refused to roll down the window. David drove away without looking back.

Standing in the empty driveway, Nina felt abandoned. David had left with her luggage, return ticket, everything. All she had was her purse.

Nina walked past her parents and straight to her room. She opened the door to unfamiliar surroundings. The room had been redone in bright yellow wallpaper with tiny flowers in a white border. She sat down on the queen-size bed that replaced the twin beds she'd grown up with. Nothing was the same.

Her mother waited a respectable interval before knocking.

"Are you all right, honey? Can I come in?" Nina didn't answer. Her mother stepped inside. "I thought you might want to talk." Silence. Her mother shook her head and began backing out of the room.

"Why are men such idiots?" Nina opened up.

"Women can be foolish too."

"What do you mean by that?" Nina was surprised by her mother's failure to agree with her.

"It's obvious David loves you very much. When you turned down his proposal, he was humiliated."

"Why are you taking up for him? You don't even like him."

"That's not true. I've always liked David. I didn't like your living arrangement. It was all I could do to keep my mouth shut. I knew you'd make the right decision. A lot of women go through a period of not listening to their mamas. I did the same thing when I was your age, only I was totally out of control. David reminds me of a man I knew years ago, before I met your father." Her mother smiled.

Nina was uncomfortable. She couldn't imagine her mother with another man. Her mother was the one who didn't bring up the subject of sex until Nina's second semester in college. Fortunately, Nina had taken the precaution of visiting Planned Parenthood the moment sex became a concern.

"He was bold and handsome, like David. The kind of man that gives parents the blues. I was forbidden to see him, which made him even more exciting. I would've gone to the end of the earth and back if he had only asked me. Fortunately, he dumped me before too much damage was done. My parents were relieved. I was heartbroken. I moped around for almost two years before I snapped out of it. You were wise to give David a breather. You know the saying about the milk and the cow."

"Please don't repeat that lame ditty."

"I won't repeat it, but it must've sunk in somehow. You had to make your own mistakes. It killed me, but I stood back and watched it."

"Why would you agree to me marrying him now?"

"The way I see it, you'll end up together one way or

another. When you introduced us to Nathan, I knew David wasn't out of your system."

"How did you know?"

"A mother knows. Nathan was nice, but he was boring."

Nina cracked up, laughing so hard she needed a tissue. She blew her nose and dabbed the makeup stinging her eyes. "I guess I messed up."

"Not necessarily. Sometimes it's good to make 'em wait. Let him stew for a while. If he's serious, he'll come around."

The women emerged from the crowded bedroom smiling. Nina's father couldn't figure out what happened.

"Did I miss something? One minute, yelling and screaming, smiles and happiness the next. What happened?"

Nina looked at her mother and giggled.

"It's a secret," Nina answered, then waltzed into the kitchen to make a sandwich. She was suddenly hungry beyond belief. Nina ate like a pig, but nothing could fill her up, except David.

He was banging the keys on the much-used typewriter when he heard the knock at the door. "What is it now?" he grumbled, flicking the off key.

Nina knocked a third time before he slowly unlocked the door.

"I forgot to leave your ticket and clothes," David said without inviting her in.

"That's not what I came for. May I come in?" she asked, then hesitated. "I should have called first to make sure you didn't have company."

"Come in, Nina. You know I don't have company."

"Everything looks the same. I can't believe it." Nina walked over by the window, examining a plant in a large ceramic pot. "This can't be the same plant I left here." She turned to David.

"It's the same one. I saved them all, except the rubber tree. It was too temperamental. Can you believe I developed a green thumb?"

Nina touched his face with her fingers. David didn't respond.

"How'd you get here?" he asked.

"Borrowed my father's car."

"Your bag is in the trunk of the rental car. I can transfer it over," David said, putting his hand on the doorknob.

Nina grabbed his hand, turning him around to face her. David looked past her, his habit when upset.

She put her arms around his neck and tried to kiss him. When he turned his head away, she purred in his ear, "I love you, David. Can you love me, just a little?"

"It won't work," he said, backing away. Nina closed in until she trapped him against the door. She opened his shirt and ran her fingers across his chest. He closed his eyes and pretended false resistance.

Nina stepped back, pulling the cord on the suede wraparound skirt she was wearing. It dropped to the floor, revealing nothing underneath. One by one, she undid the buttons on her blouse. It slipped to her feet. She bent over and pushed it into the corner. When she stood up, her perfect breasts leaped out.

David's eyes were glued to her smooth and sexy body. High-heel shoes and no stockings made her legs reach to the sky. She gave him a few seconds to appreciate the scenery. David followed willingly up the stairs and into the bedroom.

He tried to touch her, but she pulled his hands down and pushed him back on the bed. She removed his slippers and pulled his pants and underwear down. Nina toyed with her willing subject, bringing him to the point of ecstasy, pulling back and making him wait.

"You're teasing me, baby," he said, not the least bit complaining. As she eased down his muscles tensed, his insides were about to quake. She lay still to keep him from coming, held her breath, and tried to push away. David gripped her arms. She was the last life raft on a sinking ship and he was determined to be saved.

"Aw, baby. Right there. Give it to me," he said as Nina

caught the wave. When he started to relax, she threw in a few short strokes for good measure.

"Where have you been hangin' out?" David asked suspiciously.

"We agreed not to ask those questions," she reminded him. "I need to call my parents."

"Now?" he asked, looking down at their naked bodies.

"It'll only take a second." Nina grabbed the phone from the nightstand and pulled the sheet from the end of the bed.

"Hi, Daddy. I'm at David's and everything is fine. I didn't want you to worry."

"Your mom is right here. Do you want to talk to her?"

"No. Just give her the message."

"What time are you coming home?" Nina's father asked.

"Howard, hand me that phone," Nina's mother said, yanking the phone away.

"Pardon him, sweetheart. He has a hard time remembering you're not a baby anymore. Everything okay?" Mrs. Lewis asked, unable to contain her own curiosity.

"Yes. We're fine. Is it all right if I keep the car overnight?"

"No problem. The station wagon is here in case we need to go out. Enjoy yourself. . . . Ooh, I didn't mean to say that. What I meant to say is, we're happy that you're happy. See you tomorrow."

David ran his finger down her spine, intentionally making her shiver. "Mommy and Daddy worried about their little girl?"

"Don't make fun of my folks," Nina cautioned.

"I'm not making fun. I think it's wonderful being close to your family. My situation was so different from yours. Your mother and father seem content. I want the same thing for us."

"I hope you feel that way when I'm old, gray, and thick around the middle. You'll probably start chasing eighteen-year-olds."

"Is that what's bothering you? Look at me. I don't want anybody but you. I've had plenty of time to think about this. I'm the one who should be worried, hooking up with a younger woman whose libido is in overdrive."

"Ready for the second course?"

"Are you trying to kill me? How old was that Nathan dude?"

"No discussions of Nathan, especially while we're in bed." Nina slid her hand up his thigh and watched the cover rise between his legs.

David pulled the sheet up below his chin and said, "Remove your hand. I'm saving myself for marriage."

"Start saving yourself tomorrow. Right now, this little piggy is mine. And this is how I want it," she said, crouching on her hands and knees.

"Keep socking it to me like this, you may never see Laguna Beach again."

Chapter Twenty-three

DAVID WAS QUIET as they sat in the airport lounge.

"The weekend's only three days away," Nina said, trying to cheer him up.

"I hate going back to an empty house. It feels like I'm losing you again. I made all these assumptions about how things would fall into place."

"They *are* falling into place."

"I wouldn't say that. You turned down my proposal, breezed into my house half naked, and took advantage of me."

Nina laughed, but David looked serious.

"You didn't propose, David. You made an announcement without consulting me. I realize you were trying to do the right thing, but you caught me off guard. I didn't turn you down. I said I needed a minute to think. Will you ask me again?"

"No . . . I've had enough rejection. Someone somewhere wants to spend her life with me and have my babies," David said.

"You want babies? What brought this on?"

"I'd be a good father. I know exactly what not to do. I don't want to wait until my kids have to wheel me around."

"How many babies are you talking about?" Nina asked.

"Two boys and two girls."

"What!"

"I'm open to discussion."

"You'd better be or the deal is off."

"We don't have a deal, remember?"

Before Nina could respond a young woman approached their table.

"Are you, uh ... David Hamilton?" she asked, holding up *Beyond the Fire*.

David smiled and said, "Yes, I am. I see you're reading my book. Thanks."

"I'm almost finished and I'm loving every word. Would you sign it for me please?" she asked, thrusting the book and a pen in his direction.

As he was signing, the public address system announced that Nina's flight was boarding.

"Sorry about the interruption," he apologized after he finished.

"No, you're not. You were gettin' off on that young woman fawning all over you."

"It was flattering. No one's ever recognized me, except at book signings."

"Getting back to what we were talking about ..."

"Didn't they announce your flight?" David changed the subject.

"They did, but you were about to ask me something."

"No, I wasn't," he said flatly.

"Well, be like that," Nina said, grabbed her bag and stomped over to the boarding gate. David followed, smiling smugly.

Nina stood in line, looking straight ahead at the attendant collecting boarding passes.

He waited until she was next in line, then pulled her aside and said, "Before you go I have something for you."

David reached in his shirt pocket and pulled out a gray velvet pouch. He opened the drawstring and fished out a brilliant diamond solitaire. Nina squealed so loudly, everyone near the boarding gate looked at her.

"When did you get this? How did you hide it from me?" Nina asked, jumping up and down.

"Let me pop the question before you cross-examine me." David held her hand and asked, "Will you marry me, Nina?"

"Yes, yes, yes," she shouted. The ring fit perfectly on her finger. Nina hugged him so hard he could barely breathe. A few people applauded, others smiled, as the couple celebrated.

The final boarding call was announced.

"You make it hard to leave," Nina said, clinging to him.

"I don't want you to go, but the sooner you get squared away, the sooner we'll be together."

"We have so much to talk about. What about my job? Where will we live?"

"We can't decide all that if you want to make your flight."

"I'll call you the minute I get home. I love you, David."

"I love you too."

He watched as she walked down the ramp to the airplane. David stationed himself in front of the floor-to-ceiling window.

A little boy with saucerlike eyes asked, "Are you waiting for your mommy too?"

David laughed and said, "No, I'm seeing my baby off."

"You let your baby fly by himself on an airplane?"

"Not baby as in little one. Baby as in girlfriend. No, make that wife."

Nina's plane taxied down the runway and took flight. David's heart floated on the wings of a metal bird that took her away and disappeared behind the clouds.

The John Wayne Airport was teeming with travelers. It wasn't a holiday, so Nina couldn't understand why. Everything took longer than expected. An extended delay at the baggage claim area had Nina pacing around the empty carousel. The shuttle bus was lost, hijacked, or out of service. She spent more time in the airport and parking lot than she did on the short flight home.

The phone rang as she opened the door to her bungalow. Nina dropped her bags and rushed inside.

"Hi, sweetheart," Nina answered breathlessly. She heard nothing and then a click on the other end. Disappointed, she grabbed her bags and closed the front door. Nina changed clothes quickly and sat down to call David.

"Did you call me?" she asked.

"No, I was waiting for you to call me."

"That's strange. Somebody hung up when I answered the phone a few minutes ago. Probably a wrong number. Oh, baby, I'm so happy. I showed my ring to all the flight attendants and half the passengers. My hand was elevated during the whole flight. I couldn't stop looking and checking to make sure it was still there. They probably thought I was nuts. You miss me yet?"

"Do I miss you? I'm going crazy."

"I'm worried about something."

"Don't start," David cautioned.

"I've been on my job for less than a year. If I quit, they'll think I'm flaky."

"I'll move down there, if you want me to. I can write anywhere."

"You would do that for me?"

"Of course."

"What about the house? I know you love the Bay Area."

"I do, but I'm flexible. We can put the house on the market, get a bigger one. Whatever you want. Let's talk about it more this weekend. I want to remember how good it was last night."

In the low, sultry tone of lovers, they basked in intimate memories. Half an hour into the conversation Nina realized she had a lot of calls to make. There was her mother, Estrellita, and of course, Sheila.

The engagement had reached the point where the women would take over. David slipped happily into the background.

"Tell me the date, the time, and put me in front of the preacher" was all he asked. "As long you're there, I won't sweat the details."

Chapter Twenty-four

DAVID PACED OUTSIDE the Mills College Chapel, waiting for Nina to arrive. The ceremony was scheduled to begin in twenty minutes, and no one had heard from the bride.

"Did anyone call the house?" Mrs. Lewis asked.

"Won't do any good. She took the phone off the hook. People were calling at the last minute asking for directions to the chapel, instead of reading the invitation. My people, my people . . ." Sheila said.

"Was everything cool when you left?" David asked Sheila.

"Everything was fine. Nina was more relaxed than I was on my wedding day. Of course, Estrellita was getting on her nerves. That's why she kicked us out."

"Wait a minute. Your nonstop complaining was what did it." Estrellita defended herself. "If you hadn't been griping about how huge this dress makes you look, Nina would be here. It's that extra layer of fat, and not the dress, you should be worried about."

"I beg your pardon." Sheila's head bobbed indignantly.

"Ladies, ladies. We're all nervous. No more squabbling," Mrs. Lewis said. "Do us a favor and check on the guests."

The argument escalated as Estrellita and Sheila entered the chapel.

"She'll be here, don't worry," Mrs. Lewis reassured David.

"I have this strange feeling."

"That's typical on your wedding day."

"My feeling has nothing to do with getting married. I'm

not confused or having second thoughts. This is what I want."

Nina's mother looked at him, concerned. "Why don't you wait inside? It's bad luck to see the bride before you reach the altar." Mrs. Lewis put her hand on the shoulder of his off-white silk suit. The collarless suit was his compromise with the tuxedo Nina had wanted him to wear.

David looked down the road leading to the chapel. Except for cars lining either side, the road was empty. A long white limousine boldly displayed a "Just Married" banner. Peaches and cream carnations lined the walkway to the chapel. Everything was in place, except the bride, who had chosen a bad time to be late.

David exhaled his anxiety. In a fog he walked past guests, trying to get his attention. He acknowledged only his mother, sitting anxiously in the front row. He nodded but didn't stop to talk.

Word spread through the chapel that the bride hadn't arrived. Hopeful women wagered that Nina would be a no-show.

The organist began the fifth song in his limited repertoire.

Estrellita's daughter, Carmen, methodically plucked the tops from the spring flowers in her basket. Estrellita shrieked, startling the little flower girl, who let out a nerve-shattering wail. The sound carried through the stone chapel and vibrated.

David bolted to his feet. The best man restrained him.

"It's Nina," David said.

"No, man, it's just a baby crying. Let me check it out. I'll be right back."

Nina grabbed a few items and set them down at the door. She did a final run-through, making sure she had everything. Sheila and Estrellita had left a trail of clothes and assorted gadgets. Nina tried not to notice. She had everything important, except Estrellita's present—"something old" as required by tradition.

The silver and turquoise bracelet she found buried beneath a jacket. Nina fastened the delicate bangle around her bony wrist. She kissed it for luck then took a second to put the phone back on the hook.

As Nina opened the door the phone rang. "Shit." She considered not answering it. It was probably David. He'd been a wreck since they set the date. After frustrating weeks of making wedding plans, Nina argued for elopement.

Her mother begged when she got wind of the plan, "Please do it for me. I didn't have a fancy wedding when I married your father."

David sided with Mrs. Lewis. "We waited this long, we might as well do it right."

Overruled, Nina fell in line with the program. Now all she had to do was get her late butt to the chapel.

Nina grabbed the receiver. Out of nowhere a hand materialized, clamping over her nose and squeezing her mouth. Blunt fingernails dug into her cheeks. She was lifted off balance, flailing and trying to spin around. Unable to land a punch or connect with an elbow, Nina sank her teeth into her attacker's hand. A swift blow to the back of the head disabled her.

Nina crumpled to the floor and was pounced on immediately. Although her chest was pinned, her fingers inched toward the receiver. It was twisted viciously from her hand. She tried to scream, but the fall had taken her breath away. Her head was snatched back and a white rag crammed into her face. Nina gasped for air, certain she was smothering. Putrid fumes from the rag sent her sailing. Her eyes rolled back, her head fell limp. Nina was out of it.

From the dangling receiver David's voice begged, "Nina . . . Nina, pick up the phone."

"Something's wrong."

"Man, you're overreacting. She's probably on her way now." David's best man tried to calm him.

"No. The phone rang, she didn't say anything, but I heard noise. Give me your keys. I've got to get over there."

"You can't leave."

"Give me the fucking keys. If I'm not back in twenty minutes, call the cops," David yelled over his shoulder.

"What about the guests?"

He didn't stop to answer. He dashed down the center aisle of the chapel, surprising everyone, including his mother. She had survived the dreaded plane trip; now David was on a trip of his own. David's mother turned to Mrs. Lewis and commented, "He's my son, but I have no idea what he's doing. Would somebody fill me in? This is the strangest wedding I've ever been to."

Mrs. Lewis slumped in her seat and buried her face in her hands. The stress had gotten to her. Her dream wedding was turning into a nightmare.

"I'm telling you for the last time. When I got here the door was open. Nina's bags were sitting right here in the entrance," David explained.

"Maybe she got cold feet. Brides-to-be are known to be skittish," the policeman speculated.

"No, no. That's not Nina. She would've taken her purse, if nothing else. The car is still parked outside."

"You said yourself she made her friends leave ahead of her."

"They were getting on her nerves. Nina needs quiet when she's under pressure. We're wasting time standing here talking," David said impatiently. His mother tried to calm him.

By now the entire wedding party was back at the house. Dressed in formal wedding attire, they looked lost and out of place. Sheila nervously began picking up the trail of clothing.

"Don't anybody touch anything. Let's try to reconstruct what might've happened. You called the house several times and got a busy signal. Right?" the officer asked.

"Right. Then the phone rang and someone picked up but

didn't say anything. I thought I heard scuffling sounds. After a while the phone went dead."

"Where are the phones in the house?"

"Upstairs and in the kitchen."

David walked into the kitchen. The receiver dangled to the floor. "Someone grabbed her before she could answer."

David picked up the silver bracelet from the floor.

"Whose is it?" the officer asked.

"I don't know," David said.

"I do," Estrellita answered. "I gave that to Nina for the wedding. The clasp is broken." She started to cry.

Sheila babbled, "This can't be happening. It can't be happening."

Nina's mother withdrew from the conversation and started talking to The Man Upstairs.

The policeman asked, "Is there anyone who didn't want to see this wedding take place?"

"About four years ago she had a run-in with a woman named Brenda Hill. Brenda was never charged. Nina ended up in the hospital."

"Address? Phone number?"

"I don't have either. Brenda lived in Oakland with her husband, Roland Hill, but they got divorced. I don't know where she lives now."

"Pete, run a check on Brenda Hill. See if you can get an address," the office instructed his partner.

David's muscles twitched involuntarily. He shifted from side to side, barely able to contain himself. "I have to find her fast," he said.

"The best thing you can do is wait and see what we come up with. We may need your help when we get a line on Brenda Hill." The policeman turned his attention to the crowd gathering in the kitchen. "Okay, everyone in the living room while we check the rest of the house."

Brenda answered the door wearing a housecoat and looking haggard. She was shocked to see two uniformed officers at her door.

"What is this?"

"Miss Hill. We'd like to ask you a few questions about Nina Lewis. She's been reported missing."

"I thought she left town a long time ago. Whatever it is doesn't concern me."

"Let us in, Brenda." David stepped forward in the doorway.

"What the hell is he doing here?" Brenda asked.

"May we come in?" the officer asked.

"Not without a warrant."

"All right. If you want to handle it that way. Pete, go down and call this in. Tell them we need an emergency warrant to search these premises."

"Wait. I don't want trouble. I don't know where she is."

"Can we come in and take a look? This gentleman is upset about his fiancée's disappearance."

Brenda threw open the door and stepped aside.

"You stay here," they instructed David, entering the living room. One officer headed to the back room.

The apartment was dank and eerily quiet. There was a cheap, vinyl dining set in the kitchen and a worn-out couch in the living room. A half-empty bottle of vodka sat on the counter next to a tall drinking glass.

Nothing was as oppressive as Brenda's appearance, which had undergone a radical transformation. Her long hair was now short and painfully uneven. She had put on substantial weight and generally let herself go. David hardly recognized the prima donna who wreaked so much havoc a few years ago.

Within minutes a quick inspection of the apartment was completed. David wasn't surprised when one of the officers announced, "She's not here. Do you have any idea where she might be?" he asked Brenda.

"Of course not. And if I did, why would I help find her? She's the last person I want to help."

"We understand you were quite obsessed with her at one time."

"I wasn't obsessed with her. I was obsessed with him," Brenda said, pointing angrily at David.

"Talk to us, Miss Hill," the officer asked. "Miss Lewis could be in danger."

"Why should I talk to you? Nobody listened when my name was being dragged through the mud. Nobody cared when Austin was fired."

"Who's Austin?" the policeman asked.

"Austin Greene was the campaign manager for Brenda's husband. He was constantly at odds with Nina," David answered.

Brenda interrupted, "Get off Austin's case. The poor man couldn't find work after Roland finished with him. He moved to Houston to start over again."

"Is there anything else you can tell us, Miss Hill?" the officer asked.

"Yeah, I've got plenty to say. I never hurt Nina. I confronted her, woman to woman, and told her exactly what was on my mind. They tried to make me out to be a crazy woman. I wasn't crazy, just looking for a way out of a miserable marriage."

"Are you saying you weren't responsible for Nina's accident?" David asked.

"I'm saying it now and I said it then. I wasn't driving that night. Roland took the keys to the Porsche when I filed for divorce. Maybe I went too far trying to keep you. I thought Nina was a passing thing like everything else in your life. But I'm over it. I don't want to be messed with by you, the police, or Roland. Ask Roland where she is. He's the one obsessed with Nina."

"I can't listen to this," David said. "Does Roland live in the same house in Oakland?"

"Oh, yes. He got the house, the cars, and custody of Matthew. I was too stupid to know that all the property was in his parents' name. You have to give him credit for being slick. The court wasn't sympathetic to a wacko wife. All I got was chump change. Roland gave me the shaft, but I'm glad it's over. I was sick of being abused."

"Are you telling the truth, Brenda?" David asked.

Brenda bit into her dry lower lip and looked at David obstinately. His eyes searched for the truth.

"Yes. The only thing I was guilty of was wanting you too much."

"I'm sorry. Sorry about everything. Thanks for helping." David left quickly with the police.

"Pete, call Mr. Hamilton's house to see if the young lady showed up. We'll look like idiots if we go running all over town for nothing. Then run a check on Austin Greene. Make sure he's still in Houston."

The policeman turned to David. "You're lucky I'm a sucker for weddings. Most guys would treat this as an ordinary missing person's situation. She's been missing less than twenty-four hours."

"Can't we go any faster?" David asked as the patrol car entered the freeway. He checked his watch, as he had done every minute since getting back in the car. Almost two hours had passed since Nina's disappearance. The patrol car, the investigation, everything moved in slow motion, except time.

"No. We're already taking a risk going to Roland Hill's house. The man's a prominent attorney. He'll have my badge if we screw up. When we get to the house, you wait in the car."

"You'll search the house, won't you?" David asked.

"That depends entirely on Mr. Hill. We don't have a search warrant, and I don't think he'll be as cooperative as his ex-wife."

"Can you get a warrant?"

"On what basis? There's nothing connecting Roland Hill to your fiancée's disappearance. You need probable cause, and we sure don't have it here. Brenda Hill didn't look too reliable."

"I think she was telling the truth."

"Yeah, right. Every con in San Quentin says he's innocent. Their problem is that they don't have a rich husband to keep them out of the slammer."

Chapter Twenty-five

NINA WAS BACK in the hospital surrounded by doctors, whispering and shaking their heads. In tandem, they backed away, dissolving into transparent walls. A gangly man with a prunelike face and hooks for hands stepped forward and pulled a white sheet over her head.

Her throat was raspy from constant screaming. Her voice was trapped deep inside. Nina struggled to move her arms and legs weighted down by invisible resistance. Nothing worked, except her mind perceiving everything happening to her.

"Are you awake?" a voice asked softly from outside her dream.

Her heavy eyelids labored open. She wasn't in the hospital or trapped in a dream. One by one, strange objects came into focus: a dying ficus crammed into a corner, blinds closed against waning sunlight. Roland sat perfectly still on a high-back loveseat.

Nina sat in the middle of a room with her mouth taped shut and her arms tied behind her. A rope secured her waist to a straight-back chair. She tried moving her legs, but her ankles were bound.

Painfully, she started to remember the phone ringing, a blind struggle followed by a fast journey into darkness.

A low guttural sound escaped from her throat as she bucked to move the chair.

"You might as well relax, Nina. You're not going anywhere. I hate doing it this way, but you left me no choice.

You said you were coming back to me, but you came back to marry David."

Nina prayed to pass out again. She couldn't face the sick reality. She counted the times she'd been alone with Roland, trusted him as a friend. Why did he wait until now?

Roland walked to the closet and pulled out a shoe box. "I have a present for you. Slip these on." He opened the box, displaying black stiletto heels—the kind Brenda used to wear.

Roland studied the tape around her ankles. "It could be tough putting them on with your feet tied." He dropped down on one knee. When his fingers encircled her ankles, Nina cringed.

"Don't be afraid. I want to love you, not hurt you. I'm sorry I had to tie you up. You have such beautiful skin."

Slowly he unwrapped wide electrical tape from her ankles and massaged areas chafed by the tape. Roland slipped the stilettos on her feet.

Nina grunted to get his attention.

"What's the matter? You want to talk? Behave and I'll take the tape off your mouth."

Nina nodded.

"Don't do anything stupid like screaming. It won't do any good. The house is well insulated. Brenda loved to scream."

In one continuous motion he yanked the tape from her mouth and left it hanging from a corner.

Nina took deep expunging breaths. "What about my wrists?" she asked. "They're hurting me."

"Sorry, sweetheart. You've endured more pain than this. Compared to the car accident this should be a piece of cake."

"You were in the laundry room that night."

"I was confused. I needed comfort. All I wanted was to hold you, but you dashed like a scared rabbit into the street. The notes, the phone calls, nothing I did could get you away from him. The irony is, I didn't know you had already left David."

"You set Brenda up."

"It was easy. I drove her car to Sheila's apartment. When I saw you go in the laundry room I pulled a fuse. Don't feel sorry for Brenda. She's nothing but a washed-up whore."

"I always wondered how she knew where to find me."

"Now you know—she didn't. You left a message at my office that you were at Sheila's. I'd driven you there the week before. David ruined my life, Nina. He stole my wife and destroyed my campaign. He's the reason you went away from here. When you left him, I was almost satisfied. That hurt him more than anything I could do. But I couldn't stop thinking how it would feel to touch you."

"Atlanta was no coincidence."

"Of course not. I wanted you here with me. When you said you were moving to Laguna I decided to wait. I've been too patient with you, Nina. You said you'd call, but you never did."

"I thought we were friends."

"We are. We'll be even better friends. You can have whatever you want, if you give me what I want," Roland said, placing his hand on her leg.

"What are you doing?"

"Don't make me force you. Give it to me the way you gave it to David. You like being on top, don't you, Nina?"

Nina was stunned.

"That's right. I climbed up on the balcony at David's. Didn't think I was that athletic, did you? I had a great view from every angle. The dimples at the top of your ass turned me on."

He forced her legs apart and pulled up her skirt.

"This is crazy, Roland. You'll lose everything. It's not worth it."

"David thought it was worth it. White panties. Are these your wedding panties? Don't tell me you planned to wear white."

He leaned his chest between her legs. She tried to stop him by burrowing her butt into the chair.

"Don't fight me. I'm warning you—I'm a little nervous. Call it honeymoon jitters." Roland laughed like the demented creature he had become.

Nina stopped resisting. He pulled her panties down over her knees and feet.

He stood up and circled the chair.

"Roland, please, please let me go. I won't tell anyone."

"Tell them what? That we did what they thought we did years ago? I enjoyed them thinking I was sleeping with a young, beautiful woman. Watching David squirm every time you came near me made my dick hard."

Nina schemed. "Untie me so I can give it to you the way you want it."

Roland's clenched fist stopped within centimeters of her jaw. "Don't try to con me."

Nina winced but didn't cry.

His hand slid down her body, grabbed her bra hook, and tugged until the straps dug into her skin. The hook wouldn't give.

"Stubborn bastard," Roland said, snapping the hook with such intensity that it flew against the wall and left an imprint.

Her eyes closed, her head turned away. When he touched her breast, Nina screamed louder than a siren signaling the end of the world. Her cry drowned out the doorbell buzzing downstairs. Roland grabbed her shoulders and shook her violently. Nina's cry subsided into a moan. When he realized they had company, he sealed her mouth with his rough hand. His viselike fingers laced around her neck.

"Make a sound and it's your ass," he warned, securing the tape over her mouth.

Skirting the walls, Roland slunk downstairs and peeked through the peephole. It was getting dark outside. Distorted faces of two uniformed police officers stared back. Roland leaned against the wall to quiet his breathing. He looked out again. The officer in charge directed his partner to check around back.

After a quick search the rookie rejoined his partner at the

front door. "Nothing, man. There's a car in the garage, but no sign of movement inside," he reported.

The police rang the doorbell one last time, then walked away empty-handed.

"Let me try. I know she's in there," David pleaded from the squad car.

"You know what we agreed to. Without a warrant or permission from the owner, no one's going inside."

Roland watched through the peephole until the patrol car pulled away. The floor above him shuddered as a thundering noise rang through the hall. Upstairs, he found Nina on the floor, still tied to the chair.

Roland jerked her upright. "You shouldn't have done that," he said, slapping her full force. "Thanks to the cops, we'll have to party somewhere else."

"Without more information, we've gone as far as we can. Your fiancée might have chickened out at the last minute. It happens all the time. We'll drop you off at home and call if anything develops. The best thing you can do is wait."

The policeman talked. David didn't listen.

They warned him not to play hero as they pulled away from his house. David started up the stairs past the "For Sale" sign planted in the yard. The instant the black and white was out of sight, he turned and sprinted to the T-Bird.

David parked the car a block away from Roland's house and started walking. Three houses away a fox terrier raced from the driveway, yipping at his heels. David shooed away the pesky animal and placed his hand over his racing heart.

Beside the solid wood fence next door to Roland's property he stopped and peeked around the corner. Inside the garage, Roland slammed the trunk on his Volvo. David's head jerked back. Roland looked around nervously, then headed for the driver's side door. David peeked again. Nina was nowhere in sight. He sprinted back to his car and waited until Roland backed out and drove in the opposite direction.

The Volvo lumbered onto the freeway as David followed from a safe distance.

David glanced down at the gas gauge. The red needle bobbed around empty.

"Not now, not now," David agonized, pounding the steering wheel. He cruised for miles with nothing to go on, except fumes in his gas tank and blind faith that Roland might lead him to Nina.

The Volvo led him southeast, toward the Valley of Windmills. Days earlier David had told Nina how the windmills reminded him of aliens from outer space. Towering, cold, and seemingly indestructible, the windmills looked like invaders from another planet coming to take over the earth. Nina kidded him about his wild imagination. Under current circumstances, space invaders didn't seem so farfetched.

"Nellie, don't fail me now." David patted the dashboard of the Thunderbird as it hummed down the highway. "I hope he's not headed to L.A." He grimaced at the thought.

Roland passed exit after exit, showing no sign of slowing down. Suddenly the right blinker flashed on Roland's Volvo. A sign ahead read "Gas, food and lodging—next exit." David slowed to avoid detection.

Roland stopped at the end of the off ramp, turned right, and drove into the E-Z Motel parking lot. David pulled into an adjacent fast food restaurant, got out, and watched as Roland entered the motel lobby. He waited an excruciating eternity until Roland reappeared and got back in the car, started the engine, and drove to the other side of the motel.

David positioned the T-Bird in front of the motel lobby. When the lights faded on Roland's vehicle, David cut his headlights and eased around the corner. The trunk of the Volvo was open. Roland was dragging Nina, hands tied behind her and mouth gagged, into a motel room by the neck.

David revved the T-Bird's engine. Roland looked up, recognized David, and pushed Nina to her knees inside the room. Without hesitation David floored the accelerator and drove the T-Bird full blast toward Roland. The car crashed into the room's door before Roland could close it. Roland backpedaled, tripping over Nina's foot.

David vaulted from the car. He dived on top of Roland and pummeled him with his fists. Defensive blows from Roland's hands had little impact on David. Roland caught hold of a cord, which he yanked continuously. A heavy-based lamp fell within his reach. He grabbed the neck of the lamp and struck David in the temple. When David didn't go down, he struck him again on the back of the head. Stunned, David collapsed on top of Roland.

Nina struggled to gain her footing without the use of her hands. She rolled to the bed, pressed her back against it for leverage, and slowly rose to her feet.

Roland was on the brink of pushing David off him. Before he could do so, Nina raised her foot and stomped down hard with the heel of the stiletto. The stiletto penetrated Roland's palm, lodging between the bones of two fingers. He screamed in agony. Then, as shock set in, Roland calmed down like an animal stunned by a powerful tranquilizer. He tried to crawl. Nina kicked him in the side with the shoe's pointed toe. Roland went down, curled into a ball, and whimpered.

When David came to, Nina was standing over Roland, poised to do more damage. David staggered to his feet, warning Roland, "Make a move and I'll put you out of your misery."

David removed the tape from Nina's hands and mouth. Gasping for breath, he asked, "You okay, baby?"

"He locked me in the trunk. I thought I was going to die," Nina blurted as she began to tremble.

"I've got you. You're all right now."

"But you're not. You're bleeding." Nina placed her hand at the back of his head where blood was spurting. It ran down his neck and the back of his ear, saturating his clothing.

"It's not that bad. Call the police."

Within minutes the previously deserted parking lot filled

with spectators. Nina and David leaned against each other, waiting for help to arrive.

Lights, sounds, and sirens signaled the end of Roland's obsession. He tried to talk to Nina as they took him away.

"Nina, tell them you came here voluntarily. I'm a respected member of the community. They can't put me in jail. Help me," he pleaded.

Nina wanted to spit on him, but her mouth was dry, her lips chafed. An all-over lifeless feeling gripped her, as if the fluid had been drained from her body. Fear, temporarily abated, reached out and took control. Nina shook as she climbed into the ambulance with David.

"I'm okay," David said.

Nina held David's blood-soaked jacket in her arms. She knew his wound was serious. The lamp had shattered into jagged pieces when Roland struck him in the head. Beads of sweat had formed on his forehead minutes before the ambulance arrived. David fought to remain alert until police took Roland into custody.

"Miss, if you could move out of the way, it would be easier for us to treat him," the ambulance attendant suggested.

"I love you, Nina," David said in slurred speech. He was getting woozy.

Nina moved to the end of the cot and held on to his fingertips. She rested her head at his feet until they arrived at the emergency entrance. The attendants wanted to wheel her in, but she insisted on walking. David was taken into a room for immediate attention.

They placed her in a separate room where she waited for several minutes. Being alone was the hardest part. She wasn't hurt, at least not physically. She rubbed the bump on the back of her head and felt the bruising where Roland had slapped her. Anger rose up inside her. She wished she could get her hands on Roland one last time. There was one more place she needed to kick him. Finally, a nurse came in with news.

"He's okay. They're treating his wound and monitoring his vital signs. He required a few stitches, but he should be fine. He's lost some blood and has a concussion, so he needs to rest."

"I want to see him," Nina insisted.

"I know. We need to finish up with Mr. Hamilton, examine you, and then you can go in and see him. I'm sorry to have to ask this, but may we examine you for evidence of sexual contact?" the nurse asked.

"You can examine me, but he didn't get that far. He slapped me around and terrorized me. He was planning on"—Nina couldn't get the words out—"but David saved me." She started crying again. The ordeal kept hitting home.

The nurse patted her hand. "You're safe now. Would you like to lie down?"

"Not until I see David."

When they finally let her in to see him, David was propped up in bed.

"I was wondering where the other half of the tag team was," David said.

Nina hugged him and asked, "Are you okay, David?"

"I feel fine until I try to stand up and the room starts spinning."

"You warned me about him, David, but I didn't listen. You could have been killed."

David pulled her chin up with his hand. "He could've killed you. But let's not talk about what didn't happen. It's over."

"How could I be that stupid?" Nina asked.

"You weren't stupid, you were trusting. Don't let him lay the guilt on you. Did he hurt you, Nina?"

"He hit me on the back of the head and slapped me. He used some kind of drug to knock me out. Every time I think about it, it makes me shake. Roland was trying to get freaky when the police rang the doorbell. The man is sick."

"I was sitting in the police car while that maniac had you," David said, disgusted.

"This is unreal, like it happened to someone else. If it wasn't for you, I wouldn't be here. How did you know it was Roland?"

"We paid a visit to Brenda, the first person I suspected. When she started talking, I believed she was telling the truth about what happened five years ago."

"She was. Roland admitted setting her up. He was the one in the laundry room that night. I spent all this time blaming Brenda while the real enemy was right in my face." Nina's voice cracked.

David held her tighter. "It'll be all right. We'll make sure he doesn't hurt anybody else. . . . Did you call our folks?"

"Yes, they're on their way."

"They should've waited at home."

"When the doctor said they were keeping you, there was no way to make them wait."

"Keeping me? I'm supposed to be on my honeymoon," David protested.

"You're not going anywhere. They're keeping you over-night for observation. Your blood pressure was elevated when they brought you in."

"A hole in the head is enough to elevate anybody's blood pressure."

"It's just a precaution. The police have a couple of questions, then you're off to dream land. You're running on fumes."

"Speaking of which, remind me to lecture you on the dangers of running the car on empty."

Nina nuzzled his neck. "I screwed up all around. I'm sorry about the T-Bird. You think they can fix it?"

"I doubt it, but I'm not trippin'. You're okay; that's what's important."

"What were you thinking when you crashed the T-Bird?"

"I wasn't thinking. When you're dealing with a madman you have to act as crazy as he is."

Nina laughed, then turned serious. "I feel like I lost a friend."

David frowned. "You mean Roland?"

"No. I hope that bastard rots in hell. I mean the Thunderbird. It was part of our history. The T-Bird was there when we first met."

"I don't know why I didn't take the other car when I came after you. I'm sure Roy Rogers preferred an aging Trigger over all his other mounts."

"I'll buy you another car."

"The T-Bird and I had a good time together. Some things can't be replaced. When the cops told me to go home and wait, that was out of the question. I'd come too far to let it end like that."

Nina checked his wound. "He got you pretty good."

"Yes. I owe him one."

Nina walked toward the door, looked back, and said, "I can't imagine what would've happened if you hadn't been there."

"I'd be talking to the walls in a padded cell. Hurry back."

Within an hour the complete wedding party had assembled in the hospital corridor.

"Everybody's here. You feel like getting married?" Nina asked.

"I'm ready. What about a preacher?"

"We've handled bigger problems than that."

Fifteen minutes later, inside his hospital room, David and Nina became husband and wife. David's mother beamed throughout the ceremony. Nina's mother cried.

"Mama, I hope you're not disappointed." Nina tried to console her.

"I'm crying because I'm so happy. When David found you all my prayers were answered. God is good."

The celebration was brief out of necessity. The bride and groom were too exhausted to entertain.

"I hadn't planned on spending my wedding night alone in the hospital," David said.

"Who said anything about being alone? I'm spending the night with my husband."

"How'd you swing that?"

"I promised them free autographed copies of your books."

David smiled and looked at the ring on his finger. He was drifting, but fought to stay awake while Nina said good night to their guests.

Nina hand delivered the bridal bouquet to Estrellita. "I'm not risking anyone else catching this."

By the time she returned David's eyes were closed. Nina curled up behind him. She had everything she wanted and more. With her hand securely inside of his, they rested.

Amanda Wheeler brings your dreams to life
in a romance you can call your own....

ARMS OF THE MAGNOLIA

Rae Montgomery is a sharp, ambitious young lawyer
whose corporate office has become a prison. She is
black and female in an all-white male world. She
feels trapped by her job—and by her fervent, secret
love affair with a man who belongs to another
woman. Trying to make it in a cold northern city, she
longs for the strength she drew from the beautiful
magnolia tree she used to call her own.

ARMS OF THE MAGNOLIA

Published by Fawcett Books.
Available in bookstores everywhere.

For a tantalizing glimpse of ARMS OF THE MAGNOLIA,
please turn the page....

Precious moments had passed since the bartender signaled "last call" to the nearly empty room of dreamers. She lingered in the tavern long after hope had turned to gloom. The waitress glanced sympathetically at the proud, dispirited lady languishing in a shadowy corner. The door would soon close on her secret rendezvous.

They had not spoken of him specifically, but the waitress knew him well from the many hours the woman had waited for him to come and cool the fever that engulfed her. She longed for him in a way that left her open to abject emptiness. She could not recognize herself, sitting and waiting interminably for the man who had stirred the sleeping sensuality within her soul.

The million excuses imagined for his absence did not alleviate her misery. "You know there is less than ten feet of visibility in this heavy fog tonight," a compassionate patron reassured her. With drooping eyes she nodded "yes," but she did not speak. They sensed her sadness and quietly hoped for a happy ending to the long vigil. Their eyes followed with anticipation the headlights that occasionally appeared on the sleepy road beside the tavern.

The concierge at the inn had warned Rae that the fog rolling in was extremely hazardous, particularly on the narrow, winding road leading to the Tavern By The Shore. The danger was inconsequential, as she had committed herself to a far more dangerous adventure when she agreed to meet Daniel.

Rae had known him for months, but kept him at a distance until their kiss, a friendly kiss, turned to passion. They had avoided each other's eyes, refusing to acknowledge their mutual attraction. To look would have caused them to commit an indiscretion in their hearts, if not in their lives.

Her plan was to depart swiftly, assuredly, to indulge no more in the sea of pity. Two captain's chairs in her path barred her exit, intensifying her sense of humiliation. The waitress asked if she needed a taxi, but they knew no taxi would come to claim her in the fog. Rae bid them farewell and stumbled to the gravel-covered parking lot, which was almost completely deserted. She wished that the fog would consume her and save her from the reality of having acted as a fool. But the fog was like angel hair on a Christmas tree, surrounding, adhering, then floating away.

The room at the inn was close and warm as Rae plummeted into an uneasy sleep. She spiraled into a world of paradoxical dreams. Running through thick fog, she tried to anticipate the invisible water's edge. An unevenly shaped boulder loomed out of the darkness. She opened her mouth to scream, but terror muffled the sound into a hollow echo. Rae struggled to awaken from the nightmare, but the fog compelled her, like ropes, to remain against her will. An undecided knock at the door released her.

His apologies for being late and his explanation of how the waitress told him where to find her were lost in the joy she felt now that Daniel had come to be with her.

Without asking, he slipped the velvet nightdress from her shoulders and held her, very still, against his body. Tears filled her eyes as she rationalized that this was right. His kiss alone filled her up, shook her foundation, and caused her to shudder uncontrollably. Thinking that she was chilled by the air, he picked her up and carried her to bed.

Daniel undressed in silence, unbuttoning his shirt to reveal a well-toned chest speckled with soft, curly hair. The pants and underwear were removed at once, but his back was to her. She studied the definition of his smooth, tight behind before he turned to unveil the crescendo of his desire.

Wanting to feel the full length of his body, Rae slipped from beneath the covers and stood to embrace him. His tongue found her mouth, sensitive hands cupped her bottom. Daniel positioned her against the wall and secured her long legs around his waist as they unleashed months of repressed passion.

Sounds of ecstasy made them laugh between deep kisses. He came quickly, but she did not mind because he belonged to her completely, if only for the moment.

The wine and spirits consumed before their union betrayed love's unspent passion, and so they slept, coiled together, holding on to the intimacy that would be relinquished just after dawn.

As sunlight filtered through the fabric of the curtain, solitude enveloped Rae like a shroud. Perhaps the dread of this aloneness had caused her to sleep longer than was customary. Surely she felt him slip from her embrace, heard him shower before leaving. He had kissed her neck, her back, and gazed upon her delicately sculpted body. His kiss was not one of good-bye, but a reminder of moments to come. They knew it was not over.

Still feeling the imprint of his body, she lay there smelling his scent, pulsating at the thought of Daniel, knowing she had surrendered far more than was prudent. He was betrothed and could not avoid his commitment without loss of honor. His sense of honor drew her to him.

ARMS OF THE MAGNOLIA

by Amanda Wheeler

Also available at your local bookstore